RESOLVE

Colin Green

2QT Limited (Publishing)

First Edition published 2021 by
2QT Limited (Publishing)
Settle, North Yorkshire BD24 9BZ United Kingdom

This is a work of fiction and any resemblance to any person living or dead is purely coincidental. The place names mentioned may exist but have no connection with the events in this book

Cover Design by
Hilary Pitt

Printed in Great Britain by IngramSpark UK

Cover images: shutterstock.com and iStock by Getty Images

A CIP catalogue record for the paperback format book is available
from the British Library
ISBN 978-1-914083-44-0

This book is dedicated to my two current grandchildren, James Edward, (Jimmy) and Olly Jack (Olly).

They have arrived in the world at such a difficult time, yet in their presence everything is forgotten other than the ability to laugh and smile. Thank you.

Acknowledgements

To Marje, who continues to advise and support when faced with the roughest of manuscripts!

To Rachy, for her review and diligent suggestions.

To Ruth, not only for the many cups of tea and coffee supplied, but also for the patience, (which I sadly lack), and continuous encouragement.

Without their contributions RESOLVE would never have been written.

To everyone who purchases and reads RESOLVE – Thank you.

1

Toni

It was a warm Saturday evening in late August, the final bank holiday weekend of the summer. Toni Galloway had finished painting her nails. The garish purple matched her eyeshadow. The twenty-two-year-old was wearing skintight white trousers, a bright pink low-cut blouse and high heels, all purchased from Gucci, her favourite outlet of choice.

Not that money was a problem for Toni, because she was heavily financed by her doting mother. Her biggest problem was rapidly approaching: how to get out of the house without the usual confrontation over her appearance. She gave Bones the family boxer dog a loving pat, while upstairs she could hear water running, filling her mother's en-suite jacuzzi. It presented an opportunity not to be missed.

'Bye, Mam.' Toni deliberately spoke at a volume level that may or may not have been heard. There were only the two of them in the house. Her father had died in a workplace accident. She would never forget the day of his death, which had happened on her twelfth birthday.

Toni opened the front door and pushed Bones back inside, carefully avoiding the dog's ever-present spittle. Her taxi would be at the end of the drive. It would never dare to be late for the daughter of Wendy Galloway. She walked down the floodlit driveway, which was monitored by a state-of-the-art CCTV system, while struggling to stay upright as her stilettoes slithered across the uneven pebbles. Meanwhile, back at the house, her mother, armed with a large Hendrick's Gin accompanied by an obligatory Fever-Tree tonic, tested the hot perfumed water in the jacuzzi. She was blissfully unaware of her daughter's quick exit.

Two minutes later Toni was on her way. While sitting in the back of the taxi she reflected sadly on the fact that Wendy had insisted that she return home when her elder brother Matt had run off and finally joined the Royal Marines after yet another argument with his mother. Both Matt and Toni, although never particularly close, had worked in the family building business, but Matt knew that the company was a front for his mother's other activities. Joining the marines was a long-held ambition as well as a desperate attempt to distance himself from the notorious Galloway name. The soured relations between them now made any domestic conversation concerning Matt forbidden, while Toni remained as a secretary for Galloway's Building Services.

Some ten minutes later she enviously looked out of the taxi window at the exclusive waterfront East Parton Apartments. One of those luxurious units had previously been her home. The new quayside development really was the place to live, surrounded as it was by modern bars and high-quality restaurants yet still close to the city centre. Nevertheless, as her mother had paid for the property, Toni had no option but to return home when Wendy had placed it on the market without her daughter's knowledge.

With little effort Toni placed those thoughts to the back of her mind. Time to party, and a bank holiday party at that. She was meeting the girls for a few shots at Boston's on the waterfront before heading up town. Toni had a wide social circle. Being a member of the Galloway family had many benefits, and Toni attracted more than a few hangers-on. Not everyone liked Toni Galloway, but there were many who wanted to be seen with her.

It was now 8.30 p.m. and there were a dozen or so of her friends gathered in Boston's. It was their second round of drinks. Both had been purchased by Toni – another benefit for her acquaintances. She was extremely generous with her money, most of which was supplied by her mother. The night was young, the alcohol was taking an effect and music was blaring out in the background. Life was good for the group.

An hour or so later they had migrated to Lucifer's, a popular venue in the city centre. After a couple more drinks the girls, all still as a group, went downstairs to the nightclub's dancing area. It was 1.30 a.m. when Toni decided to have a smoke. It was an opportune moment because the guy she had been dancing with was obviously far too pissed and had staggered into another couple, causing a drinks spillage and some disorder. A couple of punches were thrown before the bouncers intervened and ejected them. She had witnessed the action and liked the look of one the bouncers. Toni would pursue this interest over a fag break. It wasn't just money that she was free and easy with. However, the problem with anyone wanting to partake of Toni Galloway's favours was the knowledge of the existence of Mother Wendy. And her notoriety.

As soon as she was outside she immediately recognised

the object of tonight's desire. Underneath the fluorescent tabard, from what she could see, he cut a muscular, athletic figure standing outside the glass fronted doors.

'Like a fag?' Toni slurred as she joined him outside.

No, thanks. I don't smoke,' came the polite and well-spoken reply, in an accent that Toni didn't recognise.

'Do you live locally?' she enquired, desperately trying to keep her balance as her heels and the consumed alcohol betrayed her. 'Haven't seen you before.'

'No, I'm a student at uni. Just came back early for preseason football training and to earn some cash,' he said politely.

Toni made her move and shuffled up close to the young doorman. 'I like you,' she said bluntly. He smelt both the alcohol and the cigarettes on her breath and took a step back to rid himself of the fumes, before he bent down to take a mouthful of strong black coffee replacing the polystyrene cup on the pavement.

She was drunk. But when it came to men, Toni Galloway usually got what she wanted. At twenty-two years of age, her life experience was way beyond her youthful years. And not just when it came to matters of the opposite sex.

Toni repeated her actions but this time she placed both arms around the doorman's neck and kissed him full on the lips, pushing her body against him. He resorted to the small amount of training he had received for his role and removed her arms from around his neck while stepping back at the same time, before requesting assistance via his small pocket radio. As he stepped away from her Toni lost balance and fell to the ground. Given her alcoholic state reaction time was slow, and the hands that would normally break such a fall failed her. She slowly got to her feet, sporting a small but noticeable graze to her right cheek.

'Fuck off, twat,' Toni Galloway screamed and spat at the young doorman, who had now been joined by his supervisor. The two door staff turned away and ignored her abuse. *Just another unhappy drunk*, they thought.

Totally humiliated and now crying, Toni made her way along Trent Street to the nearest taxi rank. Back at Lucifer's, the young doorman updated the licensed premises incident book. The management ordered him not to report the incident to the authorities, as it would create another unwanted police statistic attached to their premises.

On the way home Toni tried to compose herself. It was 2 a.m. and she hoped that, given her current appearance, she wouldn't have to face her mother. The heel of her right shoe had snapped and the small but noticeable graze on her cheek, as well as the smudged mascara, were all telltale signs of another drunken night. She burst through the front doors. Bones, drooling as ever, barked loudly. It was only seconds before her mother was downstairs.

She stood in front of her daughter, inwardly seething. Toni looked the worse for wear – a direct opposite to Wendy, who was as immaculate as ever, despite having had her sleep disturbed. The lack of make-up only enhanced her high cheekbones, piercing blue eyes and beautifully styled grey hair. A pair of pink silk pyjamas covered her tall, slim figure. Wendy Galloway had beauty but, more importantly, presence.

The fact that Toni was drunk didn't concern Wendy. It was a regular Saturday night occurrence. She studied Toni more closely and noticed both the graze on her right cheek and the smudged mascara.

Wendy questioned her daughter. 'What happened, Toni?' For a moment Toni ignored her mother and made for the sink, stumbling around as if she was having an audition for Bambi trying to skate in the Walt Disney film. Part of her thought she would throw up, but she desperately needed a drink. 'Toni, what happened?' Wendy repeated her question, but this time in a voice that demanded a response.

'I've been punched, Mam.' Toni said. Despite her drunkenness, she never missed an opportunity to innocently explain away her circumstances. She was a good liar. But, then again, her mother would believe almost anything Toni recounted. Without prompting and because now, armed with a glass of water, she just wanted to go to bed, she told her mother half the truth. It only took a minute or so to tell her that a bouncer at Lucifer's had punched her. That was enough for Wendy. She didn't hear the remainder of Tina's short and slurring cock and bull story about why she had a graze on her cheek. She had heard enough.

Toni went to bed via the bathroom, from where her mother could hear her being violently sick. Meanwhile Wendy Galloway poured herself another gin.

'No one messes with the Galloways,' she said to herself, and took a large sip of gin. 'No need to panic, though. No knee-jerk reaction.' She was experienced, a cool operator. For the remainder of the night she remained downstairs, drinking the occasional gin and formulating a plan. It would require some preparation, and the background enquiries would take a couple of months at least. The sun began to rise as she made her way up the stairs to bed.

2

Robbie

One month later

It was late September, and Robbie Hanson was looking around his recently purchased two-bedroom flat. The block had been constructed close to the city centre for key workers. The new-build had been facilitated through some Help to Buy scheme. It was a five-minute cycle to work for Robbie. The young police constable refused to take the risk of travelling in his second-hand Audi A3 Sportback.

When he looked back on his first three years of police service, Robbie realised that he couldn't have been happier with his choice of career. He was fortunate in being stationed in Parton city centre. Having spent his childhood on his parent's dairy farm, in the rural part of the county, he wanted to be near the action. The city centre station was widely recognised as the busiest in the force.

Previously Robbie had turned down the opportunity to continue in his parent's once successful farming business and had left that to his younger sister, Alice. Athletic and talented, Robbie was also a keen rugby player with Upper Parton RFC, who he had played for and supported from mini junior level.

Following good A level results, he had gone to one of the London universities. He loved the big city. And playing student rugby not only meant that he improved in terms of his playing ability, but it also introduced him to some raucous social nights. After graduating he achieved his lifelong ambition in joining the police service. A 2:1 honours degree in his chosen subject, law, made him an ideal candidate.

Unfortunately, life had now changed course, due to his mother's recent diagnosis of motor neurone disease. Parton Constabulary now had to be his preferred choice of force. Robbie not only wanted to assist at home, but he also desperately wanted to be near his mother. He loved her dearly and spent most of his spare time exploring Internet sites about MND research.

Despite the difficulties at home, Hanson had returned to playing at Upper Parton RFC and, when shifts allowed, he was an automatic choice in the first team's back row. Playing rugby was a welcome distraction. He had taken to his chosen career like the proverbial duck to water and had flown through his two-year probation, thanks in part to his excellent tutor constable and a young enthusiastic sergeant, Steve Barker.

The newly promoted Barker was obviously going places and took a special interest in developing his staff. He was the ideal mentor for young Hanson. The young officer was one of the stars of A relief who were regarded by their area commander as the highest-performing shift in the city centre. Robbie Hanson was making excellent progress, unlike his mother, whose mobility continued to deteriorate. This triggered many severe bouts of depression that were only offset by Patsy, the loyal family cairn terrier, who never left her side.

After the successful completion of his probation in early March that year, Hanson had been specially chosen to perform additional duties to those of his primary role as a response cop. These duties were the force's response in their push to reduce violent crime. This was the single category that they had failed to meet government targets. It was a remarkable turnaround in the fortunes of Parton Constabulary, given their most recent history.

In the spring, Chief Constable Chris Mayling had personally chaired a licensing meeting of all Pubwatch members within the city centre radius. She persuaded them to extend their current scheme. The result was that each city centre shift had nominated one officer whose remit was to ensure that all door supervisors underwent further training and maintained their accreditation, and that each premises kept an updated incident book where they recorded any relevant incidents. The timing was carefully planned, and the initiative was well underway before the busy Easter period and the upcoming summer bank holidays.

Thanks to the diligence of officers such as Robbie Hanson, the police maintained the pressure. They implemented stringent background checks, plus they had the power to immediately remove any door staff who overstepped the mark. The system was working, and early indications had shown a noticeable reduction in violent crime.

Away from their policing duties, the first Friday in September was a shift night out for A relief. It fell on one of the two weekends in Robbie's four-week duty cycle when he and his team were clear of both night and late shift duties.

He had spent the day with his mother at the farm. She was propped up in her chair, receiving some oxygen support. As ever, the loyal and devoted Patsy lay curled up on her lap.

To make life easier for their mother, Robbie and his sister Alice had spent time planning modifications to the farmhouse, while his dad distracted himself with milking their herd. Sadly, he and Alice had had yet another argument regarding the alteration costs involved.

The continual competition with the local supermarkets over the price of milk was a battle that the family business was losing. Although both siblings had their mother's interests at heart, arguments were becoming a regular occurrence. Robbie was deeply upset and left the farmhouse in tears, but not before he had given his mother a long and loving embrace.

He drove home in deep contemplation. More overtime or selling the Audi would only be the proverbial drop in the ocean, considering the building work required to meet his mother's increasing needs.

By 6 p.m. Hanson had returned to his apartment. Being sociable that evening was the last thing on his mind, but Robbie forced himself to go on the shift's night out. It was expected. After all, he was a regular member of the Friday Club. Hanson, shaved and showered by 7.30 p.m. Robbie was off to meet the other members of his team in the local pub, the Red Rooster, which had the added bonus of being close to the police station as well as other nightclub venues. The Rooster was very much a police watering hole. It was on old-fashioned premises with wooden flooring and hand-pulled draught beer, the background music allowed for conversation. The pub was always the starting point of their evening.

There was a total of fifteen PCs on Hanson's shift, plus Sergeant Steve Barker and Inspector Dave Atlee, and usually there was a hardcore of eight who attended the Friday Club.

Unfortunately, part of that hardcore was Bill Rudding. He was the archetypal disgruntled cop. Always moaning about this and that, with a continuous hotline to the police federation. Rudding was rightly regarded as a complete gobshite who, despite being encouraged by supervision to apply for some other role within the force, seemed glued to the city centre. Even the positive Sergeant Steve Barker had failed in his attempts to change the attitude of PC Bill Rudding.

The A relief shift had a youngish profile apart from the soon-to-retire Inspector Dave Atlee, whose main topic of conversation was his planned world cruise beginning the next January. There were always the regulars in the Friday Club and along with Rudding, Sergeant Steve Barker was always one of them. The club's get-togethers were the only opportunity where Hanson could call Barker by his Christian name. The thoughtful sergeant always made an exit after about three or four pints, just before the alcohol began to loosen lips. It was a practice that had so far served him well. As far as life and his work were concerned, Steve Barker was experienced beyond his years.

Four of them remained in the Rooster till 10 p.m., naturally, Bill Rudding was in full flow. They were well served, and soon the talk turned to the drunken question, 'Where next?' It was decided they would go clubbing, something they rarely did, and for Robbie Hanson it was the first time, but after such a crap day he was now a man on a mission.

Another drink was consumed while Bill Rudding, always the loudest, took control and decided it was time to head off to the Dart, a nearby nightclub within walking distance of any city centre venue. The wisdom of four off-duty city centre officers attending a city centre nightclub was always debatable. However, the Dart had a reasonable reputation. It was also easily walkable from the Rooster, despite the amount of alcohol they had consumed.

The journey was uneventful, although Hanson needed some persuading that it was too early for a kebab. He would also fail to notice how much time Rudding was spending studying his mobile. Unknown to Hanson and the other Friday Club members he was under surveillance, but not from any law enforcement agency. Constable Bill Rudding had been on Wendy Galloway's payroll for a couple of years, and tonight he was working under her instructions.

They approached the Dart around 11 p.m. There was the usual queue, monitored by door staff, who were all wearing the newly provided fluorescent tabards. Despite his inebriated state Hanson smiled inwardly at the security measure that he, in some way, had made a small contribution. Rudding had other thoughts on his mind. He was a heavy drinker and had a greater alcohol tolerance than Hanson. He was focused, and his night's work was just beginning.

Prior to leaving the Rooster, as he had been ordered, Rudding sent a text to his taskmasters informing them of their proposed destination. As they walked to the Dart he observed one of Galloway's boys walking on the other side of the street.

There was never a chance that the group of four

off-duty police officers would consider that their evening's activity might be subject to surveillance. They arrived outside the Dart. Rudding, on a normal night out with his other mates, would have flashed his warrant card to gain immediate entry. Tonight was different, and he knew that the other members of the group, unlike himself, were dedicated coppers. What was more important was that any such action would attract un-wanted attention to Galloway's plans and, for Rudding, would place an excellent payout in jeopardy.

It was a cold fifteen-minute wait while the queue shortened. There was a general discussion about who would be their next inspector when their boss, Gentleman Atlee, retired. The chat always naturally turned to work. It was the very reason they all came together. Rudding didn't concern himself in the conversation. He was more concerned with what was to come. He didn't have to wait long, and it developed naturally.

They passed the point of no return. There was just a casual nod from the last outside member of the Dart's door staff before the group descended the dozen or so stairs into the basement area, which was the Dart's nightclub.

Rudding was last to enter. Hanson briefly looked back to see him in conversation with the same bouncer who had given them access. As planned, Rudding was providing a brief description of Hanson's clothing. The cave-like nightclub consisted of a raised dance floor at the rear of the premises and a long bar running the length of the left-hand wall. It was the usual nightclub environment and was packed with revellers. The loud music made any conversation with anyone other than the closest individual nigh on impossible.

The other two officers made their way to the bar while Hanson waited for Rudding. 'Bill, I'm dying for a piss. I'm off to the bog,' Hanson spluttered into Rudding's ear.

'I'll join you, Robbie,' Rudding shouted back. He sensed the opportunity and again reached for his phone, praying he would find a signal in order to send the necessary text.

It was never an easy journey at that time of night. Half-jostling, half-barging, the officers made their way through the mass of people heading towards the neon flashing light indicating the ladies and the gents. Such was his haste that Hanson ignored the sight of two males loitering around the single swing entrance door of the toilets.

He entered the gents, and the immediate stench of the strong urinal disinfectant cubes infiltrated not only his nostrils but also travelled directly to the back of his throat. It was a hit similar to the strongest of mints but without the associated pleasant taste. He desperately tried to hold his breath as Rudding followed him through the swing door.

After turning slightly to his left he saw where the individual porcelain urinals were located against the back wall. The cubicles were along one side, opposite the handbasins. Hanson, closely followed by Rudding, found the toilets empty. He chose an empty urinal and was immediately aware of company in the form of Bill Rudding, who was occupying the next available place in the row. The glare of the white porcelain stared back up at him as he unzipped his trousers.

With both hands occupied, Hanson was grabbed from behind and pulled backwards towards the nearest cubicle. He was twisted around in the same movement. Hanson had been forced into the cubicle and was facing the toilet bowl, legs astride. It was a violent but at the same time well controlled move. There were two of them – both males, from the glimpse of their footwear. He felt the full weight of one of them pushing him over the toilet and up against the wall. Robbie was literally going nowhere.

'Get your fucking arms up,' one of them said, harshly spitting into Hanson's right ear. The urinal smells were now being challenged by the aroma of some cheap aftershave.

'Piss off,' Hanson shouted back, after quickly coming to his senses. 'Bill, get these bastards off me. Call the troops,' Robbie screamed, as operational mode kicked in. His instructions fell on deaf ears. Bill Rudding had just made a sharp exit and had left the toilets and joined Wendy Galloway's lookout man, who had been waiting outside in the gloomily lit corridor.

'Excuse me, mate. The toilets are out of order at the moment,' Rudding said to a disgruntled patron as he approached the toilet entrance.

'Take a look at this, Hanson,' said the other male, this time in his left ear. He then reached inside his jacket pocket and removed a mobile phone underneath Hanson's extended left arm, then brought it back up in front of the young constable's face. 'Look, you bastard.' He forced the phone screen up in front of his face while the other member of the team increased the weight and therefore the pressure upon the obviously lighter frame of PC 305 Hanson, who closed his eyes and looked down and away from the screen in an act of brave defiance.

Robbie felt a hand on the back of his head pulling his hair backwards and forcing his face upwards. Hanson's heart was pounding when he heard the words,

'Nice figure, your Alice?' It was said, almost as a polite enquiry, a considered observation. The impact of those four words had the desired effect as far as the members of the Galloway team were concerned. Hanson opened his eyes and stared at the screen before him. It showed his sister Alice pushing his stricken mother in her wheelchair around the farmhouse garden. As always, Patsy, her adored pet, was lying contentedly on her lap. It had obviously been taken during the hot spell immediately following the August bank holiday weekend. Alice was dressed in red shorts and a black vest that showed off her fit, tanned physique.

There was silence as Hanson tried to come to terms with his situation. He thought about screaming to no one in particular, and about kicking back against his captors. But that would have been absolutely useless.

Robbie Hanson had no control whatsoever of the situation. He did nothing. He didn't need to do anything, as far his captors were concerned. Their job was almost complete. The male who had showed him the picture on the phone neatly placed that same item in Hanson's pocket together with a folded package. As he did so he whispered the words, 'We will be in touch.' It was said not as a threat but as a promise. Robbie Hanson knew immediately that it wasn't the end of his ordeal, merely the beginning.

There was a final push back against the wall as the two henchmen exited the toilets. Hanson locked the cubicle and sat back on the toilet seat. He removed the burner phone from his jacket pocket and, heart still pounding, stared at the picture. With the index finger of his right hand he traced a line across the screen as if he were lightly brushing the hair on his mother's head.

Then Hanson heard footsteps and realised that the toilets had been reopened for business. Now was not the time to study the contents of the package. He unlocked the cubicle door and went to the sink, ignoring anyone present. As he washed his hands Hanson looked up at the mirror. Looking back at him was an ashen face and an abruptly aged individual. He was instantly sober. Hanson noticed a small graze above his right eye, but other than being slightly dishevelled he was physically unscathed.

He walked out of the toilets. No sign of Rudding. 'The little shit has long ago made his exit,' he said to himself.

Some thirty minutes later Hanson had returned to his flat. He hadn't bothered to try and trace his other colleagues in the crowded nightclub. There was something more important he needed to do. It was approaching midnight, and with some trepidation he phoned Alice. The phone rang and rang.

'Al, it's Robbie. You OK?' he said with some urgency in his voice when he finally got an answer.

'What time do you call this?' came the sleepy and slightly annoyed reply from his sister.

'Just checking on you and Mum,' Hanson said. His voice now sounded less urgent after hearing the reassurance of his sister.

'It's after midnight, so you must be pissed. Bugger off, Robbie,' Alice, now awake from her slumber, said vehemently, and she put the phone down.

Hanson took a deep breath. His next call would be to Steve Barker, his sergeant and mentor. Robbie knew he needed to report the matter, and who better than Barker to advise him? Before he did so, Hanson opened the package that had been delivered to him in the nightclub toilets. With trembling hands he unfolded the bundle. The banknotes fell out like confetti, together with a photograph of Patsy and a superimposed gun on the image pointing directly at the dog's head.

There was no message. There didn't need to be.

In an instant an emotional PC Hanson forgot about the planned call to Barker. In his mind his mother's needs dominated priorities.

He was awoken at 8.30 a.m. by a loud ping emanating from the jacket he'd been wearing last night. He removed his newly acquired burner phone and studied the text, which read, *It was a good night, last night, Robbie. Let the fun begin!*

3

Wendy Galloway

And the fun had already begun for Wendy Galloway. She sat back in her study and smiled contentedly. 'Preparation is the key,' she said to herself. It was a mantra that had served her well.

She scanned the photographs on the walls of her special room. There was only one of her late husband and none of her children. Being a mother had been a complete failure, with neither Matt nor Toni having any real purposeful relationship with their mother.

'Look what you have missed, Ted,' she said almost contemptuously as she reflected back to those years when her late husband had launched his small building business, with Wendy in charge of admin. Ted was always on the tools and would do anything to save money. But it was Wendy who drove the business. When Ted died after falling while cutting corners during a roofing job, it wasn't a surprise to Wendy.

Instead of wallowing in grief she took full control. The company had a small, reliable workforce, which she slowly expanded. When she heard that a few of the younger labourers had begun to work the doors at weekends, Galloway's Building Services diversified. Within a few years most nightclubs in Parton city centre employed door staff associated with the Galloways. Those who didn't were greeted with threats and intimidation. With their own door staff in place the Galloway empire then took another important step forward, although outwardly it still operated as a legitimate building company.

Wendy tasked a couple of her most tried and trusted men who were regularly working the doors. It wasn't difficult for them to put the squeeze on a couple of the drug users who were regular nightclub attenders. Use of violence was actively encouraged, and the names of drug suppliers soon followed. Naturally, it wasn't long before Wendy got the supply of the drugs she desired so that she could secure a successful network of distribution via nightclubs. The money then flowed in.

As she approached her fifty-fifth birthday Wendy reflected that she had seen off many younger rivals and wasn't about to give up. The Galloway team maintained a large presence on the doors, and naturally continued to be a major issue for Parton Constabulary.

The name of the person responsible for the assault on Toni had been supplied the following day. Wendy still possessed the necessary contacts on the doors to obtain the intelligence that would enable her to carry out the job she had in mind for Toni's assailant. In addition, the recruitment of police officers had always been an important tactic for Wendy, a fact well noted by both her children.

Some officers were more highly prized than others. PC Bill Rudding was a foot soldier who was rightly regarded by Galloway as a lazy police officer, and someone whose access to the intelligence Wendy required was likely to wane in line with his lethargic career. She needed some foot soldiers and some frontline officers.

Hence the successful recruitment of PC Robbie Hanson.

Galloway's background enquiries had revealed that the young officer was in many ways the opposite of Rudding. He was enthusiastic and hard-working and was currently dedicated to Parton Constabulary. He was everything that Rudding wasn't. Yet, by cleverly using Rudding, Galloway had found out that Hanson was highly thought of and, crucially, was the shift liaison officer for nightclub venues.

The current problems surrounding the health of Hanson's mother were common knowledge among his shift colleagues, and they were also aware that her deterioration had caused Robbie and his sister to consider building work to the farmhouse. Crucially, Hanson could never mention his mother without referring to her beloved dog, Patsy. PC Robbie Hanson was the proverbial open book, and he was always the first to put his name forward for any overtime going. It was Hanson's profile, supplied by Rudding, which convinced Wendy that the officer was worth recruiting. Anyway, Galloway had a particular task in mind for PC Hanson.

Since the first incident at the Dart she had kept up the pressure on Hanson. A few more covertly obtained pictures of Alice or Robbie pushing their wheelchair-bound mother with her faithful terrier were supplied back to Hanson via his gifted non-attributable burner phone. Then came the first direct request from Galloway, with the promise of £1,000. Hanson was to identify a member of the door staff at Lucifer's. Lucifer's was a city centre nightclub that Wendy Galloway was struggling to have any representation. The actual tasking arrived with another menacing picture – this time featuring Patsy, snared in some superimposed basic game trap.

Robbie Hanson was in absolute turmoil. The longer he procrastinated the less likelihood there was of him doing the right thing: going through the official channels and reporting the blackmail attempt.

He returned to his apartment from another visit to the farmhouse and the inevitable argument with Alice over his mother's needs. The money for the alterations was rapidly becoming a necessity.

'Time to bloody do something,' Hanson said to himself. Work had ceased to be the enjoyable focus of his life. He swore inwardly. 'Bloody Rudding.' The mere thought of his name made his skin crawl, but Robbie knew he couldn't avoid Bill Rudding.

***

It was just after 1 p.m. when his burner phoned pinged. This time it was a single picture of his ailing mother and Patsy. Hanson wiped away the tears and had a quick shower before cycling to work.

The 2 p.m. parade was professionally conducted by his mentor, Sergeant Steve Barker. Unusually, there was an absence of wisecracks from Rudding, who Barker hated with a vengeance. Far more worrying was the fact that the young sergeant had recently noticed a distinctively different atmosphere in the parade room. He considered informing his inspector, but Dave Atlee wouldn't be interested. 'Too busy planning his cruise and his retirement do,' Barker said to himself. This was Steve's problem.

In accordance with his new role and responsibilities, Hanson was allocated some nightclub venue visits during the last hour of his shift. Lucifer's was due a visit.

It was 9.30 p.m. when PC 305 Hanson walked into

the venue. 'Coffee, Robbie?' Andy Smeaton asked. He had met the club manager at a couple of Pubwatch meetings.

'No thanks, Andy. I just want to check the incident book and see who you've got on duty,' he said in a professional manner. He scrutinised the book and noted the name of the newly appointed senior supervisor of the door staff. Although he maintained a database, one of the major problems with the developing scheme was that staff moved around the various premises so quickly.

After obtaining the information he needed Hanson returned to the station and completed his shift. 'Good night, Robbie,' Sergeant Steve Barker said as Hanson mounted his cycle, although his young officer appeared distracted as he set off for home at the end of his shift. Hanson hesitated. He stopped his bike, half-dismounted and looked directly at Barker. It was as if he was about to engage with him but then decided otherwise. There was a token nod from his helmeted head before cycling away.

An hour later, in the safety of his apartment, Hanson sent the required information to his blackmailers by means of a text from his new phone. The message was relayed back to Wendy Galloway, who was still in the confines of her study.

'There are bigger things to come, young Robbie,' Wendy said to herself, easing back on her leather swivel chair.

A day later, while off duty, Hanson received instructions to collect his money. A bank transfer would leave a trace. One of Galloway's staff observed Hanson outside any CCTV coverage as he cycled to Admiral Park on the outskirts of the city, which was not one of the most scenic areas, populated as it was by alcoholics and druggies who were too stoned or pissed to notice others around them.

As directed, he collected the hidden envelope. He found it as instructed, behind the only bin located in the remotest part of the park, before making the return journey home. With gloved hands he counted the money. There was no need. It was all present and correct.

Hanson destroyed the envelope. He knew that he would have to provide Alice with a reason for giving her cash for the building work. But he also knew that the cash would be gratefully received with few unwanted questions, such were his mother's circumstances.

4

Kev Stryker and Jonta Roberts

One month later

Outside it was a cold Friday November evening but Wendy Galloway was warm and settled in her study, her mini control room. 'All systems go,' she reminded herself. A glass of gin and tonic was all she needed, other than her own non-attributable phone, which was used strictly for her special operations.

Although there was never a hope in hell that they would be able to confirm the person behind their mission, both Kev Stryker and Jonta Roberts knew the hallmarks of a hit authorised by Wendy Galloway.

They stood together in the small lock-up.

'It's fucking freezing in here.' Kev stated the obvious. It was 9 p.m., and the job was planned for 10 p.m. The timing was crucial. Stryker was wearing his Thinsulate black gloves. He checked and rechecked the Ruger SR40c handgun with the Smith & Wesson ammo. 'Perfect. Fucking perfect,' he repeated to himself. He had collected the paper bag package containing the weapon and ammo earlier that day from a waste bin at the given GPS coordinates.

Stryker had travelled to the destination alone and

had walked the final half-mile, which was out of view of any camera system. Kev Stryker was the chosen one. Not only was he being well paid for the job, but Wendy Galloway had specifically requested his services. Indirectly, of course.

Kev, having burnt the package containing the firearm, was now eulogising over his best ever toy.

'She's a beauty, Jonta, a fucking beauty, son.' Jonta ignored his comments. Stryker's partner in crime was busy with his own preparations.

Kev Stryker was familiar with weapons. It was a natural progression after convictions for assaults, robberies and other offences where extreme violence was the consistent theme. Two other strings to his bow were the athletic build and striking good looks that made him a total winner as far as the local girls were concerned. It was a pleasure that Stryker pursued with some vigour. He was the original Jack the Lad. Outside these interests he was a judo black belt, competent enough to be an instructor in the sport at the local leisure centre.

Kev finally managed to avert his gaze from checking the Ruger handgun and looked across at Jonta Roberts. When Stryker received the request there was only one person he would ever choose as his accomplice.

Roberts was standing astride the red Harley-Davidson 1200 cc Sportster motorcycle. He was as much as an anorak for motors as his good mate Kev Stryker was for firearms. Jonta was a trained mechanic. Committing crimes provided some much-needed added income.

Kev and Jonta had grown up together and had attended the same martial arts club before crime became their drug of choice. Yes, there had been a few hiccups along the way, and Stryker had spent periods of incarceration, which gave him the opportunity to refine his skills, as he learnt much from the experience of other inmates. He did, however, achieve an instructor's qualification in self-defence.

As for Jonta, he had luckily avoided prison by always playing a lesser role in the offences he committed and by readily admitting his involvement at the earliest opportunity. This approach, coupled with a first-appearance guilty plea, had contributed to various non-custodial punishments.

'It's the last chance saloon,' his solicitor kept reminding him.

Although the pair had always remained good mates, Jonta's life was now a complete contrast to Stryker's. He had regular work and a long-term partner – and now a two-year-old daughter. He was dedicated to them both. The thought of custody struck him with fear and panic. He would not only risk losing Gemma, but the thought of not seeing and holding his daughter Kate was unbearable. Jonta was constantly faced with the same dilemma: cash obtained from crime, or the worst scenario … prison.

'We just need the off,' Kev said quietly. He had been informed that they were to await their final instructions, which would arrive at 9.30 p.m. His pay-as-you-go phone illuminated and rang. An unknown caller appeared on the screen.

'Get the fucking phone,' a nervous Jonta said to his close friend.

'He's on at 10 p.m. at Lucifer's, wearing a black North Face fleece, police tabard number 10.' The numbered fluorescent tabards had been purchased and introduced by Parton Constabulary. Little did anyone know that in these circumstances it made the individual as clear as the proverbial sitting duck.

The call ended almost before it began. Kev didn't recognise the caller's voice.

Kev and Jonta knew exactly how long it would take to get to Lucifer's. They knew it would be a city centre job and had therefore pre-planned a route that would take into consideration not only the camera coverage but also any potential automatic number-plate recognition (ANPR) sites. The journey to their destination needed to be at a pace that didn't attract unwanted attention. After the hit, the gun and the burner phone would be deposited in the River Part. The bike and the clothing would be burnt. The costs were all incorporated into the job.

The final checks had been made. After securing the false number plates they placed the dark-coloured crash helmets on their heads and noted the time. It was 9.50 p.m. From head to toe there were absolutely no distinctive marks on their clothing.

No words. They embraced like brothers in arms, then Jonta started up the bike and Kev climbed on board. After a quick time check and a thumbs up they exited the lock-up at 9.53 p.m.

Despite their crash helmets there was a sharp intake of breath as they hit the fresh fair. Jonta was in his element. The traffic was light as they made their way to the target premises. By slowing down and accelerating he anticipated the traffic lights and made perfect time. Travelling at speed would come later, after the deed was done. With his heart beating fast, Kev had one hand tightly around his mate. The other was clasped around the handgun hidden deep inside his clothing.

While the pair stealthily closed on their intended target Wendy Galloway, from her study, checked the time on her phone and immediately sent a text.

Andy Smeaton, Lucifer's manager, had already greeted the reliable Steve Mather as he walked through the door of the nightclub. 'Number ten tonight, Steve. Thanks for turning in,' Smeaton added. He was always grateful to have someone so dependable.

Mather had picked up the number ten fluorescent tabard from the peg in the dirty storeroom at the rear of Lucifer's. He was just beginning his shift, which was due to end around 3 a.m. the following morning, depending on the number of revellers. The soccer-playing medical student at Parton University saw his two-night stint every other weekend as a necessary evil, in that it allowed him the funds to make the most out of student life.

As required, he signed in and noted any other relevant comments in the club's incident book. He had just seen PC Robbie Hanson leaving the premises. That wasn't unusual. He had recognised him as their liaison officer. It was early for Lucifer's in terms of footfall. The club only came alive after 11 p.m. Mather had already boiled the kettle and made himself a strong cup of black coffee in a polystyrene cup. It was probably the only perk of the job. He picked up his small pocket radio that allowed communication between him and the other bouncers and, wearing his North Face fleece underneath the tabard, began to walk through the club to take up his regular spot. 'Just a couple of hours,' he said to himself as he positioned himself just outside the large glass front doors bearing the name *Lucifer's* in large garish purple letters.

Kev and Jonta were now in the city centre, where

there was more traffic around. Jonta was riding more cautiously. The last thing they needed was an accident. Kev felt a vibration in his pocket from the soon-to-be discarded burner phone. 'For fuck's sake,' he shouted to himself. There was supposed to be no contact.

He momentarily removed his hand from Jonta's waist and saw the message of one word – *ABORT* – in capital letters as they turned left into Trent Street, where Lucifer's was located. He reached forward and put a thumbs down sign in front of Jonta's visor. The two continued their journey along Trent Street and passed Lucifer's as Steve Mather was bending down to take a sip of coffee. The nearby cathedral bells had just chimed for ten o'clock.

Meanwhile in the study Wendy drained her glass. 'Good lad, Robbie. Good lad.' She smiled to herself. Their most recent recruit had just passed the ultimate test.

Some twenty-four hours later Kev Stryker and Jonta Roberts had returned to the lock-up. It wasn't their job to ask any questions as to why last night's job was aborted, but the message was clear. The job was back on tonight, and they would receive a confirmation message via the same burner phone.

'Just as well it's bloody worth it,' Stryker said to Jonta as the pair repeated their preparations. Roberts didn't reply. He shivered, and not just because of the cold.

The phone rang, exactly on time. The only alteration to the previous instructions was that the target would be wearing the number five on his tabard.

At 9.53 p.m. they exited the lock-up and followed the same route. Jonta, as careful as ever, manoeuvred the Harley with expert care. They turned into Trent Street.

A few moments previously, Mather was beginning his

second weekend shift at Lucifer's. That night he had been allocated tabard number five. He repeated last night's signing-in process and walked outside to take up his position. Steve took a long, slow sip of his strong black coffee and spilt a few drops down the front of his tabard. He looked up at the cathedral clock as it began its 10 p.m. chimes. 'Just another five hours,' Mather said to himself and sighed.

Jonta slowed the bike as it crossed to the opposite side of the road at the same time as Kev was withdrawing the gun from inside his clothing. He had seen their target standing with his back to them and clearly displaying the number five on his vest.

They approached Lucifer's as the young, fit student was placing his coffee on the ground. 'Perfect,' said Stryker to himself. The target wasn't looking and wasn't prepared. As Mather stood upright, and from a distance of only five metres, Kev gave him three rounds, all to the head. He was keen to minimise firing the ammo as it left more potential evidence, in the form of discarded cartridges, at the scene. Fleetingly Kev Stryker saw the impact of discharging the weapon as Mather collapsed, poleaxed, and deflating like a pricked balloon. But not before the debris of his brain were splattered across the purple lettering of Lucifer's glass doors.

Steve Mather had been obliterated.

'Go, Jonta, fucking go,' Stryker screamed at his partner as the Harley's front wheel momentarily rose from the tarmac. They literally took off and Stryker held on for dear life. He had immediately replaced the weapon along with the burner phone back inside his clothing ready for the prearranged disposal.

They would not have noticed PC Robbie Hanson

who, some 100 metres further along Trent Street, had stopped in his tracks with his head dropped down and his chin on his chest. He knew immediately the consequences of that night's tasking by Wendy Galloway.

He then looked skywards, with tears streaming down his face. He could only visualise his mother's face. 'Why Mam, why?' he said, almost blaming his mother for his desperate actions. For the second consecutive night he was the nearest officer to the scene, but Hanson did nothing. Young Robbie was paralysed by his circumstances.

At the same time Jonta was speeding away from the crime, making his way towards the River Part and totally ignoring the background noise of the sirens, which faded as the pair continued their escape away from the city centre and joined a single-track road adjacent to the river. The route had also been carefully planned, although they both knew that it was virtually impossible not to have been captured on a camera system somewhere. Jonta again slowed the machine to allow Kev to throw the small handgun into the fast-flowing water.

Stryker repeated his earlier instructions. 'Fucking go, Jonta, go.'

They sped off again, then around half a mile along the road they repeated the exercise. This time the burner phone entered the water with a small splash and some accompanying ripples. Kev smiled to himself. The river was swollen due to the recent heavy rain, a fact that would create significant difficulties for any subsequent search operation. Despite there being no one around, the noise of both objects hitting the water appeared deafening to them.

So far so good, thought Jonta as they observed the river long enough to see both items disappear.

'Let's go,' Kev said, in an altogether calmer tone.

The pair continued their journey. They had been travelling for some fifteen minutes before Jonta made a sharp right turn onto a small track that gave access to remote woodland adjacent to Gerard Country Park, which was located some six miles from the city centre. They travelled directly to their destination and began to remove the branches and foliage to uncover Jonta's Honda CB1100 RS, which tonight – naturally – was displaying another set of false plates. In total silence they removed a change of clothing from a rucksack attached to the handlebars of their getaway bike.

No more than five minutes later Kev looked back over his right shoulder to see the night sky reflecting the fire burning away the evidence of their horrific crime.

'My fucking Harley…' Jonta was almost visibly upset at having to destroy such a treasured item.

'Shut the fuck up, Jonta,' Kev said, and grinned.

There would be no contact with their 'employer' which could lead to a trail of evidence that the police could exploit. Kev and Jonta knew that their reward was guaranteed. The job had been authorised by Wendy Galloway, and they would receive the necessary instructions for claiming their bounty.

***

It was 10.30 p.m. Wendy Galloway was only to be contacted if there was a problem. Naturally, she was in her study. The clock mounted on the wall told her that the shooting had been a success. The local news in the morning would confirm that the job had gone as planned.

'That will show them. An old-style nightclub hit,' Wendy said contentedly to herself, as the victim Steve

Mather lay dead on the streets of Parton city centre. He had been a law-abiding individual who had never received even a parking ticket. Welcome to the world of Wendy Galloway.

At the same time as a very smug Wendy Galloway retired to bed with a satisfied grin across her elegant features, Detective Chief Inspector Trish Delaney, the on-call senior investigation officer, was contacted. It was the nightmare phone call from the control room. A drive-by shooting in the city centre with one fatality is probably the worst news, even for the most experienced SIO.

Delaney was just recovering from the stress and anxiety of Operation PROOF, and now this, with all the hallmarks of a gangland job.

5

Geoff Sutton

Pressure was mounting for Parton Constabulary following the shooting. No early arrests and a whole host of media hype.

'No story unless it's a bad story,' said Geoff Sutton to himself while munching on his toast, which was coated with peanut butter. Unusually, he had tuned into a local radio station. He still needed to keep updated on another high-profile Parton Constabulary investigation. He remained a very dedicated employee and couldn't help himself.

'I'm off, love.' Sutton gave Debbie a long embrace to accompany a lingering kiss, before reluctantly heading to work at the police headquarters based in the city centre.

Sutton stood rather than sat in the waiting area of the chief constable's office. It was a cold November Wednesday morning, some four days since the nightclub shooting at Lucifer's. He was early for the appointment. Unusually, he had considered wearing a suit. But, if he were to lose his job, what did it matter? No, it was his normal mode of dress: plain shirt and dark chinos. Naturally his green Barbour was hanging over his right arm. As far as the former detective chief inspector was concerned it was his uniform, his identity. Even in his current role of civilian support officer, Sutton's approach to police work remained unchanged.

While he waited Sutton briefly thought about last Saturday's poor round of golf, which he had played with his lifelong friends Pete McIntyre and Stew Grant. Yes, the three of them had had their ups and downs. It was only natural. Pete and his family had moved away for a couple of years and had lost contact without a word being said about their move, but after a surprise return to the area and a quick catch-up it was if he'd never been away. Stew had dropped out of the group when he first met Tina, who seemed to dominate his every move. Then as a couple they had admirably embarked on fostering. Inevitably, this had brought along understandable problems when one of their protégés was either detained in some police station or had absconded to another part of the country. But throughout these trials and tribulations their friendship had survived and was stronger now than ever. There had been a fourth member of their group, and the recent loss of Roger Strong dominated their conversations.

'Roger stories,' Sutton said, quietly lamenting his friend. 'Why, oh why, Rog?' he asked himself repeatedly. The late Roger Strong had tragically taken his own life. Sutton, Pete and Stew had their own real problems in coming to terms with the fact that none of them had been able to recognise any signs of Roger's mental frailties. He was so missed, and their own recriminations remained.

Sutton smiled to himself as his mind kept wandering back to the previous Saturday. After golf, their day had continued as normal when they had gone to their beloved Upper Parton RFC to witness another home league win. A few beers afterwards made for a near perfect day. Particularly as Sutton ended the evening in the arms of Debbie, who had recently moved into his house on the Springfield Estate – another significant development in their relationship. Sutton was rapidly coming to the conclusion that life without Debbie was becoming unthinkable. He briefly thought back to that lingering kiss.

'I love her. I really do,' Sutton said to himself, almost in a trance-like state. He stood still and stopped his daydreaming when reality and his current surroundings returned, like the first surge from an injection following the plunge of a needle.

Sutton had been summoned before the chief constable. He believed the appointment was because of Operation PROOF, the police response to a series of violent robberies on the elderly. Ultimately the operation had proved successful. However, as part of the investigation there had been a misguided deployment of a young probationer constable, Dominic Charlton. It had initially been Sutton's idea, even though the final authorisation had come by the way of Assistant Chief Constable Ron Turner, who had already had in his own words, received the bollocking of his life from Mayling. Sutton was under the impression that the Charlton issue, together with more reported austerity measures, was the reason behind his appointment with the chief constable. His final goodbye to Parton Constabulary beckoned.

Margaret, the chief constable's secretary, approached him. 'Geoff, the chief will see you now.' She used his Christian name because they had known each other for years. Margaret was the second longest-serving member of Parton Constabulary and had joined the force a month after Sutton. He paused at the chief's door momentarily. Despite his length of service he was extremely nervous. You only ever attended this office as a result of a promotion, or for a private briefing on some secret intelligence. Despite his apprehension he knocked firmly.

'Come in.' Geoff got a very confident reply. Chris Mayling had now been in post for nearly two years. Her assignment from the Home Office, to restore confidence in Parton Constabulary after Operation TRUST, had rapidly been recognised as an inspired decision. The former Met officer had made a considerable impression on the force and had made some key appointments, most notably Ron Turner's promotion to assistant chief constable. A distinct improvement in force morale had led to an overall reduction in crime and a recent significant increase in public confidence, partly due to the recent success of Operation PROOF.

Mayling, in full uniform, rose from behind her desk and greeted Sutton with a warm handshake. 'Good to see you again, Geoff. Please take a seat,' she said brightly. She cut an attractive, slim figure and her hair was tightly pulled back, revealing kind but also determined features. According to Sutton's sources down south, Mayling had risen through the ranks the hard way. Not for her had there been any accelerated promotion. A two-year probation and a first-time failure at the sergeant's exam had only hardened her ambition. It was the only blemish on a career that had taken her through the ranks with roles as senior investigating officer and borough commander before reaching the pinnacle of her career.

'Thank you, ma'am,' Sutton said respectfully. Al-though she was known for being personal Sutton firmly believed that it was the end of his career. But this was a million miles away from the introduction he had expected.

'Geoff, we have a significant problem,' Mayling said. The word *we* was emphasised, despite the fact that he was technically a non-operational civilian support staff member who was currently working reduced hours. 'It is a problem that could bring us national headlines again, and for all the wrong reasons,' Mayling continued, as a deep frown appeared on her forehead. 'The fallout would cause significant embarrassment to the force and a massive blow to public confidence. It is the last thing we need, particularly after the embarrassment of Operation TRUST.' The chief constable had again emphasised the word *we*.

There was a quiet knock on the door. Without any invitation Margaret appeared, carrying a tray of coffee. After she placed the cafetière, cups and milk on the table she gave Sutton a sly wink before making her exit. 'What she doesn't know isn't worth knowing,' Sutton, momentarily distracted by Margaret's appearance, said to himself. Geoff wondered where the hell this conversation was now going as Mayling poured coffee for them both.

She then took a deep breath and focused her eyes on Sutton. So far there had been no mention whatsoever of Operation PROOF and the misguided deployment of the young cop. Certainly, there was no sign whatsoever of him being 'encouraged' to resign.

'Geoff are you aware of Operation RESOLVE, the name of the investigation dealing with the recent drive-by shooting of Steve Mather in the city centre last Saturday night?' This was Sutton's first day back to work following Operation PROOF and Roger's funeral, but he would have had to become a Trappist monk not to have seen and heard the subsequent media coverage of the incident.

'I am, and it has all the hallmarks of an organised hit,' Geoff said with some confidence. 'Wendy Galloway is always the prime suspect. As a force we have tried and failed repeatedly to get her convicted and to do some decent time,' he added, with some personal disappointment.

'Well, I'm still catching up with the history, but some intelligence has been brought to my attention by Assistant Chief Constable Ron Turner that causes some serious additional concern,' Mayling said firmly. 'Among the deluge of reports we have received follow-ing the incident there is an item that stands out. We have an anonymous report that a police officer is supplying intelligence to Galloway. He or she is on Galloway's payroll, and apparently a serving officer was involved in the shooting.'

Sutton's expression didn't alter. 'You're not surprised, Geoff?' Mayling asked.

'I'm not, ma'am. Shame it's anonymous,' he said, with some scepticism. 'I'm not sure what sort of credence we should give to this intel. You always get these reports with incidents such as this,' Sutton added, speaking from personal experience.

'You do.' Mayling nodded her head in agreement, 'But we need to know if there is any substance in this claim, given the potential damage this could do to the force if there is an involvement from within.'

Sutton started to dig. 'Does the intel give the name of the officer concerned?'

'No, but we are making some discreet background enquiries. We need to keep this really tight. Trish

Delaney, as SIO, is obviously aware, as are Ron Turner and me...'

Mayling paused. 'Now, the reason I have briefed you with what we have so far is that I want you to take this forward. You will report directly to ACC Turner. You can't do this on your own, though. Who do you want as your partner?' Mayling asked, already predicting that Sutton's answer would be a formality.

'Detective Sergeant Jo Firth,' Sutton replied immediately, without considering the implications of his new assignment.

'Not a problem. I will get Ron to sort that out,' Mayling said. 'Geoff, I need to know if this is going to come back to bite us. And I need to know quickly,' she added finally.

Sutton walked out of his short briefing with the chief, his mind in a state of confusion. 'What the hell have I done now?' he said to himself. He knew full well that this could develop into another highly stressful investigation that he really didn't need, nor did he have to involve himself. After all, he was a civilian investigator, not the detective chief inspector of former years... Yet recently Operations TRUST and PROOF had both seen him play significant roles.

'Get a grip of yourself, Sutton,' he said to himself. 'The chief constable has asked you, and there was never a single doubt about how you would respond.' He hadn't even consulted Debbie. Because he had his head down Sutton was unaware that ACC Ron Turner, the man who had recommended to Mayling that Sutton's involvement in Operation RESOLVE was essential, was approaching him.

'I've contacted Jo Firth, Geoff,' Turner said confidently.

Typical, thought Sutton. There wasn't a hint of any introductory small talk. Knowing Sutton well, Turner had already second-guessed Geoff's reaction to the chief's request. 'Brief me tomorrow at 5 p.m. in my office,' Ron Turner continued as he walked in the direction of his office. Sutton saw him disappear. He was as immaculately dressed as ever in his normal style of dark pinstripe suit, white shirt and, on this occasion, a deep red tie. Geoff noted that Turner didn't walk. It was more of a march.

Sutton's phone rang. It was Jo Firth. 'Hi Geoff, what time are we meeting?' she asked in a professional tone.

'Half an hour in the canteen,' Sutton said instantly. He checked his watch and immediately punched in Debbie's name under his contacts. She had now become such an important person in his life – his first real relationship since the tragic death of his wife following a prolonged cancer battle. Their only child, Maggie, currently lived in London, and was delighted that Dad had finally fallen in love again.

Not that it had been plain sailing. They had met when Sutton had frequented the Parlour Cafe, which was owned by Debbie. She had recently broken free from an abusive relationship and had promised herself that men were a thing of the past...

And then she had met Geoff Sutton. While the scars of Debbie's past had proved a major hurdle to overcome, some recent successful counselling had enabled them to move forward to the point where Debbie, despite her previous thoughts about the male species, had moved into Sutton's comfortable semi only last Friday.

'Hello, gorgeous. How did it go?' asked Debbie, referring to Sutton's earlier meeting.

'Hi, Debbie. She never mentioned Operation

PROOF, but she wants me to investigate some intelligence regarding the shooting at the weekend,' Sutton replied. 'I could have some long work hours coming, depends on how things work out,' he added.

'All that matters to me, Geoff, is that you keep yourself safe,' Debbie said without prompting, not realising how important her words were to become.

'I will, Debbie. I love you,' Sutton replied. It was a totally natural response from Sutton as he ended the call.

He paused for a moment and then realised that it was the first time he had told Debbie he loved her.

6

Jo Firth

Sutton walked into the force's canteen and scanned the area. It had once been a busy venue, buzzing with officers on various training courses, but was now a rarely used facility. The training department had suffered more than most from the recent and ongoing austerity measures. Now only those on probationers' courses frequented the facility, and that was only when the force was recruiting.

He saw Jo Firth sitting on her own, studying her phone. He sighed with relief when he noticed that there were two mugs on the table. It saved him trying to operate the coffee machine, which was a step too far for someone with Sutton's lack of practical capabilities. Firth looked up as he approached.

'Coffee, Geoff? Milk, no sugar, as I recall,' Firth said politely as she pushed the white mug towards him. It was half a question from the detective sergeant, but Firth had guessed correctly.

Sutton smiled as he took a seat. 'She always had the ability to dress down,' Geoff thought to himself, noting her simple black trouser suit and plain flat shoes.

'This could be seriously bad news for the force,' Sutton said, after briefing Firth. Not that there was a great deal for him to update her on. They were only armed with the anonymous report of a police officer supplying intelligence for Wendy Galloway. That same individual was on her payroll and would have been directly involved in the shooting.

'Mud never sticks to Wendy,' Firth said, and sighed. She was yet another officer with first-hand experience of a failed Galloway enquiry.

It took them only ten minutes to decide on a course of action. Firth went to the incident room to glean information about the current state of the investigation at first hand while Sutton went to the complaints department, which was known as professional standards. Having worked previously in the department, Sutton knew they had a large amount of Galloway intelligence that had police links. The rank-and-file officers who sailed close to the wind always looked upon the department with some degree of suspicion.

Sutton stood in front of the forbidding grey door. The words *Professional Standards*, displayed in large white letters, clearly announced the name of the department. He ignored the keypad, which had been placed on the door for added security, and rang the bell. Shaun Adams, the department's long-serving secretary, answered after reviewing Sutton's well-known image on the CCTV camera above the entrance.

'Hi, Geoff. The boss was expecting you. ACC Turner has been on the phone. I've got what you need,' Shaun said enthusiastically, shaking Sutton's hand as if he'd just won the lottery.

'Good to see you, Shaun,' Sutton said, as he followed Adams to an empty interview room with a single computer terminal. The walls of the room were lined with boring dark brown soundproof panels. It had no atmosphere whatsoever and was often used to formally question officers who had fallen under suspicion.

Sutton placed his Barbour over the chair and logged on with a new secure password that had been supplied by Shaun. This enabled him to gain access to the department's stand-alone intelligence system.

A couple of hours later, two cups of warm filter coffee supplied by Shaun were the only evidence of his endeavours. He had formed the impression that there were more intel reports on Wendy Galloway than on Al Capone. He was able to discount most of the historic stuff and some apparently meaningless sightings.

For example, this had been reported by a traffic officer: *At 5.30 p.m. on 5/6/2017 saw Galloway single-crewed in her blue Land Rover cruiser, GAL 55.*

No doubt an officer eager to hit his target for intel sightings, Sutton thought about the reporting officer.

Such was Galloway's supreme confidence that she would never be caught, a personalised number plate was merely a show of complete arrogance towards the authorities. But repeated stops had caused Wendy to abandon identifiable plates, and she opted for pool cars as her preferred mode of transport.

Then something that caught his eye. It was a short report on an investigation concerning PC Bill Rudding, who was currently posted to A relief in the city centre.

It had begun with the receipt of an anonymous report of Rudding, while off duty, being involved in a city centre fight during early January of that year. The report had come to professional standards, who initially studied Rudding's previous history. It didn't make good reading. He had a record of three unsubstantiated complaints within the past twelve months. All three had a common theme: excess violence during arrest. Rudding's prisoners had sustained minor fractures. Fortunately for the officer the complainants were unaccompanied, all had previous convictions and were drunk at the time, making any subsequent statements unreliable.

'This is more like it…' Sutton looked further into Rudding's file to examine another three anonymous reports of Rudding being associated with Wendy Galloway.

Sutton's scrutiny was interrupted by the head of department, Chief Superintendent John Dexter, who had entered the room. There was no knock. Dexter had a rank and an attitude to go with it. In his current role he had regular contact with the chief constable and her team.

Sutton always thought that Dexter acted with a certain amount of arrogance and that he was a frustrated chief officer. He was probably right. Ron Turner's surprise promotion had hit Dexter hard. He always considered himself the next in line for the post of assistant chief constable. John Dexter had become a bitter man.

'Geoff, you might like to look at this.' Dexter handed over a buff folder marked *STRICTLY CONFIDENTIAL* in red lettering. There was no handshake or small talk. As Sutton studied the contents he realised that it again concerned Bill Rudding. On Dexter's authority, professional standards had undertaken a proactive investigation into the officer.

It began with some discreet enquiries with the federation office, where it became known that Constable Rudding was the proverbial pain in the arse. He was always making formal complaints about his supervision regarding shift changes, staffing levels and the allocation of overtime. Cleverly, he had a sickness record, mostly self-manufactured, that, due to timescales and police regulations, only just avoided further investigation and him being placed on half-pay. These were some of the common issues that typically arise from a disgruntled officer.

The investigation into Rudding's conduct developed by way of background profile enquiries. The purpose was to ascertain whether he had assets above and beyond what would be expected from a cop with nine years' service. The fact that nothing was found only increased suspicion. Finally, the department undertook a week's surveillance on the officer, which was a resource-intensive exercise. Again, nothing was found to justify further use of their resources, and Rudding's investigation was held on file.

Sutton was impressed by the thoroughness of the enquiry, given that the intel provided was anonymous. 'What do you think, sir?' Sutton asked Dexter respectfully, as he closed the folder.

'I think Rudding is a real headache for the force and will continue to be until the day he retires, but so far we have found nothing to suggest he's become corrupt. Sadly, there are a few of them about,' Dexter said.

Dexter took the Rudding folder and exited the interview room. He was very much in the Ron Turner mould: smartly dressed and always wearing a collar and tie to match a high-quality suit. He was known throughout the force for his love of fast cars and his office was filled with Grand Prix photos, a hobby he followed all over the world. He currently drove a newly purchased top-of-the-range black BMW X5 that was large enough for the family and his fishing equipment and was fast enough to fulfil his passion.

Sutton thanked Shaun for his hospitality before leaving the department. He and Firth were due to meet up mid-afternoon.

***

Since accepting their roles, Turner had allocated Sutton and Firth a small office at the force's headquarters. The fact that the room was on the same floor as the command suite reflected the importance of their task. One large desk, a force computer terminal and a couple of chairs were the only furniture. Turner had insisted on a secure keypad lock and had texted them both with the relevant code.

It was around 3 p.m. when they met up at their new office. Firth had managed to find a spare kettle from her CID office while Sutton had managed to sweet-talk the canteen staff into letting him borrow some mugs when he purchased coffee and milk.

Armed with coffees, the two discussed the information from their morning's work. Sutton began. He had identified a possible in PC Bill Rudding, who was stationed in the city centre and disillusioned with the job. There was more than one report of him being connected with Galloway and, even though they were anonymous, there were some indications that they came from separate sources from the manner in which they had been forwarded to the police.

'I've just done a little more digging, Jo.' Sutton was finishing his summing-up. Like a barrister in court he momentarily paused for effect, saving his best to last. 'Bill Rudding was on duty the night that Steve Mather was shot.' He looked directly across at his partner.

'I recognise Rudding's name from somewhere, Geoff.

Just can't place where at the moment.' Firth looked up at the ceiling as if seeking some divine assistance before providing Sutton with a report from the Mather murder incident room. 'Trish Delaney's really got her hands full on this one. Nothing forensic. Only a couple of bullet casings, some CCTV, and a host of anonymous intelligence claiming that Galloway was responsible. But not a shred of evidence to connect her to the crime. Background enquiries show that Mather had no criminal connections whatsoever. He was a lovely lad, a student earning some pocket money,' she said, frowning.

Firth's face then lightened. 'However, I have studied the CCTV and extended the search as the motorcycle left the scene. The closest officer to the incident is a PC Robbie Hanson. He is one those recently appointed nightclub premises liaison officers. The investigation team have got what they believe to be an identical motorcycle, albeit bearing different plates, completing a dry run the night before. The same time and route. And another thing: PC Robbie Hanson is again close to the scene.'

'I know Hanson from Upper Parton Rugby Club. Not a bad player, and I've heard a few people say he's making a good impression as a young cop,' Sutton added.

Firth took a large mouthful of coffee, 'There are two things I don't understand. If it is the same people on the bike, and it certainly looks likely, why would Galloway risk a dry run? And also, is it just coincidence that Hanson makes an appearance on both nights?' She looked directly at Sutton, who immediately remembered why she had been his first choice of partner after their experience during Operation PROOF. 'She always asks bloody good questions,' he said to himself.

'In his role Hanson would have good reason to be

there.' It was a statement from Sutton, and not a question.

Firth, looking directly at him, came straight back. 'On consecutive nights? Lucifer's isn't the only nightclub he has responsibility for. Plus…' Firth momentarily hesitated. 'He didn't call it in, Geoff,' she said emphatically, her eyes never leaving Sutton's.

There was a prolonged silence between them before Sutton spoke. 'Hanson needs eliminating, as does Rudding, who's a continual problem to the force. Even if we don't find a link from our enquiries into the shooting, we might find something that puts PC Rudding on a firm discipline route,' Sutton said.

He glanced across at Firth. She was a dedicated officer with a conscience that allowed her to immediately know right from wrong. Although he had never worked with her prior to Operation PROOF, Sutton's many force contacts had provided excellent references for the forty-five-year-old divorced detective sergeant.

Firth returned his glance. 'Fancy another coffee, Geoff?' she asked as she drained her cup.

'Not for me,' Sutton said, as Firth made herself another drink. Drinking multiple cups of coffee was a coping mechanism to hide an ongoing illness. Other than professional counsellors, Firth's sister was the only person who was aware of her battle with alcoholism. The bottle of vodka she had kept next to the toothpaste in her bathroom cabinet had been thrown out some ten years previously.

A couple of hours later, after a visit to the force's personnel department, they were sitting in what was often referred to as the lion's den, facing ACC Ron Turner in his office. Here there was no hint of any coffee being offered, and his desk was immaculate as ever – no sign of notes, files or paper. Turner operated a total clear desk policy.

Sutton expertly summed up their investigation while Firth looked on. Turner's face changed only once, when Sutton mentioned the fact that PC Robbie Hanson appeared on CCTV footage on consecutive nights. It was Sutton using the phrase *going forward* that caused Turner to lean forward in his chair, as if there was ever a chance that he was going to miss some important detail.

Their proposals were simple. Although it had proved negative previously, lifestyle surveillance on Rudding might provide some crucial evidence, particularly if he was involved in the recent shooting. His previous history would guarantee the authorisation, which Turner was more than happy to sign. Furthermore, they would look at Rudding's finances, to view any recent suspicious activity. As for Robbie Hanson, he needed to be either eliminated or implicated, and a complete profile was required.

Turner ended their meeting. 'Thanks for that. Just thinking about the surveillance, I think we should use a team from Borrington. It will assist the integrity of the operation. I will try and get Rory Lomas and his team, who worked for us on Operation TRUST,' Turner said, thinking out loud.

Borrington was the neighbouring force to Parton, and it wasn't unusual for them to call upon each other for mutual aid. 'I will brief the chief. Meet tomorrow around the same time. I will require an update,' he said with authority.

7

Stew Grant and Pete McIntyre

It was gone 6.30 p.m. when Sutton left Parton HQ, his hands dug deep in the pockets of his coat. *Winter is rapidly approaching*, he thought, hunching his shoulders as protection against the cold. On his way home Sutton made a short stop at the golf club to meet with Pete McIntyre and Stew Grant. It was a regular Wednesday evening get-together. There was only thing – or, in this case, one person – missing: the late Roger Strong.

The purpose of the golf club meeting was a quick pint, some chat, and the main objective – to put their names down for Saturday morning's club competition. Saturday was their day: a round of golf, then down to watch the rugby at their club, Upper Parton RFC. A few beers around their table … what could be better?

Some ten minutes later they were discussing Roger Strong's recent funeral. Sutton's phone rang. He ignored the call, as he was leading the conversation about Roger's first rugby tour. Stew ended the story with the time-honoured phrase, 'What goes on tour stays on tour.'

The three of them finished their drinks and left the club as always in fits of laughter, but not before securing a 9 a.m. tee-off time on Saturday. Significantly for Pete, Stew and Geoff, it was the inaugural playing of the Roger

Strong Cup, a three-person team event in memory of their great friend. While driving back alone their laughter abruptly ended. All three were still haunted by the guilt surrounding Roger's death.

Once he was safely home, Pete McIntyre began the pre-read for his mental health counsellor's course, which was due to start the next evening. Later that year Stew Grant would be an attendee at his first session after qualifying. He was having similar issues.

Tina, Stew's wife, had decided that enough was enough. 'You need professional help,' she had said. The 3 a.m. nightmares were becoming a regular occurrence for her husband. Stew had promised Tina that he would seek counselling as the guilt concerning the circumstances of Roger's death, rather than fading, just became more acute.

Some fifteen minutes later Geoff Sutton arrived home. He'd forgotten about his earlier missed call. A bottle of an Australian Shiraz was strategically placed on the kitchen island next to two glasses. After so much time living alone Sutton didn't recognise the smell of home cooking.

'Dinner will be in ten minutes, Geoff.' Debbie turned from the oven and walked towards him wearing an old flowered apron – which, due to its age and condition, Sutton rightly guessed must have belonged to Maria, his late wife. This caused him to hesitate as Debbie approached.

The hesitation was only momentary. Her gorgeous eyes were dancing as she drew closer. He could smell the perfume that permeated her hair. She kissed and held him close, before she drew back. 'Enough of that, young Sutton. Pour the wine,' Debbie said. Geoff did as he was told, like an obedient student on his first day at school.

The lasagne washed down with the wine was punctuated by the experiences of the day. The time they spent together passed so very quickly. The conversation between them resembled the banter between eager adolescents, not the serious discussions that might be expected of people of their age. Sutton's phone rang. He chose to ignore the call. His priority was Debbie, and he was engrossed in a story concerning one of her Parlour Cafe regulars.

While Sutton was enjoying the perfect evening, Sergeant Steve Barker was having one of those late shifts he wanted to forget. 'What next?' he said to himself.

His career as a constable had begun with the trauma of Operation TRUST. Despite the upheaval caused to the force Barker had excelled on a personal basis, and it had proved to be an excellent grounding when it came to promotion boards. After passing the necessary exams and gaining his sergeant's stripes he was posted to A relief in the city centre. His potential for further promotions was emphasised during Operation PROOF.

'Why did I pass those bloody exams?' Barker continued moaning to no one as he sat alone in the shift sergeant's office.

His current 2 p.m. to 10 p.m. duty began dealing with another messy complaint concerning Bill Rudding. He managed to get the matter informally resolved, mainly because the complainant was so unreliable. The injured person was a habitual drug user with numerous convictions for theft. Steve summed up his investigation by saying, 'Yet another Rudding case of unnecessary violence on arrest.'

Barker really wished that the allegation would stick

but the complainant had changed her account and failed to attend prearranged meetings on three separate occasions, making the whole process a meaningless paper exercise. It would require an inspector's signature, but it had reached the stage where Dave Atlee merely endorsed his comments. Steve even doubted if he would actually read through his report. Barker sighed deeply, frustrated that there wasn't a different outcome, one where he could have alerted professional standards. Like many others within the organisation, he hated everything about Bill Rudding.

He turned up the volume of his Airwaves radio. 'Sarge, supervision requested to attend an unexplained death on The Counties estate…'

Barker was on his way.

At the scene he found a deceased twenty-one-year-old female who had been found in the bath, and one of his probationer officers being sick in the toilet. The experienced tutor constable outlined the circumstances to Barker.

No forced entry, a sad background of mental health issues and a note, presumably written by the deceased. Baker confirmed the thoughts of the tutor constable, who quite rightly had asked supervision to attend.

Barker updated the control room before returning to the station, where he hoped to grab a coffee. 'No suspicious circumstances. An unexplained death.'

He parked the supervision car in the allocated bay. For a moment he considered hanging the supervision car keys on the vacant peg, just on the off-chance that Inspector Dave Atlee required transport. He thought again and put the keys back in his pocket. Atlee never ventured out. Nature called and Barker walked through to the toilets.

'You're a bastard, Rudding.' Robbie Hanson's face was white as a sheet. He had one hand gripped around Rudding's throat and had pushed the back of his head hard against the toilet wall. Rudding's face was the opposite colour to Hanson's and was deeply flushed. His wide eyes were staring at his aggressor. Yet although Rudding was powerless against the young, muscular athleticism of Hanson he was still able to talk. He always could.

'Piss off, Hanson. Piss off,' Rudding spat back at him.

Barker was rooted to the spot, unable to believe what he was seeing in front of him. But the moment of inaction didn't last. He grabbed Hanson's arm and expertly pulled it down, back and behind the young officer's back in a well-practised move that had been finessed in the many hours of tedious self-defence classes he had attended. Hanson immediately relaxed his aggression as Rudding coughed loudly before recovering. 'Do him, Sarge. Fucking do him,' he repeated.

'Rudding, my office now,' Barker said, without shouting and in a controlled voice, as he released his grip on Robbie Hanson. Bill Rudding, without uttering another word, walked out of the toilets.

'Robbie, what the—?' Barker began. He hated bad language but, given what he had witnessed, he was momentarily at a total loss how to continue the conversation.

'I'm sorry, Sarge. I'm so sorry,' was the only reply Hanson could muster as he looked down and tried to avoid his sergeant's gaze.

'Look, Robbie, are you all right?' Barker said with empathy. He instantly knew it was a stupid question. Barker knew Hanson well enough by now. Something was radically wrong with the young officer, who had become a shadow of his former self over the past couple of months.

Robbie refused to look up at his sergeant and kept his hands defensively behind his back like a schoolboy receiving a bollocking from the head teacher. Without any response from Hanson, Barker had to act. 'Go home now. Take some time off. I will cover that and will ring you later,' Barker said, recovering some composure, but not having a clue as to how to deal with this scenario.

Hanson turned on his heel and, careful to avoid any shift colleagues, made off to the locker room.

'That was the easy part,' said Barker to himself, as he made his way back to the office to deal with Rudding.

Through the open door he saw Bill Rudding, looking as slovenly as ever, slouched in the seat opposite his desk. He had quickly recovered from his encounter with Hanson. Even before his sergeant had closed the door and sat down Bill Rudding had started his agenda.

'What are you going to do with him? He's bloody mad.' Rudding was on the attack and wasn't about to stop. 'You witnessed the assault,' he continued, deliberately rubbing his neck to increase any potential bruising. 'And I am willing to be photographed.'

Rudding was quick to realise what he considered to be an opportunity while Barker looked down at his desk and desperately played for time, time that would give him options. The buff folder marked *CONFIDENTIAL* in red looked back up at him as if returning his gaze. It contained the recently resolved informal complaint against Bill Rudding, which he knew should have been locked away securely. His mind had been distracted when he had responded to the recent high-priority incident.

'Bill, you need to think very carefully. I couldn't persuade this one to go away,' Barker said, making a direct reference to the most recent complaint against the officer. Steve said the words, feigning concern, as he looked down to the folder in front of him.

'Bollocks. She's bloody crackers.' Rudding made the condescending remark towards the absent complain-ant. Typically, he gave absolutely no indication of his guilt or otherwise.

'There's an independent witness, Bill,' Barker said, although this was a lie. He was desperately thinking on his feet and hoping, more than anything, that Rudding wasn't secretly taping his remarks. Surprisingly, Rudding said nothing in response. He was obviously considering Barker's response and the implications. Both of them knew that taking the matter to their respective supervision in the form of Inspector Dave Atlee was a complete waste of time. Steve Barker ran the shift.

'I'm going to speak to the federation,' Rudding eventually said and stormed out of the sergeant's office, rubbing his neck and slamming the door behind him. It was a typical response from Rudding, but it did give Barker time. He would use it wisely. A relief were due two days off at the end of this shift.

Their tour of duty had ended when Steve Barker first rang Geoff Sutton. He rang again at 10.30 p.m. There was no reply on either occasion, despite him having requested Sutton to return his call on the second attempt. Barker had specially chosen Sutton. The experience of working with him during Operations TRUST and PROOF had made him the go-to person as far as Barker and work issues were concerned. The respect was mutual.

***

The following morning Sutton was woken by his alarm. It was 7 a.m. He looked over, but Debbie had already gone. The opening times of the Parlour Cafe varied, but today it was a 6.30 a.m. start. Thursday was always busy, and an early start was necessary to prepare the breakfast orders for the building contractors working on the estate.

Sutton knew he had a long day ahead. He studied his phone. It was highly unusual for him not to return missed calls at the earliest opportunity, but the events of the previous night had overtaken him. He saw two missed calls from Steve Barker. He listened to the message from the second call. There was an urgency in the request to call him back and Sutton responded immediately, ignoring the time.

'Steve, I'm sorry. I've just picked up your message,' he said sympathetically.

'Geoff, can we meet asap? But not in a police building,' Barker said in an urgent tone. He had hardly slept the night before. Although Sutton was due to meet Firth, after she had briefed the surveillance team, he instantly recognised the urgency in Barker's voice.

'What about the Costa at the retail park?' Sutton asked the young sergeant.

'Thirty minutes,' came Barker's immediate reply.

Barker was already in the cafe when Sutton arrived. He had ordered tea and a blueberry muffin for him and a coffee for Sutton. They shook hands. *Barker has a presence*, thought Sutton. Even though the twenty-eight-year-old looked stressed, the slight bags under his eyes took nothing from his good looks. And even though it was an early start, Barker had obviously taken time over his trendy appearance, wearing skinny jeans and white trainers. His hair was groomed and well cut. Barker looked a complete contrast to his experienced colleague.

Once he had sat down Geoff took a welcome sip of his tepid Americano while Barker picked at the cake. Quietly he relayed the assault that he had witnessed the night before between Hanson and Rudding.

'Geoff, any thoughts?' Barker said, with a certain amount of desperation as to how he should deal with the matter.

'Do nothing, Steve. Do nothing. Let the whole thing pass,' Sutton said in a reassuring voice, his eyes widening at the result of this new information.

'Rudding could have taped me. I certainly wouldn't put it past him,' Barker instantly replied, still agitated.

'Steve, you currently don't need to know any details, but I have an enquiry ongoing at the moment. It is in its early stages. This scuffle between Hanson and Rudding may or may not be part of that investigation. In the meantime, anything you observe involving them, either on their own or together … make sure that you record it and ring me immediately, at any time,' Sutton said. 'I will ensure that nothing will come of Rudding's complaint, even if he contacts the federation.'

Geoff knew that a quick call to Ron Turner would bring an abrupt end to Rudding's protestations, and that any complaint to the federation would go absolutely nowhere.

Sutton took another mouthful of coffee. The incident that Barker had witnessed could have been just a minor scuffle between two shift officers. It wasn't a unique occurrence, but that sort of incident usually took place off duty after a certain amount of alcohol. Yet the timing of this incident, because it involved the two officers potentially linked to Operation RESOLVE, was of massive interest to Sutton. Another major plus was that he now had someone of Barker's reliability close to both Hanson and Rudding. He drained the dregs of his coffee and reached for his green Barbour.

'Geoff, just another thing regarding Robbie Hanson ... he's a cracking lad. He flew through his first two years, but the past couple of months ... he's changed. I can't get to the bottom of it. I've tried putting an arm around him, have given him a bollocking, but no change. He has a few problems with his sick mother but that has never affected his work. No, he's definitely changed, Geoff,' Barker said, this time with confidence. 'It's just an observation.' This last comment caused Sutton to momentarily stop in his tracks.

'Thanks, Steve, that's really useful.' Sutton rose from the table and repeated himself, 'Ring anytime, and apologies for not coming back to you last night.' They shook hands again, 'He'll making a cracking inspector soon,' said Sutton to himself as he made his way out of the cafe.

Just before he drove off Sutton rang Ron Turner on his personal mobile. There was no hello. 'Yes, Geoff?' It was short but never a sweet conversation. But Bill Rudding was sorted, for now...

8

Rory Lomas

Six nondescript vehicles, including an unremarkable motorcycle, made up the surveillance team supervised by Detective Sergeant Rory Lomas. The members of the team had been briefed via secure video link by Jo Firth from their Borrington Constabulary location, which in their particular case was a unit on an out-of-town industrial estate within easy reach of the major road networks.

The necessary authority had been sent electronically, together with a current photograph of their target, PC Bill Rudding. There was a unique relationship between the two forces, Borrington and Parton, which were two of the smallest in the country and which regularly used each other's resources when required. This mutual aid agreement had proved crucial in preventing Home Office plans for amalgamation.

Lomas was parked opposite the entrance to a new housing estate. He had reversed their silver Astra behind some old dilapidated garages. 'This will do, Joan,' he said to his partner for that day, DC Joan McDonagh. The vehicle was now well out of view, but in a perfect position to respond.

Following the briefing, a study of Google Maps had given them a complete overview of Rudding's home address.

***

It was 9.30 a.m. on a miserable Thursday morning in November, with rain beating down on the windscreen. Their target, a man on a mission, was busy cleaning his teeth. Rudding placed his electric toothbrush back in its charger. It looked a miserable day outside but that didn't matter to him, not the way his mind worked.

Rudding smiled to himself. Another opportunity to cause the force some aggravation.

He was distracted by a text on his other phone, the pay-as-you-go one, which had been supplied by one of Wendy Galloway's team. He was expecting a call and was due his monthly salary payment. The message informed him that he would receive further contact later that morning.

Rudding carried out a final check of the house and paused for a minute in the second bedroom of his small semi. He looked down at the cartoon figures on the duvet, which was a souvenir from the trip to Disney World in Florida, where he had taken his now estranged daughter for her ninth birthday. Wendy Galloway had financed that trip, but Rudding managed his corrupt gains with care and the trip had been organised as part of his main period of annual leave.

'He might not move a muscle in this,' said DC Joan McDonagh to her sergeant, who was mesmerised by the wipers on the windscreen. 'It often happens,' she said to herself, 'on the many occasions when surveillance work becomes the most boring job in the world.' She pulled out a cold bacon roll and took a large mouthful.

'Shit. It's an off, off, off,' McDonagh spluttered,

dropping the sandwich into the footwell, as she spotted Bill Rudding's red Ford Focus making its way out of the only entrance to the estate and onto the main road. The remaining members of Lomas's unit were immediately alerted. They had parked and plotted around the target in similar strategic positions over a wide area. They reacted immediately and made up the ground quickly and safely, in line with their intensive training.

The target's car made its way towards the city centre. McDonagh called up the motorbike to take the lead as the traffic became heavier. Within a few minutes Rudding was pulling into Parton Constabulary HQ and the surveillance team sat back and plotted, then waited.

Rudding was back in his car within ten minutes. Unbeknown to the surveillance team his trip to the federation's office had been less than successful, and he sat in the driver's seat contemplating his next move.

'I've got the eyeball. It's no change, no change,' was the periodic call from a member of Lomas's team. Then there was an update. 'He's just received a call at 9.50 a.m.,' the same voice shouted in, ensuring that today's surveillance loggist would record their subject's every move. This in turn would prompt an enquiry, in the hope that it may become evidence. In this scenario the call could assist the investigation team in terms of Rudding's phone records.

'Exhaust smoke visible. He's starting up,' the commentary continued. 'It's a left, left, left, and a loss from me.'

The commentary was again taken up by the motor-cycle as Rudding's vehicle threaded through the city centre towards the marina area of Parton. The marina consisted of two distinctly different sections. The west side had been redeveloped with expensive modern apartment blocks overlooking the water, and housing what the locals would consider as Parton celebs. In addition the area was populated with sophisticated bars and restaurants. On the boundary of the west side, approximately another mile away from civilisation, there was a quiet and well-kept area for conservation, where the land eventually fell away into the sea. With a toilet block and a few benches, it was the usual developer's sweetener to the community.

The conservation area could be accessed either by car or, for a walker, along the newly constructed boardwalk. The area, which was cared for by volunteers, was most often frequented by birdwatchers.

In marked contrast, sitting almost directly opposite and separated by the large expanse of the estuary, the east side of the marina was run-down and completely underdeveloped. The only seemingly active industry was the ever-dwindling fishing fleet, which only survived to supply the smart eating places on the west side.

Rudding headed to the east side and parked in the large, desolate car park full of potholes. The rain continued to hit the windscreen, and the sound of raindrops was drowning out his current playlist. There were a few old and battered vans parked haphazardly around the immediate area. One, with flat tyres, was seemingly glued to the tarmac.

The target's new location caused Lomas and his team some operational problems. When it became obvious that Rudding was committed to the car park he ordered his team to hold back as they frantically sought a covert view of their target. Had he or any of his colleagues entered that location, they might as well have done so in a liveried police personnel carrier with its blues and twos blazing: a direct compromise.

'I've got a visual,' DC Helen Ives shouted in, and

Lomas quickly breathed a sigh of relief. One of his officers had set off on foot after rummaging through the boot of her nominated vehicle that day. She had found enough items to use for a disguise that would at least give the impression that it wasn't the first occasion she had been birdwatching. High-powered binoculars and a camera, which were prerequisites on any surveillance deployment, gave added credibility to her appearance.

Ives walked along the boardwalk, desperate to find an observation point that wouldn't seem obvious. A couple of vehicles were parked in the small conservation area car park, one of which was a black BMW X5. But Ives had more pressing issues to address than recording vehicle details.

The surveillance officer looked far from out of place as she used the binoculars to scan across the water from the west to the east side. There were only a couple of like-minded individuals in her vicinity. There was no doubt that the heavy rain had kept away all but the keenest of twitchers. Ives would only call in when the opportunity arose, and as far as the other members of the unit were concerned it was a case of watch and wait.

Meanwhile, at the almost empty car park on the east side, Bill Rudding's pulse was racing as he sat in the driver's seat. He had turned off the radio and now it was the turn of his heart to pound in time with the incessant rain. As promised, he had received the call, and had travelled to the location as instructed. Since becoming enlisted onto Galloway's payroll Rudding had only been summoned to a meeting on two previous occasions, and never with Wendy Galloway herself. She had decreed that he didn't warrant her presence. Every contact Rudding received contained instructions about where and how he was to collect his reward. They arrived via a burner phone, which was then immediately replaced.

He stepped out of the car to find that the rain was easing, giving way to a sea mist as the tide turned, and he headed for the shore. 'Bloody freezing,' Rudding muttered to himself. He zipped up his black Superdry overcoat, dug his chin deep into his chest and walked towards the harbour area. It was surrounded by small container units and garages, most of which were either unused or had fallen into disrepair. It was a walk of some 300 yards from where his car was located.

'Target has exited his vehicle and is on foot, walking towards the harbour area.' Ives stepped out of earshot from her newly found bird-loving friends in order to make the call. 'Sarge, I have a problem. Visibility is poor, and getting worse.'

'Helen, keep it going. You're the only one with any sort of visual,' Lomas said in encouragement, while looking around at any other possible options of maintaining the surveillance. 'Shit. There's bloody nothing, Joan,' he said to his partner. He had already decided to stand down his motorcycle asset, purely on the grounds of safety, given the poor weather conditions.

Helen Ives stared through the binocular lenses, desperately trying not to blink. 'It's a loss, a total loss. I got the target on foot walking towards the harbour. There appears to be about half a dozen garages built into the rock and some containers on the south side of the harbour. Can't see a thing now, not even his vehicle,' Ives continued, as the sea mist descended. Gone was the previous calm commentary. Hers was now a voice of sheer frustration.

The orders that Rudding had been given were perfectly clear. He was now looking for a sky-blue garage with a distinctive up and over door partially hanging from its hinges.

'Bastard,' he screamed inwardly in pain. A twisted left ankle from one of the many potholes had stopped him dead in his tracks. Bent over in pain, his hands on knees, all nerves about the forthcoming meeting were banished. 'Shit,' he screamed to himself, biting down on his bottom lip, while desperately trying to flex the joint.

Rudding placed his foot back on the ground and tried to put some weight on the injured ankle. Finally he limped on, his joint pulsing as the swelling began. It looked similar to the inflation of a small balloon. 'Shit … bastard…' Every possible expletive was used by Rudding as he hobbled on to his destination. He was now walking on an uneven cobbled path as he approached the harbour. It only increased the pain.

Rudding finally reached his intended destination. The paint was flaky in parts, but he could see it was definitely the distinctive sky-blue door of the disused garage that he was looking for, which became part of a cave as it backed into the cliff face. Half the door projected outwards and bent downwards, yet there was still enough space for someone to gain access. For a moment he forgot his own agony and listened for any sound, any indication that someone was present.

Assisted by the blanket of fog there was a stillness, almost a complete silence. The only interruptions were the sounds of regular saltwater deposits dripping from the mangled door. It was a scene reminiscent of an epic horror film. Rudding, in considerable discomfort, bent down and peered inside.

The moment he bent forward was the same moment that Rudding was dragged inside. A gruff voice greeted his appearance and said, 'Welcome, shithouse.'

He screamed out in pain, an automatic reaction. Not that it mattered, because there was no one to help him. The shout was greeted with a kick directly into the deepest part of his core. Struggling to breathe, he collapsed to the ground. Rudding spluttered as salty water leaked into his open mouth.

'Your fucking time is running out, Rudding. Lazy shit.' An envelope was thrown down onto his prostrate body.

He looked up. There were two of them. One he instantly recognised as one of Galloway's crew, the other... Rudding looked once, then squinted. The salt entering his eyes was causing more pain.

He looked again as Chief Superintendent John Dexter, head of professional standards, stood over him. Whether it be Parton Constabulary or the Met, every officer would recognise their head of complaints. Despite the surroundings, Dexter was dressed in typically smart manner, an expensive light-coloured long raincoat that no doubt covered an equally expensive suit.

His breath returned but Rudding still couldn't speak. 'Dexter, bloody John Dexter.' He tried unsuccessfully to mouth the words as his two captors made their exit.

John Dexter had phoned work earlier that morning and reported that, after a disturbed night's sleep, he had arranged an urgent dental appointment. The loyal Shaun Adams took the call, and nothing further was said. 'Typical Shaun,' said Dexter to himself. 'He would believe anything.'

In awful weather and using his own car, Dexter drove out to the quiet conservation area on the affluent west side marina. After being met by one of Galloway's cronies in one of their work vans bearing false plates, they then drove around the estuary to the east side before parking and walking to their destination to await their guest.

Despite the fog DC Helen Ives had tried to maintain her position. An extremely basic knowledge of bird-watching, which initially had been of benefit, had now become more problematic. 'That well-known saying, "A little knowledge is a dangerous thing," is so very true,' said Ives to herself, as after the mist came down the small group of twitchers had gathered together and made small talk, mostly about their optimistic hopes of a change in the weather. Using some charm, Ives had scrounged a cup of coffee, but the bird questions kept on coming.

She had tried to change her location, in the unlikely event that she would need to alert the team – but Ives was constantly followed by a young male sporting various lapel badges, all depicting different species of bird. She resorted to desperate measures, and finally managed to shake off this young enthusiast after having emphasised the need for a wild pee. 'I don't do public toilets,' she said in explanation.

A few minutes later and with the fog beginning to clear, Ives, now happily alone, shouted up. 'I can just see some fog lights appearing,' she told the remainder of the team. 'It's definitely not the Focus,' Ives said, disappointedly.

Some five minutes later Lomas and McDonagh were sitting, bored, in their Astra. They had parked in one of the restaurant car parks on the west side. Lomas had a decision to make. For all he knew Rudding could have gone fishing and might have had some kit in one of the harbour lockups. They could be there for hours, but the idea of deploying someone on foot had too great a risk of compromise.

He then observed some headlights pass their stand-off point, heading out to the west side and the conversation area.

McDonagh dropped the newspaper crossword and stared through the lightening gloom. She scrawled down the reg number, which she hoped was correct. She didn't bother the loggist. It merely fell into the something to do category at this stage.

Meanwhile, some thirty seconds later DC Helen Ives became aware of a vehicle with its fog lights illuminated entering the small car park at the conservation area. She pulled out her small notebook and became immediately aware of yet more company – a fellow birdwatcher.

'I think it might be getting better. Seen anything yet?' A hooded and heavily bearded twitcher, recognising the early signs that the mist was lifting, looked upwards. Over his right shoulder Ives noted a white van pulling up next to a black BMW X5 in the car park. What did surprise her was the sight of a rather well-dressed male emerging from the tatty white van before driving off in the smart Beamer. Both vehicles disappeared.

'No, nothing, just updating yesterday's sightings,' Ives said. She moved away from her new unwanted friend and noted what she hoped was the correct number of the white van. Her position made it impossible to note anything other than colour and make of the other vehicle.

Another five minutes passed and, with the fog still clearing, Helen Ives, who had excused herself for yet another wild pee, resumed her commentary. 'I've got a visual. Subject returning to his vehicle. He's limping.' A short silence followed. 'Lights and exhaust. It's an off, off, off.'

Lomas and McDonagh took over the commentary at this point.

***

It proved an uneventful journey for Rudding back to his home address. He parked and limped into his house while the surveillance team returned to their early morning positions. His ankle injury slipped into insignificance as he remembered the words, 'Your time is running out.' His employers weren't known for idle threats.

As Rudding was going home John Dexter went back to his desk at professional standards. It was only the ever-attentive Shaun Adams who noted the time.

Dexter's phone rang. 'John, it's Ron Turner.'

'Ron,' Dexter said sharply. 'Good to hear from you,' he said, lying.

'Just to let you know that that lad Rudding, from A relief in the city centre, has been to the federation office wanting to make a complaint of assault by another cop. He got short shrift but, just to mark your card, he may come to you,' Turner said.

'Thanks Ron,' Dexter said and smiled, the call ended. He refused to call Turner *sir* – which would have been appropriate, given Turner's superior rank.

He reached inside his suit jacket and felt for his engraved silver fountain pen. He then checked the inside pocket on the other side of his jacket. Other than the crumpled brown envelope containing the package he had received an hour or so earlier the pocket was empty. He knew exactly what was in the envelope. In one particular aspect of her life Wendy Galloway was true to her word. But where was his pen? Dexter was becoming concerned.

'Shaun, you haven't seen my pen lying around, have you, by any chance?' he called out to the dutiful secretary.

'No, I haven't, sir,' Adams replied, as respectful as ever.

Meanwhile Turner smiled ironically as he thought back to his recent phone call. 'There haven't been many occasions in the last year or so when Dexter has said thanks to me,' he thought to himself.

9

Matt Galloway

Toni Galloway stood in the kitchen of her mother's house. It was early afternoon and she had finally decided to rouse herself. She had spent the morning in bed, skiving off work, feigning another bout of sickness and viewing a series of *Love Island* on her iPad. The only incentive to leave her current location was the fact that she had left her charger downstairs.

The atmosphere in the house was never convivial. Even Wendy would have to admit that, after having engineered Toni's return home. Domestic life was far from a bed of roses. Parenthood had been one of the few failures in Wendy Galloway's life.

Toni had heard about Saturday night's shooting and knew her mother well enough to suspect who was behind the murder. She had forced herself downstairs, collected the charger and buttered a slice of toast when her mother entered the kitchen.

'Sleep well, love?' Wendy asked, in yet another attempt at a conversation that Toni had consistently avoided.

'Yes,' Toni replied curtly. It was another one-word dismissive answer.

'Fancy dinner later?' her mother asked, even though her piercing eyes were diverted to a large wall-mounted

TV screen showing a press conference on the Mather murder. There was no answer from Toni as the two of them stared at the screen. She reached for the remote and turned up the volume.

They both stood and stared while Olivia Mather, in tears, made a heartfelt appeal for witnesses to the shooting of her murdered son, who had been callously shot down on the streets of Parton city centre. Olivia was flanked by Trish Delaney, in her role as senior investigation officer, and ACC Ron Turner. It was all over in a matter of minutes. Olivia, leaving the platform, was assisted by family liaison officers when her legs gave way.

'You're a real bastard, Mam, a real fucking bastard.' Toni spat out the words with venom and averting her eyes from the screen as she looked directly at Wendy, who grabbed the remote and changed channels.

Wendy was about to give her a hard slap but thought better of it. 'Nothing whatsoever to do with me,' she lied earnestly. For her the accusation was like the proverbial water off a duck's back. Lying was a character trait that came naturally to both of them.

Toni ignored her completely. Armed with her toast and her charger she returned to bed, knowing only too well that her mother's actions were a direct result of her own drunken false allegation of assault, which in turn had led to the shooting of a totally innocent person. Like mother, like daughter. As far as Toni Galloway was concerned, Steve Mather's death had absolutely nothing to do with her.

The doorbell rang, an unusual occurrence in the Galloway household. Toni hesitated and dived back underneath the duvet. There was no way she would rush to answer. She waited for her mother to break the habit of a lifetime by answering the door.

Matt Galloway took a deep breath. 'Last chance saloon,' he said to himself, and dropped his kitbag on the doorstep. Matt's world had fallen apart. His Royal Marine ambitions were in tatters. He didn't yet know if there would ever be the possibility of a return to his initial training. He had been obliged to leave after a diagnosis of a degenerative shoulder condition, which despite his young age, had been caused by a rugby injury suffered while playing for Upper Parton RFC.

With his life in turmoil, Matt was in total confusion. He dossed about for a couple of days with his newly acquired friends from the marines, but he knew he was imposing himself on them. He was caught between a rock and a hard place. Where was he supposed to go? Sadly, for Matt, he had few options.

While standing outside his mother's house, he was already having second thoughts. 'Why I am I here?' he said to himself as he tried to rationalise his confusion.

It had been an awful few days for the twenty-four-year-old. His mind drifted back to that fateful meeting with the commandant. The injury received during the final phase of training had caused him to fail the final, most gruelling exercise. Subsequently, following diagnosis, Matt was unable to pass out as a member of syndicate 3/2019.

Wendy reluctantly made her way through the hallway as the doorbell rang again. She glanced up at the viewing monitor. 'Who the hell?' she muttered inwardly. The monitor gave a visual on whoever had arrived at the Galloway residence, a necessary security measure following several credible threats against her life.

She had to look twice at the screen to confirm it

was her son Matt. 'What on earth does he want?' was her instant reaction. Wendy glared at the monitor. A fit and groomed marine stood before her. His choice of profession was a blatant V-sign to his mother's empire of crime and intimidation.

Upstairs, Toni had heard the doorbell ring again. Out of sheer curiosity and boredom she forced herself out of bed and looked down from her bedroom window, 'Shit, Matt,' she said, as she smiled to herself mischievously and wondered how this scenario might play out. Her own relationship with Matt was only slightly better than her mother's and, for Toni, her brother joining the marines wasn't a great loss. However, they did tolerate each other and had one thing in common: a dislike of their mother.

Wendy glared again at the monitor. 'You're not a Galloway,' she shouted, loud enough to be heard outside, and turned away. She was never going to open the door. Wendy Galloway no longer had a son.

Matt turned around and retraced his steps. 'Bloody stupid idea in the first place,' he said to himself. It had been a visit made in desperation rather than hope. Matt failed to look up and notice his sister, who had her hand over her mouth and was trying to stifle her giggles at the scene she had just witnessed.

Matt Galloway stood at the end of the driveway and stretched his injured shoulder. He deliberately turned his back on the house and made a plan. He scrolled through his list of contacts, looking for the letter H, and cursed the fact that he hadn't considered this as his first option.

Thirty seconds later Robbie Hanson picked up his phone and studied the screen. 'Shit. Matt Galloway. Haven't heard from him in ages,' he said to himself. He took his time and let the phone ring out before checking into voicemail.

For a moment Hanson thought back to the good times that he and Matt Galloway had shared – playing rugby, touring together – before the diverse problems with their respective mothers had ensured that they drifted apart.

Before then the two had been the closest of friends. Growing up, Robbie was both patient and kind with his rugby friend, who was becoming increasingly disillusioned about life at home with his mother, while Matt was always available to console a young Robbie when the news of his mother's diagnosis became known.

It had been a couple of years since they had last met – not through any falling-out, but just because of life's circumstances. While Robbie knew about Matt's ambition to join the marines, neither of them was aware of each other's more recent exploits.

Hanson listened to the voicemail. 'Robbie, when you get this message could you give me a call … please?' It was said with some urgency. Hanson shuddered. His immediate thoughts weren't with his long-lost close friend. It was the fact that Matt's mother had become his controlling taskmaster.

'Bloody hell, Matt, long time no hear,' Hanson said, immediately thinking about the good times they had both shared.

'Robbie, I need some help. Can we meet up?' Galloway said immediately, without any recourse to small talk.

'Sure, Matt,' Hanson said without thinking.

Within the hour the two were sharing a warm embrace at a Starbucks located in the newly developed Parton city centre precinct. Time flew as the pair exchanged stories of happier times. It is in these circumstances that a real friendship is rekindled in an instant. The good times seemed like yesterday, as opposed to the years they had spent apart.

It was just a few hours later when Matt Galloway placed his kitbag on the single bed in Robbie's spare room. Hanson had a lodger ... for now.

10

Trish Delaney

At the same time that Matt Galloway was moving into Robbie Hanson's flat, Trish Delaney was making her way to ACC Ron Turner's briefing after a highly charged press conference. As senior investigating officer of the Mather drive-by shooting, Delaney was under intense pressure to produce results. She had just caught her breath after Operation PROOF, which for her had been a make-or-break enquiry, but now she had been landed with this nightmare.

'Why me?' she kept repeating to herself and, despite her carefully applied make-up, nothing could hide the darkness around the eyes – an obvious sign of sleep deprivation. 'Keep it together, Trish.' She gave herself a motivational prompt as she knocked politely on Turner's door.

'Come in,' came the immediate reply. He had been waiting.

Delaney, joining Sutton and Firth, was last to arrive. The three were lined up in front of Turner's desk, similar to a row of misbehaving school children nervously await-ing punishment. Trish took a final deep breath, pulled back some hair straying down across her forehead and looked up, desperately trying to create an expression of confidence.

'Developments…' It was a statement rather than a question from Turner, as Delaney gave an update of the enquiry to date.

Her response was both professional and thorough, but crucially there was little in terms of developments. 'Searches negative. CCTV had footage of the shooting but nothing distinctive regarding clothing or identification of the vehicle,' she began. 'Background enquiries regarding the deceased confirmed there was no criminal association or anyone who would have any grudge or motive to commit such a crime.' Her mouth dry, Delaney paused.

The pause seemed an eternity before Delaney recovered. 'We are extending the coverage by looking at private cameras that may cover the motorcycle's route either to or from Lucifer's. We have established that there was a dry run the night before the murder, with PC Robbie Hanson being identified in the vicinity on both occasions.' Her voice began to falter as she admitted they had made no significant breakthrough in the investigation.

Sutton recognised Delaney's plight, so he immediately began his briefing and tried to add some positivity to the situation. He spoke confidently. After all, he had been there on numerous occasions. He began with an account of the surveillance team.

'When the coast was clear and the weather lifted, Jo and I had a walk down to the south side of the harbour, on the east marina, and we found the containers where Rudding appeared to be heading.' He glanced across to Firth. 'There was also a white van leaving the area immediately prior to Rudding returning to his own vehicle.' Sutton continued. 'That same vehicle then made its way to the west side before dropping off a passenger, who left the area in a BMW. We have the reg of the van but not the Beamer,' Sutton said enthusiastically.

'Geoff, sorry to interrupt... I have an update on the white van. It's one of Galloway's pool cars,' Jo Firth said politely. 'The plates refer to another similar vehicle, but there've been a couple of intel reports that placed a couple of Galloway's cronies on board,' she added.

'Although we can't evidence the connection due to the surveillance loss, it's far too much of a coincidence,' Turner said loudly. 'Geoff, I want those containers and garages searched. Make sure the officers are covert, dressed up as council workers. The less attention the better. If the word gets out, Galloway will know. Sounds as though the place is almost deserted. Shouldn't be a problem, and you never know they what they might find,' he added.

'Sir, I forgot to mention that Rudding injured his ankle walking over across the car park. Did nothing for the rest of the day. I've checked with personnel. He rang in and has gone sick for a week. Suggest we bin the surveillance for now,' Sutton said to update them, before one of his two phones rang.

He always carried both, but one of them was almost redundant. It was his old informants' phone, which the force allowed him to keep on the off-chance that one of his past informants might ring. On this occasion Sutton had made the schoolboy error of not switching it off during the briefing. 'Shit. It never bloody rings,' he said to himself as he sought to apologise and cover his embarrassment.

He quickly located and switched off the offending item before continuing his update, albeit in less confident and embarrassed tones. 'What about the BMW? It was seen in convoy with Galloway's van. If we completed an extended CCTV search we might be able to identify the reg number,' Sutton said, quickly recovering his composure.

'Yes, good point, Geoff.' Turner assumed control. 'Now, PC Robbie Hanson…' he said, and glanced towards Sutton. 'In addition to him being reasonably close to the scene on both evenings we have this incident where he and bloody Rudding almost come to blows during a tour of duty. We haven't a clue about the reason for this altercation, but any potential association Rudding has needs investigating. Hanson requires attention either to confirm or to eliminate him from the enquiry.'

Turner paused and looked up at the three of them. 'Tomorrow, Trish, I want to know the forensic result from the bullet casing and anything further from the CCTV. Geoff, I will need an update from the search around the harbour area and anything on the BMW. We'll put Lomas's surveillance team on Robbie Hanson. See what that brings to the table. Right, same time tomorrow.' Turner looked down and returned to his notes. It signalled the correct time for his audience to leave.

Sutton walked back to his car while rummaging in his pocket for the renegade phone. It didn't really cause him much concern because the last five or six calls to that mobile over the past twelve months had always been someone ringing the wrong number.

As he sat in the driver's seat he looked at the screen, blinked and stared. 'Shit. Bob Hope,' he shouted to himself, immediately recognising the pseudonym (a safety mechanism was used for all registered informants).

He took a deep breath. His heart began pounding and his hands started sweating.

Vernon Edwards, aka Bob Hope, was a contact never to be forgotten. 'Vern... Vern Edwards...' Sutton repeated to himself, now shivering, but not from the cold.

Edwards had been imprisoned some ten years previously for a kidnapping and stabbing. It had followed a prolonged turf war between him and Wendy Galloway. At the time, the pair of them were each looking to rule the city centre's nightlife.

They hated each other with a vengeance. The feud had ended when one of Wendy's closest associates was left clinging to life in intensive care after a kidnap and torture crime. Death had been avoided only when the injured party managed to escape by jumping through a window minus a couple of mutilated fingers.

The crime had obviously been perpetrated by Vern Edwards, but obtaining a successful prosecution was another matter. The injured person was a career criminal who, apart from his missing digits, made a full recovery. But then, unsurprisingly, he refused to speak to the police regarding his ordeal. It was only the testimony of a protected witness, who not only had the necessary connections but also more importantly the courage to testify, that led to the conviction of Vern Edwards. That testimony, added to some forensic links and some exceptionally strong circumstantial evidence, convinced the Crown Prosecution Service (CPS) that there was a case to answer. With the help of the unknown witness Parton Constabulary were hoping that both Edwards and Galloway would end up on a charge sheet. However, the CPS had other ideas, and Edwards alone was charged with the one particular incident.

'Seems like yesterday,' Sutton mused, as he reminisced over a case that he remembered so very clearly. It had had a profound effect on him then, as it still did now. The reason was that Vern Edwards had been his informant who, when convicted, tried to cut a deal. He wanted a reduced sentence as a reward for the intelligence he had previously supplied to Sutton. But the force hadn't cooperated, and Sutton had been left with the unenviable task of telling Edwards.

'You're going down, Sutton.' It wasn't an idle threat from Edwards, thought Sutton, when the force's technical staff appeared on his doorstep to provide him with a panic alarm and some CCTV monitoring equipment.

Charging Edwards was just the start for the enquiry team. It led to a two-month-long high-security trial, where rumours abounded concerning jury nobbling.

The whole process had reached a tumultuous climax. After the final speeches the jury was sent out to consider their verdict. Tensions continued to mount, and after days of deliberations the judge finally accepted a majority 10–2 verdict. The key witness had been placed in a rarely used and highly costly witness protection scheme some months prior to the trial. This system was only used for the most vulnerable of people. Their evidence was given behind a screen using a heavily disguised voice. Edwards was sent down for a fifteen-year stretch for kidnap, assault and false imprisonment.

'Who was that protected witness?' Sutton had spent many wasted hours speculating. As far as he knew there were only two people in the force who would have known the identity of the individual concerned: John Dexter, who was at that time head of the force's intelligence, and Ron Turner, who was his deputy. For an individual to be placed in the witness protection scheme they had to enter into a contract, with their welfare being catered for by another force by way of a mutual arrangement. The whole process had massive ramifications not only for the individual but also for his or her family, and moving away from the area was just the beginning.

At that time in his career, the then Detective Inspector Geoff Sutton worked in the CID based at Parton city centre. He didn't need to know or want to know the true identity of the witness. Inevitably, there had been a few rumours flying around at the time.

This all came back to Sutton as with some trepidation he stared at the phone while at the same time working out some simple maths. 'Edwards … fifteen-year sentence with parole? No, he must still be inside. Could he have made the call?' He thought deeply. 'Could it be someone other than Edwards ringing me? Hopefully, another wrong number.' Sutton continued his deliberations. He was nervous. And yes, just a little frightened. Geoff Sutton knew full well the capabilities of both Vern Edwards and Wendy Galloway.

Sutton's sweaty palms grasped the steering wheel, but he still made no effort to start his vehicle. He checked his mobile. There had been no message left on voicemail, but Sutton knew this was no wrong number call. 'He'll call again,' he said to himself.

His heart sank.

Finally one hand left the steering wheel and grasped the gearstick. He decided to do nothing, and clung desperately to the forlorn hope that there would be no further calls from the contact known as Bob Hope. His pulse was still racing as he set off for home.

At the same time as Sutton began his journey, John

Dexter was still searching everywhere for his engraved silver fountain pen. If he wasn't sitting at his desk the pen was always tucked into the left-hand pocket inside his suit jacket.

His mind wandered desperately, trying to retrace his recent movements.

11

Pete McIntyre

Pete McIntyre had just retired to his study. After a heavy tea of toad-in-the-hole, his wife Valerie's signature dish, he needed a comfortable seat. A final quick glance through of the pre-read course material was in order. Tonight was the first session of his mental health counsellor's course. The decision to enrol had been taken in an effort to help others, as well as being an attempt to understand why his good friend Roger Strong had taken his own life.

A quick glance to check the time was followed by a prolonged yawn. It had been a long day childminding Ben, his grandson, and now, after consuming Val's dinner, which lay like a brick on his already bloated stomach, he wondered if he could stay awake, never mind concentrate his mind. He was due at Parton Sixth Form College, the venue for that night's lecture, at 8 p.m.

Pete was awoken from his lethargy by the ringtone of his mobile. Without looking, he grabbed out, rather than search for the phone, and recovered the item at the second attempt. He smiled when the caller's name, Matt Galloway, appeared on the screen and answered immediately.

'Pete, is there any chance we can meet?' Matt Galloway

said with some urgency.

'Not a problem, Matt,' McIntyre said, without giving the question a second thought. He hadn't heard Matt's voice for some time.

'Usual place, Pete. In half an hour,' Galloway said. It was more of an instruction than a question. It was now 6 p.m., and the usual place was the city centre precinct, the Starbucks coffee house, which was approximately half a mile away from where he needed to be at 8 p.m.

'See you there, Matt,' Pete answered slowly, fully realising that his day was far from finished. He began to pack his briefcase while his mind clicked into overdrive. His semi-conscious state had by then been replaced by one of both excitement and curiosity.

Some years previously he had been instrumental in setting up Upper Parton RFC Colts section, the transition team for the under-eighteen age group. At the end of that season, the final one as junior members, the team would then move up to become senior players. As the team manager, Pete did everything for the lads. He was not only a coach, manager and principal fundraiser for their annual tours, but he shared all their trials and tribulations. Pastoral Pete was a nickname that McIntyre had earned from the members of Upper Parton RFC.

Matt Galloway had been one of Pete's boys who, despite the complete lack of interest shown by his parents, loved his rugby. There were many occasions when McIntyre's vehicle was to be seen dropping off young Galloway outside the parental home. Matt was made captain of his particular age group, with his good mate Robbie Hanson the obvious choice as his deputy.

Starbucks was one of the few premises that hadn't moved location when the precinct was developed, and

Pete had always used the premises as a meeting place with captains, disgruntled parents and other Colts volunteers. It was also Val's favourite coffee spot after a long day's shopping. Tonight the venue was ideal for Pete McIntyre, given his tight schedule, with Parton Sixth Form College only around half a mile away.

'Val, I'm off,' Pete shouted through to his wife, who was still in the kitchen scouring the baking tray and desperately trying to remove the last remnants of her latest culinary exploit.

'But it's only just gone six. You will miss *The One Show*,' came the reply.

'Matt Galloway just phoned, out of the blue. He wants us to meet up before I go to the college,' Pete said, grabbing his coat, briefcase and beloved blue and white Upper Parton RFC bobble hat.

'Good luck, Pete,' Val said to no one in particular, as Pete had already closed the front door. He slowly reversed his silver VW Golf out of the driveway.

It was a cold and dark November evening. The only brightness came from the early signs of Christmas decorations. He made the short journey to the city centre multistorey car park. Due to the time of day, most office commuters had already made their way home, and he easily found a spot on the second floor. There were a few early Christmas shoppers keeping him company. 'A dwindling generation,' said Pete to himself, a reference to those who still preferred a trudge around the shops to the ease of online ordering.

After he had parked, Pete ignored the lift and risked the cold, barren concrete staircase, plastered with obscene graffiti, that accompanied the constant smell of stale alcohol. He instantly regretted choosing this route. But, then again, from past experience, the lift was no more appetising. Once out of the car park he took a deep breath of fresh air as he entered the city centre precinct. It was a welcome relief from the multistorey.

New lighting and a pedestrian walkway created an upbeat atmosphere. He walked past a few street traders doing their best to raise interest from the pedestrian traffic. He made his way to Starbucks, and it was only a matter of a minutes before he sat down at what he referred to as their table, a window seat looking out onto the pedestrianised area.

The fact it had taken him longer to order the coffees than to walk from his car wasn't lost on Pete McIntyre. Patience had never been one of his virtues. The drinks arrived and he took a sip of his espresso. It was not his normal choice, but it had been specially chosen to give him the necessary hit and to aid his concentration through tonight's lecture. He took a freebie magazine from the rack and failed to notice his former Colts captain as Matt Galloway entered Starbucks.

At six feet tall and with a muscular build Matt was dressed very casually, in a similar way to an American college basketball player. He was wearing a navy-blue Nike hoody and grey shorts, despite the cold. His trendy white trainers completed the outfit. The only identifying feature of anything that would associate Matt with the military was his closely cropped hair, partially hidden under the hoodie. He pulled back the seat opposite McIntyre.

'Cheers, Pete.' The athletic Matt Galloway sat down, looked at his coffee and removed his Sony headphones.

'He looks the part,' thought Pete to himself.

'Glad you got rid of them. You looked like a Martian,'

Pete said, referring to Matt's headphones and chuckling as the pair shook hands across the table. 'Really good to see you again,' he continued. 'Thought you would be deployed somewhere. Keeping the likes of me, picking up my pension, safe and well.'

'I've had a bit of bad luck, Pete. Bloody rugby.' Matt looked down, hoping that his one-time mentor would not see the disappointment that he felt in being sent back from his initial military training etched upon his face. He was still in shock and coming to terms with his circumstances.

Young Galloway then explained to Pete the issue with his shoulder problem. The fact that he didn't have a clue how things were going to work out – or if they ever would – had clearly upset him. McIntyre didn't talk. He just listened. Being a good listener is a quality that few possess, and Pastoral Pete had it in spades. In effect this was why Matt had suggested they meet – so that he could share his recent disappointment with an adult who he respected. Obviously his mother was completely out of the question.

Pete McIntyre was well aware of the history between mother and son. Indeed, he had been a key sympathetic ear for Matt when he sought someone to confide in. Matt hadn't held back in giving McIntyre more details than he needed to hear about the ongoing turf war between his mother and Vernon Edwards. They had also spent some time discussing his lifelong ambition to join the marines.

'For many reasons, leaving Parton would be a good idea.' It was one of the few pieces of firm advice that Pastoral Pete had given Matt Galloway. 'You might not see it now, Matt, but I do believe in fate. Everything has a reason,' McIntyre said compassionately, taking another sip of espresso. The black treacle hitting the back of his throat acted like a jet stream. Pete would never realise the significance of the words he had just uttered to the young Matt Galloway.

Matt sat back. A studious look appeared on his face. He changed the subject to a topic he wanted McIntyre to comment upon. 'But, Pete, I know my mother is corrupting police officers. I feel there is unfinished business—' Matt said, lowering his voice.

'Stop there, Matt. I don't want to hear about it,' McIntyre said to interrupt him. For once he was no longer Pastoral Pete. This subject was taboo as far as he was concerned.

The two of them then spent the remainder of their time together discussing old rugby stories and the infamous Amsterdam Easter tour. And then, as Matt attempted another graphic description, Pete reminded him of the age-old saying, 'What goes on tour stays on tour,' and glanced down at his watch. He was conscious of the time, given his imminent mental health counsellor's class at the nearby college.

'You have somewhere to go,' Matt said, observing Pete. It was now his time to listen as McIntyre quickly described Roger's suicide, and hence the course he was attending at Parton Sixth Form College. The pair stood up and shook hands again. 'Where are you parked?' Galloway asked.

'Just along the precinct in the multistorey,' Pete replied, carefully restoring his Upper Parton blue and white bobble hat back on top of his balding head.

'I'll walk along with you. I'm staying with Robbie Hanson at the moment. He dropped me off. I'll get a taxi back from the rank at that end of the precinct,' Matt added.

'I've got him back playing. I sent him a text when I heard he transferred to Parton Constabulary and got him playing for the club, shifts permitting,' Pete said, combining a direct reference to his love of Upper Parton RFC with McIntyre's lasting interest in his former Colts players. 'Then I heard about his mother,' Pete continued, with some concern and disappointment. 'Sorry I can't give you a lift, Matt. I'm in a bit of a rush,' McIntyre added, wishing to change the subject as Galloway rummaged for his phone.

'Speak of the Devil. It's a text from Robbie wondering what time I will be back. He's trying to be the mother I never really had,' Matt said, laughing, as he began typing. Galloway had thought about walking but didn't trust the dodgy weather. *I'm leaving Starbucks now, getting a cab*, he wrote, and sent the text with an obligatory emoji.

The pair of them made their way out of Starbucks. Pete led the way. The shock of the cold air in his mouth mixing with the espresso he had just consumed made him stop suddenly, like a startled rabbit in car headlights. With wide-open eyes he finally began the short walk along the precinct accompanied by his young friend, who bounced along beside him with his over-ear headphones around his neck.

A moment or two later a tall man limped out of the Crop public house located directly opposite Starbucks and glanced across at the two of them walking towards the taxi rank. He turned and smiled to himself, then cursed the pain as he limped away in the opposite direction.

It was only a matter of minutes until Pete and Matt approached the multistorey entrance and said their final goodbyes. 'Same time next week, Matt,' were Pete's final words. This time there was no shaking of hands. It was a caring embrace between the two of them before Matt, hoodie down, replaced his headphones and disappeared into a world of music that Pete would never have wanted to be introduced to.

Pete stood and watched Galloway bounce along the pedestrian-only paved area as he made his way towards the taxi rank. 'A great kid,' he said and sighed to himself. He was about to open the door to the multistorey when he first heard and then saw…

Kev Stryker and Jonta Roberts weaved their way through the stationary taxis at the rank and headed towards their intended victim. They had recently received the information that their target would be making his way along the precinct from the direction of Starbucks. Jonta gripped the handlebars and slowed on the cobbles, ensuring that he and his pillion passenger not only remained upright but that the manoeuvre would also assist a very accurate shot. On this occasion he was astride a Triumph rather than his favoured make, a Harley-Davidson. Kev, his passenger, had his hand grasped around yet another weapon, this time a Browning Hi-Power handgun. Stryker slowly removed the weapon from inside his leather jacket.

Pete McIntyre was rooted to the spot. It was one of those instances when you knew full well that something was about to happen, but also that there was nothing in the world you could do to prevent the inevitable. McIntyre saw the gun momentarily glisten against the background lights as it was brought out into the fresh air. Matt Galloway, head down, immersed in his music, was totally oblivious to the sound of the fast-approaching high-powered motorbike. Like a snake slithering to its unsuspecting prey, Stryker and Roberts hunted down their target. Their task could not have been easier. Three shots rang out and Matt Galloway dropped like a stone before McIntyre could finally respond.

'Matt, Matt,' Pete screamed, and ran the thirty yards or so to his former player and young friend. The blood from Galloway's wounded body had already begun to pool on the cobbled street as the few late-night shoppers slowly began to take in the macabre incident they had just witnessed.

'Stay with us, Matt, stay with us,' McIntyre repeated. He was now on his knees, cradling Galloway's stricken head. The bullets had all been body shots.

McIntyre heard a trembling voice. 'I've called an ambulance.' He looked up to see an ashen-faced mother trying to soothe her hysterical daughter, whose idea of a pleasant shopping trip and observing the Christmas lights had ended in trauma.

Stryker and Roberts were long gone. They had exited via a quiet side road in the precinct that was used only for deliveries and waste collections. By the time the emergency services arrived at the scene any potential evidence linking them to the scene had been deposited in the city's fast-flowing River Part. They then made their way to the woodland near Gerard Country Park before setting fire to the Triumph and recovering Jonta's Honda. It was a tried and tested process as far as they were concerned.

While McIntyre was kneeling over the stricken Matt Galloway, the circumstances that his lifelong mate found himself couldn't be more different, as Sutton and Debbie were wrapped in each other's arms on the living room sofa. It was their time, and they both loved this part of the day. After a quick catch-up on their respective day's highlights, it was a catch-up of a different type as they ploughed through yet another episode of *Homeland* on Netflix.

Their tranquillity was interrupted when Sutton heard again the unmistakable sound of his informants' phone. The noise hit him physically. He jumped up immediately, leaving Debbie marooned on the sofa while almost spilling his half-drunk glass of wine.

'Geoff, are you OK?' Debbie called to his back as Sutton retrieved the mobile. His heart skipped a beat. Another bloody call from Bob Hope. Disturbed, Sutton returned to the sofa. His mind was racing. The evening was ruined.

The call confirmed his fears. 'That isn't someone ringing a wrong number,' Sutton said to himself, and frowned.

12

Bill Rudding

After her early evening briefing with Ron Turner, Trish Delaney made her way to the gym. It was after all a Thursday evening, an exercise night indelibly marked in her mental diary.

Even though she was mentally shattered, she forced herself to go. An hour later a release of endorphins surged through her body just as she collapsed on the cross trainer. It was the final station on her twice-weekly cardio hour. Exhausted, she gasped and then sucked up what little air she could through her hard-working lungs. She didn't feel good at the moment, but Delaney knew she would be buzzing in another hour and reaping the benefits of her workout.

While she was recovering, ACC Ron Turner was answering an early evening call on his work mobile. His eyes glanced upwards as he looked towards his wife and headed for the study. Sheila Turner knew that dinner would be delayed or potentially postponed. After forty years of marriage the telltale signs were instantly recognisable.

'Sir, I thought you would like to be made aware of this incident,' came the nervous voice of a newly promoted control room inspector who had dared to ring Ron Turner when he was notionally off duty. Briefly the officer ran through details of the latest Parton city centre shooting. The circumstances outlined caused Turner to frown.

'I will ring you back,' Turner said abruptly. His experience had taught him to reflect and consider, maybe just for a few moments, but this short period of reflection could be crucial in arriving at the correct decision. 'Sheila, I will be fifteen minutes,' he shouted through to his wife.

While sitting at his desk he drew three columns on an A4 sheet of paper. Each column had a title: *Short-term*, *Medium-term* and *Long-term*. He started scribbling under column one: *Short-term*. The others could be dealt with in the morning.

Five minutes had passed when Turner made his call. 'Is the victim still alive?' He required the most current update.

'I believe so,' a quiet voice replied cautiously.

'Speak up.' Turner was in full operation mode now.

'Yes, sir, and the scene is secured, with the on-call senior detective attending,' came the reply.

'Authority for firearms at the hospital, and call out the armed response tactical advisor.' He barked his instructions.

'Yes, sir.'

'Who is the on-call detective?'

'Steve Orton,' the inspector said immediately.

'Change it to Trish Delaney,' Turner said without hesitation. This recent shooting had to be linked to last Saturday's incident. 'And ask her to give me an update by 10 p.m.'

Turner put the phone down. He smiled to himself sardonically as he scribbled the word *Retire* in large capital letters across columns two and three, which were labelled *Medium-term* and *Long-term*. He would update Chief Constable Chris Mayling after dinner. She needed to know.

Delaney was on her way home when she got the call from the control room. Her heart sank and the previous high from the gym session immediately disappeared, to be replaced immediately by extreme fatigue. 'No good whinging,' said Delaney to herself. Ron Turner had made the request and it made sense.

Having altered her career path and joined the ranks of the CID after several uniformed postings, she was still trying to prove herself in the eyes of Turner. Delaney was ambitious and had bottle, but first Operation PROOF and now the two shootings… She had been given a real baptism of fire.

With her hair still damp hair from a quick shower, Delaney drove to Parton Infirmary. She had replicated the conversation Turner had with the control room inspector regarding the incident and immediately ensured that force procedure would be followed. A crime scene manager had been authorised to attend the scene along with her detective inspector from the incident room to supervise, collate witnesses and ensure CCTV recovery. They were to update her before 9.30 p.m. The incident log would formally record her actions.

Delaney was ensuring there would be no comeback from Turner for her, whatever the outcome of the investigation. Her second phone call, which was no less important, was to Geoff Sutton.

While the police were responding, Pete McIntyre was grasping tightly onto some internal handles inside the ambulance transporting Matt Galloway to hospital. It was a white-knuckle ride. The vehicle was flying, rocking from side to side, with the blues and twos blaring. But Pete heard none of that and wanted to look anywhere but down towards the prone body of Matt Galloway. But he couldn't help himself, as he was drawn to look at him as if he were a macabre magnet. 'Hang on Matt, hang on,' he mouthed towards his former protégé. The monitors and IV drips were a complete blur and Pete just stared at what appeared to be Matt's lifeless body covered by bloodied clothing. Ironically, his headphones still hung limply around his neck.

'How long have you known Matt?' The voice seemed to come from a different world, but it was the same paramedic who at the scene had persuaded him to come to the hospital. 'You could help him live,' were his exact words, and Pete knew he had no choice.

The question was repeated, but again he couldn't reply. It was an eight-minute journey to Parton Infirmary, although it seemed a lifetime to Pete McIntyre. In addition to the awaiting medical staff, the ambulance was greeted by a team of heavily armed police officers swarming around in full protective equipment and brandishing their weapons in an overt show of force. Their appearance only heightened the tension. The injured Matt Galloway was whisked away at some pace while McIntyre slowly disembarked from the emergency vehicle with the blood slowly returning to his previously drained knuckles.

A few minutes had passed and slowly Pete's composure was returning. A kindly porter had placed him in a small office-type room with bare walls. Two or three reasonably comfortable chairs with old-fashioned floral cushions made up the remainder of the furniture. McIntyre had rightly guessed that the room was reserved for the close family of those gravely ill. He reached for his phone.

Sutton had just received a call from Trish Delaney. She wanted him at the hospital, and he didn't hesitate for a moment. As a civilian he didn't have to attend, but the chief had asked him to be part of this enquiry and this latest incident was an obvious escalation. He quickly explained to Debbie that their cosy evening had come to an end. When his mobile rang again, he instantly noted the caller and let it ring out. 'Bloody McIntyre, he's forgotten the golf tee time for Saturday. He always does,' Sutton said to himself.

He made a quick call to Jo Firth and gave her a briefing about what he knew so far. She suggested a visit to the crime scene if Sutton was attending the hospital. Sutton did not need any reminder that Firth was an excellent choice as partner in this enquiry.

Debbie hugged him close, too close, as he began to regret responding to Delaney's call. After reluctantly breaking free from her arms he left Debbie's warmth and headed out, thankful that he hadn't consumed any more wine.

As he made the twenty-minute drive to Parton Infirmary, Sutton reflected on his missed call from Pete McIntyre and thought back to the Roger Strong scenario where his dear mate had tried unsuccessfully to make contact, not only with him but also with Pete and Stew Grant, before taking his own life. Sutton knew they were all still having problems coming to terms with the circumstances surrounding Roger's death. Using the hands-free, he phoned McIntyre.

'Geoff, thanks for phoning. I've had an awful night,' Pete began.

'What is it, Pete? Can I help?' Sutton said without any hesitation. McIntyre told him about his meeting with Matt Galloway and walking away from Starbucks. Sutton interrupted him as he began talking about Galloway's injuries.

'Pete, did Matt contact anyone or receive any calls when you were with him?' Sutton said with some authority.

'Yes, just as we were about to leave. A text from a lad. You probably know him from the rugby club: Robbie Hanson. Matt's dossing with him at the moment. He couldn't go back to his mother's. Hey, he's one of yours now, Robbie. He used to be Matt's vice-captain in the Colts,' Pete said, making direct reference to Hanson joining the force as well as being in the same rugby team as Matt Galloway.

'Where are you now, Pete?' Sutton again interrupted him.

'Believe it or not, I'm at the hospital. Came in the same ambulance with Matt,' McIntyre replied, looking at the bare walls of his bleak surroundings.

'Stay there, Pete. I'm five minutes away,' Sutton said, and ended the call without providing any further explanation. While still on hands-free he dialled Delaney's number.

'Trish, are you at the hospital?' he said, not even giving her a chance to answer.

'Just walking in through the entrance now,' Delaney replied.

'Get Matt Galloway's phone. He received a message before he was shot. It could be important,' Sutton said quickly and with authority. 'Will see you in five,' he added in an urgent tone.

A few minutes later Delaney and Sutton joined McIntyre in the bare relatives' room. Delaney was armed with an exhibits bag. Even before receiving Sutton's call she knew that whatever the outcome of his medical condition, Matt Galloway was himself a crime scene. She had already tasked the forensic officers to attend the hospital.

After Sutton had hurriedly introduced Pete to Trish Delaney there was a polite knock on the door, one of those knocks that was merely a notification of an imminent entrance. Whoever was about to enter wasn't in the habit of being delayed.

'Good evening, I'm Doctor Anita Rogers. Who are you?' the A & E consultant said officiously. All three stumbled through their involvement with Galloway. Once she was satisfied with their credentials, Rogers continued abruptly by saying, 'Mr Galloway is currently in surgery. He is critically ill. However, remarkably the three shots all missed his vital organs. He is suffering from extreme blood loss coupled with significant trauma but he's a fit lad. It really is touch-and-go.' There was almost a touch of humanity as Roger's finished speaking. 'Family, next of kin?' Having seen him alight from the ambulance, she looked directly at Pete.

'His dad's deceased and he doesn't speak to his mother. I know he has a younger sister, but he never mentions her at all,' McIntyre said, equally abruptly, to match the doctor's manner.

Anita Rogers shrugged her shoulders. 'One other thing… Is it really necessary for the hospital to be turned into a fortress?' It was an obviously a direct reference to the armed patrols around the hospital. The doctor looked at Delaney pointedly.

'Doctor, no doubt you have a duty of care to your staff as well as your patients,' Delaney said frostily. 'Due to the obvious risk posed by the people who tried to kill one of your patients, armed police are a necessary inconvenience,' she added dismissively. Rogers didn't answer. Instead she merely turned on her flat shoes and left the room. 'Arrogant bitch,' said Delaney to herself. It was unusual for her to take an instant dislike to people.

Trish quickly reverted to operational matters. 'It was Hanson who contacted Matt immediately prior to the shooting. He knew exactly where Galloway was going,' Trish added, almost triumphantly.

'Well, that's no surprise.' For some reason Pete felt the need to interject. 'Matt was staying at Robbie's flat. He had nowhere else to go, and Robbie was doing him a favour. He's a good lad,' McIntyre added.

Delaney and Sutton both turned to face Pete as Sutton's work phone interrupted them. Geoff looked down at the screen. It was Jo Firth, from the scene of the shooting. He needed the update. 'I've got to take this,' Sutton told the other two. 'Hi, Jo.'

Firth went straight into overdrive. 'Everything is in hand at the scene, Geoff, but you need to know this. From the CCTV footage, moments after Matt Galloway and another guy leave Starbucks there's a bloke who comes out of the Crop opposite. He glances at the two of them and limps off in the opposite direction,' she added.

'The bloke Galloway is with is a mate of mine, Pete McIntyre. He and Matt arranged a meeting, which wouldn't be anything unusual. Pete was the Colts team manager and Matt Galloway was one of his former players. McIntyre was known as Pastoral Pete to the young rugby players,' Sutton said.

'Geoff, Geoff...' Firth was trying to emphasise her main point, 'The bloke who came out of the Crop was

Bill Rudding. I would recognise him anywhere. No ifs or buts. It's bloody Bill Rudding,' Jo said emphatically. Sutton's jaw dropped, and he finished the call.

'All OK, Geoff?' Delaney and McIntyre said in unison. From Sutton's reaction they both knew that the call had contained serious information.

Geoff Sutton looked directly at Delaney. 'Trish, you're never going to believe this. Bill Rudding is captured on CCTV leaving the Crop when Matt and Pete were walking along the precinct. He then clocks the two of them walking towards the taxi rank before limping away in the opposite direction. Jo Firth is positive it's him.'

'Who the fuck is Bill Rudding?' said an exasperated Pete McIntyre, purposefully using an expletive in a bid to end what was becoming a prolonged silence. For him, using foul language was a rare occurrence that was usually reserved for a poor shot on the golf course.

Delaney's fatigue returned immediately, like a punctured balloon. She almost felt tearful. 'Who the hell tipped them off? Hanson, Rudding or someone else?' she said out loud, referring to their motorbike suspects. 'I thought that the text on Matt Galloway's phone had been a major breakthrough in the enquiry, but not now. Would Wendy really arrange her son's shooting?' The sound of another mobile interrupted her thinking. Sutton knew the ringtone immediately. On this occasion it was yet another call to his informants' phone. He glanced down and rightly guessed the caller.

'I'll get that later,' he said, trying to give the impression of nonchalant irritation.

'He hates his mother and I'm sure the feeling is mutual,' McIntyre interjected, referring back to Delaney's original question.

It was nearing 9 p.m. when Delaney finished summarising the situation. 'Look, I need to update Ron Turner. There's nothing more to be done tonight. Nice to meet you, Pete. And Geoff, I'll see you in the morning,' Delaney said quietly, looking across at Sutton – who immediately thought of Debbie, waiting for him to return with a loving embrace. She had changed his life, and not just for now. Sutton really hoped forever.

'Golf is looking doubtful this Saturday, Pete,' Sutton said, awaking from his thoughts of Debbie. He knew that there would be every chance that he would be working. 'I will give you a lift back to your car,' he added. 'But not before we take your outer clothes for forensics. You were the last person in contact with poor Matt,' Sutton said, and smiled sadly.

'You're bloody joking, Sutton,' McIntyre said indignantly, but within ten minutes the pair of them were in Geoff's car. Pete was now dressed in a jumper, jeans and shoes, all supplied by a friendly hospital League of Friends volunteer.

'Just perfect.' Sutton laughed at his front-seat passenger, who was dressed in a chunky Arran sweater, maroon Wolsey trousers and black brogue shoes. McIntyre's outfit was completed with his rugby club bobble hat which, after a prolonged debate, they had allowed him to keep.

'Piss off, Sutton.' Pete said, laughing back at his good friend as the barrier lifted and the two of them exited the hospital car park.

13

Art Gormley

Matt Galloway's shooting had been planned earlier from Parton Constabulary Police HQ. That evening Chief Superintendent John Dexter had purposefully remained at work. Unusually, he was the last to leave. He had used the excuse that he was making up for lost time and had referred to that morning's fake dental appointment. He had received a call from Wendy Galloway on his unattributable phone. She was planning Rudding's exit from her operations and had tasked Dexter with getting him sacked from the force as a reward.

'Get rid,' was Galloway's final short command. Considering Rudding's previous history, Dexter considered this to be one of the easiest problems he faced. However, the Chief Super took a sharp intake of breath when he heard that Wendy's son Matt had returned. Galloway informed Dexter that she'd sent him packing, or words to that effect. That information acted as a catalyst to John Dexter.

'Shit,' Dexter said to himself. He was a worried man. Life was closing in.

Dexter thought back to the many intelligence reports during the historic Galloway and Edwards turf war. They were indelibly marked in his mind. By the time the trial ended, Wendy Galloway had become aware of Dexter's rank and his roles within Parton Constabulary.

'I need someone of rank and access,' Wendy Galloway had said to herself. She carefully considered the possibilities and began the long process of successful grooming the high-ranking officer into what would, for her, become a prized asset. Even though he was disgruntled by his perceived treatment by Parton Constabulary and had missed out on his ultimate hoped-for promotion, the ensuing benefits provided by Galloway allowed John Dexter to pursue his expensive motor racing hobby, and although this lifestyle was enough to raise a few eyebrows it never reached the threshold of an active investigation.

Matt Galloway featured in many of those intel reports, as did his haunts and associates, etc. Anything or anyone associated with Wendy Galloway would always be worth reporting for operational cops. One of Matt's most regular haunts was the Starbucks located in the city centre. Dexter considered the possible locations that young Matt was likely to frequent, given his current circumstances, and concluded, 'Starbucks is as good as anywhere.' It was an educated guess.

Dexter made a couple of calls from that same unattributable mobile phone. First he rang Bill Rudding. 'A final job for the tosser,' Dexter said to himself as Rudding limped out to his car en route to the precinct and a pint in the Crop. He had previously confirmed to Dexter that he could easily identify Matt Galloway. Every cop in the city centre knew him.

This will have come from Wendy, thought Rudding, following his conversation with Dexter. After that morning's uncomfortable meeting he was more than willing to oblige. Rudding had little option.

John Dexter's next call was to Art Gormley, a local taxi businessman known all over Parton. He had the necessary contacts. Dexter asked Art to mobilise Kev Stryker and Jonta Roberts.

He breathed a sigh of relief. It was now just a case of waiting impatiently. To occupy his mind Dexter thought again about the whereabouts of his silver pen. Not only did the item have emotional attachment, it had been given to him by his late parents at his passing-out parade nearly thirty years previously, but the pen also bore his initials. Anyone who knew or who had worked with John Dexter would have recognised his pen. It was a permanent possession. Because he had already scoured the office, his car, his briefcase – in fact, everywhere – and not found it, he came to only one conclusion. He had lost his pen early that morning while 'at the dentist'. He sighed deeply.

His unattributable phone pinged, and his sweaty hands scrutinised Rudding's coded message from his observation point at the Crop. 'For fuck's sake, it's on. Now or never,' Dexter swore to himself. He quickly breathed in and then slowly exhaled.

Shaking fingers punched in another coded text to the phone number previously supplied by Art Gormley. 'It isn't just Wendy Galloway who has people on the payroll. Art Gormley owes me.' Dexter managed a nervous smile.

Stryker's phone pinged. He studied the coded message closely at their predetermined stand-off location. The job was on and the sender of the text, John Dexter, who was trembling in his office, had another interminable wait.

He waited anxiously and examined the current chief constable incident log on his laptop. It highlighted the major incidents that had occurred within the force's area.

Since he had sent that text he had scrutinised the log continuously, eyes wide and staring at the screen.

A further ten minutes passed. This time Dexter read the narrative back to himself: *Shooting at the precinct. One male casualty. Offenders made off on a motorcycle.* He sat back, momentarily relieved. 'Turner's got another one,' he muttered in self-satisfaction. 'Serves the bastard right.' Dexter continued his jealous thoughts. He then read further down the page before the name of the injured person appeared: *Matt Galloway. No current update on his condition.*

He took a deep breath and continued reading as the incident was updated by the force's control room. They expertly summarised the comments from officers at the scene. A couple of lines down the name of Pete McIntyre appeared. 'Shit,' Dexter said. His heart began racing again. He seemed to be on a never-ending roller coaster this evening. He reached for the phone again and was forced to give Art Gormley further instructions.

Gormley was planning to exit the office when he received Dexter's first call. 'What the hell does Dexter want?' he said out loud. He breathed heavily when he saw who was ringing through his round-rimmed spectacles. He knew he had no option but to answer.

Gormley ran a successful business near the city centre precinct, with numerous delivery motorbikes and a fleet of taxis. Being a natural wheeler and dealer, he also had a small property portfolio of rented houses and apartments. Yet it was the vehicles that were the main source of his income, and *Gormley Goes* was a frequent billboard slogan around Parton city. This was in addition to his clever use of social media as an advertising tool. Everyone in and around the city knew of and probably used his prompt taxis or, if not, his delivery service.

'Can I help, Mr Dexter?' Gormley said obediently and looked around his office. He spent most of his time there, isolated from his team of twenty-four-hour despatchers. The word *office* was a slight exaggeration. Wedged behind his desk, he could just about make out his computer screen as he peered over his massive gut and heaped ashtrays. He was surrounded by half-drunk coffee cups and Post-it notes. Through his chaos Art listened intently to Dexter's instructions.

'Yes. I'm on it,' he said, and ended the call. Gormley scratched his almost completely bald head. A few rogue strands of hair caused a suitable comb-over that would have rivalled the legendary footballer Bobby Charlton. He looked down at his dark crew-neck sweater peppered with discarded ash and the day's offerings. Art Gormley was a complete mess. But he was nobody's fool, a fact not lost on Chief Superintendent Dexter.

In response to Dexter's request Art made the call. 'Kev, there's possibly a job on,' and gave him the brief.

'How much?' Stryker had heard his phone above the background noise as he completed a kick-boxing workout. The haggling over money took most of the time during the two-minute exchange. Then Stryker said, 'We're in,' to confirm participation for him and Jonta Roberts. He always did.

'Mr Dexter, it's sorted. They're available if and when.' Art spoke with a feeling of relief. It was a surprise to many that he was able to operate at all. It was well known that he sailed close to the wind. Despite his legal front he cleverly sought a low criminal profile.

For the police there was plenty of intelligence surrounding his activities, but never enough to cross the threshold needed to warrant the resources required to mount a thorough investigation. Or so it seemed, despite the council's licensing department making repeated requests to find any grounds that would prevent the renewal of Art's taxi operating licence, which he needed to run his business. The fact that the head of professional standards, in the form of John Dexter, was responsible for dealing with these requests ensured that Art Gormley could operate successfully.

He didn't enjoy being tasked and would have much preferred some lucrative low-level criminal activity with little or no chance of capture. But when Dexter called he had no option. His business depended on it. As far as Art Gormley was concerned, he hoped that would be an end to his involvement.

An hour or so later a second call from Dexter confirmed that Art was in it up to his proverbial neck. He had little or no option but to cooperate if his business were to survive.

After Dexter's second set of instructions Gormley deployed his most experienced and trusted driver to sit at the rear of the regular taxi rank outside the A & E of Parton Infirmary and not become involved in taking any fares. Art would ensure that she would be suitably paid for her time.

Rita had been supplied with a full description of the individual. When this male was leaving the hospital, she was to update her boss. Once Rita was deployed Art wasted no time in again ringing Kev Stryker with another set of Dexter's instructions, coupled with the promise of a further reward.

Jonta Roberts and Kev Stryker had thought they had finished that night's work and were about to knock off and have a pint, when on this occasion it was Jonta who received the call from Art.

'Shit. It will be a breakdown,' he said to Stryker. Jonta, being a trained mechanic, had a regular income from using those skills on Gormley's taxis.

'Just ignore the bastard. I'm dying for a pint,' Stryker said, knowing where the call had originated from.

Kev was hoping that it was still early enough to pursue some female action. They had made plans to attend their usual watering hole where the licensee, if ever required, could provide an alibi and whose CCTV system wouldn't be in operation for that particular night.

But Stryker knew that Jonta had no option but to answer. While that night's work was an excellent money-spinner, those jobs were few and far between. His work as a Gormley mechanic provided him with an income stream to support his partner and young child. Jonta took the call. He had no option either.

'It's not a breakdown. It's good money, and I need you both. Now.' Art gave no further details.

'I really wanted that pint,' Stryker said and sighed, still torn between drink, women and making more cash.

Some twenty minutes later they arrived at Gormley's garage, looking slightly harassed. This job, like the last, needed two men. Stryker and Roberts were like Batman and Robin, or in this case Ronnie and Reggie.

Art breathed a sigh of relief when the pair entered the office. Timing was key if Dexter's plan were to work. He was quickly briefing Jonta and Kev when Rita phoned from the taxi rank outside the hospital.

'Art, I'm ninety per cent sure it's him. He's in the front passenger seat in a Skoda Karoq. His clothing is totally different, but he's still wearing that bobble hat,' Rita said calmly. 'I'm just leaving the rank now, following him.' She ended the call. 'There's something familiar about this bloke,' Rita said to herself, racking her brains.

Jonta and Kev reversed out of Art's garage in the Honda CR-V with blacked-out windows. The vehicle was rarely seen outside the garage and was used only for Art's very special jobs. The seats in the rear of the vehicle had been specially altered and they now ran parallel along the two sides of the interior, similar to an ambulance. The front and rear compartments were separated by a soundproof partition. Naturally the Honda was bearing false plates, which had originally been assigned to an identical vehicle that had since been written off.

As ever, Jonta was comfortable in the driver's seat, with Kev out of sight in the rear. They were able to receive Rita's commentary via the taxi radio. Art, in his wisdom, had invested substantially in a communications system that not only could be used efficiently to communicate between the drivers but also possessed a stand-alone secure channel that only Gormley knew how to activate. He knew it was money well spent when he was faced with an evening such as this.

'The bloke has been dropped off and is on foot, walking down the cobbled area of the precinct towards the multistorey. Bit of a guess, but I can't see the point of him having a lift then getting a taxi. There is a police cordon blocking his route. Go for the multistorey.' Rita explained it to them logically, giving a full description of the man's clothing and appearance. Given the Arran sweater and the maroon trousers, it was very distinctive. 'I will try and keep you updated. He still has to walk almost the length of the precinct,' she added helpfully.

Jonta reacted immediately to the commentary. He

went through the gears of the Honda while accelerating up the almost empty five floors of the cold, stark city centre car park. Level one was clear, and level two had only one vehicle present, a silver VW Golf. It was their banker. Logically it was the nearest vehicle to the exit, and they would cover the lift.

They were relying on the fact that most people are naturally lazy as well as hoping that the Golf belonged to the subject. Furthermore, there was no visible CCTV covering this small area. If their target took a different route they would be forced to react and cover the remaining three vehicles, which were all sited on level four. Jonta parked the Honda on level two, in the closest bay to the lift doors. The multistorey staircase was only around the corner from the lifts, a matter of paces away.

Rita spoke. 'He's turned towards the car park, but that's it. I can't see him any longer.'

A few minutes earlier Pete had been sitting in Sutton's Karoq, approaching the top of the precinct and totally unaware of the Gormley's taxi that had followed their route from the hospital.

Pete turned to Geoff. 'Just drop me off here. I could do with some fresh air.'

'Are you sure? I can take you round to the multistorey,' Sutton said.

'No, I'll walk. Thanks for the lift, Geoff.' As Sutton brought the car to a halt Pete reached across and they managed an awkward embrace over the gearstick and the handbrake. It was a gesture of both warmth and care.

'You take care of yourself, young McIntyre,' Sutton added with some concern, then looking at his clothing, 'Make sure you don't get picked up. And love to Val.' He smiled at his mate.

'Bugger off, Sutton, and love to Debbie. She's much too good for you,' Pete said with a knowing wink as he opened the car door. Sutton watched him head off into the dark night and smiled again at his appearance before he drove off. His thoughts again wandered back to the gorgeous Debbie.

Pete took a deep breath. The temperature had cooled dramatically since his earlier evening visit to the precinct. The brogues supplied by the hospital were fitted with old-fashioned segs and sparks almost flew as he walked across the cobbles. He thought about phoning Val but knew it would be better to explain that night's events face to face.

He glanced at his watch. It was approaching 9.30 p.m. 'She will be halfway through a bottle of Pinot Grigio. So much for my counsellor's course,' he said to himself, 'Anyway, Val won't be expecting me home much before 10 p.m.'

He looked up. A lovely star-spangled sky momentarily distracted him before his attention was drawn to the flashing beacons of the police cordon surrounding the crime scene. Pete continued with his thoughts. *It will be a long and cold night for some. Poor Matt.*

He shoved his hands deep into the pockets of his newly acquired trousers, both to avoid the cold and to locate his car keys. He glanced across at Starbucks, which was now closed for the evening. Even though the precinct was ideally located in the city centre it had surprisingly few restaurants, and he knew that you would be lucky to purchase a bag of flavoured crisps at the Crop public house. Locally brewed hand-pulled ales and no food were the order of the day there. Pete hesitated as he passed the pub door. He really fancied a pint, just one. But then he considered his ridiculous appearance, changed his mind and continued along the cobbles to the pedestrian entrance of the multistorey.

Jonta was cold, very cold, mostly due to nerves. He and Stryker were playing blind now, with no more updates available from Rita. He looked across at Kev and immediately felt reassured by his muscular and athletic build. While Jonta was no slouch when it came to handling himself, Stryker was an expert and would always take the lead.

The pair waited at their planned location. There was no cranking lift sound or illumination of buttons. *He should be here by now*, Jonta thought.

While he was having these thoughts Pete McIntyre had entered the confines of the multistorey car park. He was contemplating the lift, which smelt of urine, or the less than welcoming graffiti-covered concrete staircase – which even though it was slightly more ventilated, still carried that unwelcome stench. It was a difficult choice. Taking his time, he took a deep breath, pushed open the heavy door and entered the gloomy corridor facing the foot of the steps.

'Fuck,' Jonta said, fumbling awkwardly for his balaclava. He looked straight across at his partner. 'The stairs,' he said, as they heard the sound of McIntyre's segs on his shoes echoing on the concrete. Stryker had already reacted. Only his eyes were showing from his newly donned headgear. He was already on the move.

Pete arrived at the heavy door of level two. There was some flaky yellow paint that created the impression of a sign. It indicated that he had reached his destination. Without looking up he yanked back the door and exhaled deeply before stepping forward in the direction of the parking bays. That was the only step he took.

In a matter of seconds McIntyre's face was hitting the concrete and both his hands were held tightly behind his back. He desperately struggled to move his face to one side, not to scream out but to breathe. With a huge effort he pulled upwards, his neck muscles straining, but just enough to allow a space between his face and the concrete floor.

He gasped once, and only once, before Jonta arrived on the scene and stuck some gaffer tape around his mouth. Any opportunity to shout out or alert someone immediately disappeared. The same roll of gaffer tape, part of the special equipment hidden in Art's vehicle, was used to secure his hands. With Stryker on one side and Jonta on the other they simultaneously lifted McIntyre up from his prone position with their arms linked beneath their captive's shoulders. As they were pulling him forward, Pete's legs had no option but to follow his body. McIntyre was forcibly dragged along and was practically running the few yards to Art's Honda. At the same time Jonta activated the key fob with his free hand.

Stryker took the lead as he approached the vehicle and opened the door, giving access to the rear of the vehicle, without releasing his grip. He jumped athletically into the car ahead of McIntyre, forcing him to follow, and almost single-handedly dragged him inside as Jonta instinctively released his grip.

Pete McIntyre felt as though his shoulder joint was being pulled out of its socket. He tried to scream out in pain but for the second time in a matter of minutes he was again face down, this time on the floor of the vehicle. His face was already heavily bruised and grazed from its earlier meeting with the concrete. His breathing, through a bloody and now broken nose, was laboured, thanks in part to a backhand reminder from Kev Stryker.

Jonta Roberts sat in the driver's seat and removed his balaclava. With his adrenaline running high, he desperately fought to control his heavy breathing. From his elevated position Jonta looked around to ensure that the coast was clear and there were no unwanted witnesses.

'Art, where now?' He posed the question via the secure radio channel, having been informed to contact Gormley only when they had secured their subject.

'Go to 56 Norfolk Street, The Counties. The keys are in the glove compartment,' Art replied.

Jonta set the satnav for the destination that Art had provided. He carefully reversed the vehicle out of its allocated parking bay. The Honda made its way methodically, circulating the two empty floors that led to the exit point. Upon entry they had obtained a prepaid ticket for a two-hour slot, which had been more than enough time for their task. Jonta fed the ticket through the machine. 'Move you, bastard,' Jonta said silently.

It seemed a lifetime before the barrier eventually lifted and they entered the main thoroughfare. The satnav indicated a five-mile journey that would take twelve minutes. However, Jonta would take an alternative route. He knew the area, and his way would avoid unwanted cameras and automatic number recognition systems.

His partner in crime, Kev Stryker, was more relaxed, and still wearing his balaclava while sitting in the rear of the vehicle. One foot was placed firmly across the centre of McIntyre's back as his captive lay prone and bound. He delved further into the equipment bag and found what he had been looking for. Stryker grabbed

McIntyre's hair and pulled it back before deftly slipping a black hood over Pete's head. He then released his grip, allowing the prisoner's head to painfully recoil. McIntyre was completely under his control.

Jonta took a right into Derbyshire Street, then a left to their destination, Norfolk Street. It was one of a series of identical rows of terrace houses named after English counties. He pulled up outside number 56, the end property. The houses were in poor repair. Many were boarded up with steel grilles, and those occupied were rented. The respective tenants paid their rent usually via fraudulent benefit claims. It was the original sink estate and everyone in Parton knew about The Counties. It was a blight on the outskirts of the city and carried with it some notoriety for its deprivation, associated drugs and criminality. 'It's Shitsville,' said Jonta Roberts to himself as he closed in on their destination.

For the residents, there was only one rule if you lived in The Counties: you never grass. Art Gormley had purchased a few Counties properties after a tip from one of his councillor contacts that they were looking at doing the place up. That had been some five years previously, but nothing had ever come of it. That lack of progress had prompted Art to drop the free taxi trips he had been providing for his councillor friend.

'Here we go,' Jonta said to himself. Roberts didn't need to look around as he jumped out of the vehicle, after having removed the house keys from the glove compartment. He opened the front door and entered number 56.

The first thing that met him was the smell of damp, which soon permeated his nostrils. Roberts first needed to ensure that no squatters or druggies had acquired a new home. He turned the light on in what an estate agent might refer to as a welcoming hallway and quickly cleared the ground floor. He began to climb the stairs. The landing light was a single bulb without a lightshade. It hung forlornly from the ceiling. 'Thank God it works,' he said out loud. Jonta was just relieved that the electricity was in working order, particularly as the banister was falling away.

The upstairs consisted of two bedrooms and a bathroom. One bedroom was completely empty, with no bulb in the light socket. There were no curtains, but Jonta could make out the rotting window frames thanks to the clear moonlit sky. A quick glance into the bathroom saw a torn, deeply stained shower curtain hanging limply over the bath. A repetitive dripping noise emanated from a leaking tap, like a consistent musical beat into a brown-stained sink.

He turned the light on as he entered the second bedroom. It flickered twice and came to life. A single dirty mattress that had once had blue and white stripes lay in the middle of the room, half-covered with a duvet matching the colours and stains of the mattress. Deep red curtains hung as limply as the shower curtain in the bathroom. They barely covered the only window.

In the corner of the room stood an old forgotten fridge. Jonta quickly opened the door. A carton of milk, a small loaf of bread and a half-opened can of baked beans were its only contents. Standing upright on the fridge was a kettle with the makings for tea and coffee. 'Luxury,' said Jonta, smiling to himself. 'But it's bloody cold in here,' he added.

With the house clear, and now knowing where their prisoner needed to be, Roberts left the front door of number 56 slightly ajar, returned to the vehicle and replaced his own balaclava. On this occasion caution got the better of him. He quickly looked around. No one in sight. Not that it would have mattered in The Counties. Nothing was ever reported to the authorities. He had expertly parked the Honda on the pavement as close as possible to the front door.

Jonta gave Kev Stryker the expected knock on the window and opened the car door. He manoeuvred Pete so that his head was hanging out of the vehicle and facing the open door of the house.

'It's an upstairs bedroom,' Jonta said to his good mate.

'I'll take him. You go to the top of the stairs,' Stryker said to Roberts, thinking that two of them trying to drag someone up the narrow stairs would be impossible. Kev faced towards McIntyre's head. He bent down and pushed his arms up and under his captive's armpits after first reaching forward and cutting the gaffer tape holding his ankles. Showing great strength, Stryker pulled Pete's prone body forwards and towards him till his legs dropped out of the vehicle. McIntyre became almost upright now in what looked like an embrace with Stryker, who then began walking backwards, pulling McIntyre, and entered the property. Straining now, Stryker dragged McIntyre step by step to the top of the stairs, forcing him to follow.

'Get in, you bastard,' he muttered quietly, dragging Pete across the landing to the designated bedroom indicated by Jonta. Kev threw McIntyre down on the grimy mattress like a discarded rag doll, while Roberts dashed downstairs, grabbed the roll of gaffer tape and locked the Honda. Finally, he re-entered the house and secured the front door.

A few minutes later McIntyre was reacquainted with the gaffer tape around his ankles and trussed up like a Christmas turkey. Through the poor light Jonta Roberts and Kev Stryker viewed their prisoner. Two pairs of black eyes stared out menacingly from their infamous headwear.

With their identities concealed, they removed McIntyre's black hood. Tonight's task was complete, and the only matter that concerned them was the money they were now owed. That would be waiting for them when they returned the vehicle and the house keys to Art Gormley. The pair returned to the Honda and removed their balaclavas. These items would be burnt at Art's small incinerator, together with the remainder of their clothing.

Kev was sitting behind the driver's seat. Jonta gave him a knowing wink in the rear-view mirror then calmly checked the mirror again, put the Honda into first gear and slowly pulled away, ignoring the sound of fireworks. Strangely, for the few residents of The Counties, firework celebrations were a year-round occurrence.

Some fifteen minutes later, having returned to the garage, they were removing their clothing while updating Art. 'Shit. Nearly forgot this,' Kev said, as he chucked McIntyre's phone into the pile of possessions that needed to be destroyed.

'I'll get someone to look in tomorrow morning,' Art said, referring to their prisoner. He brushed away some cigarette ash and the remainder of a recently consumed kebab from his heavily stained sweater. Gormley's main concern, however, was about where they would go from there. 'No doubt I'll get further instructions,' he said to himself, lighting up yet another cigarette as he handed over a package to Roberts.

'That's good,' Jonta said to his boss, having counted the bundle of notes. He nodded across to Kev, who was just stuffing his pockets with the final bundle.

'Fucking busy night, Jonta,' Kev said as they made their exit. After a quick embrace they made their way from the garage and headed in different directions. Stryker was off for that well-earned drink, and maybe he would give one of his girls a call, while Jonta was going home to deliver the news, together with a few things he was planning, that family winter trip to the warmth of the Canaries was no longer a dream.

Pete McIntyre lay on his left side. Blood was caked around his face and the gaffer tape was cutting into the corners of his mouth. Despite the violence he had remained conscious throughout, although he could hardly feel his fingers. He hadn't recognised the voices of his captors, but each time he closed his own eyes McIntyre saw theirs.

It was a nightmare that would always remain with him. Pete was of an age to be able to remember the fear and intimidation caused when the IRA would appear before the media, anonymised by identical headwear. He didn't bother trying to make a noise. He had enough to do with trying to breathe through the confines of the tape and his broken nose. But, above all, it was the bloody cold that caused his body to ache and tremor.

Pete looked around his room. It was shit. Despite the problems with his nose he kept getting a fair whiff of the disgusting duvet, which in turn caused his stomach to churn. He moved his head slowly from side to side to stop himself retching. Given the tape around his mouth, vomiting was the last thing he needed.

McIntyre was sore – yes, very sore – but he was very much coming to terms with his situation, and even his closest friends were unaware of just how resilient he was. In his rugby-playing days he had been an uncompromising second-row who never took a step backwards. Quiet and unassuming, he was a hard player, light years away from the reputation he had gained as the caring Pastoral Pete, the Colts team manager.

Desperately trying to dismiss the eyes of those who had captured him, he tried to sleep. Pete McIntyre knew that whatever was coming next was likely to be the biggest possible test of his resilience. He knew he was fighting for his life and although his mind was wandering, unlike Kev and Jonta, or even Art Gormley, McIntyre was almost certain that he knew the reason why he had been kidnapped.

As Pete was trying desperately to find a comfortable position to lie in, Geoff Sutton was making his way back from the precinct. Walking through the front door he called out, 'Sorry, Debbie.' Geoff smiled contentedly as the warmth of being indoors worked its way through his body. There was no response, no sign. He made his way to the living room before calling out again.

'Up here, silly bugger,' Debbie replied as he raced up the stairs. 'Love you, Sutton,' she said as he entered the bedroom. His glance met her gorgeous eyes shining out from under the duvet.

Geoff Sutton knew he was in love.

14

Val McIntyre

Val McIntyre was fast asleep on the sofa. Earlier she'd grabbed a spare duvet and snuggled down for the evening on her own. She was now knocked out, both by a series of *Made in Chelsea* and more than three-quarters of her bottle of Pinot. She awoke around 4 a.m., half-asleep and half-drunk. Though her thinking was blurred, she thought that Pete had been very considerate in not disturbing her and that she would do the same.

Still drowsy, she made her way as quietly as possible to the spare bedroom – which Ben, their grandson, occupied on his frequent sleepovers. While trying to undress, Val knocked over the small bedside lamp. 'It's only me, Pete,' she said, slurring loudly. Grateful for no reply, she finally made it under the covers.

***

The alarm sounded at exactly 6.45 a.m. on the Friday morning. Sutton moaned and rolled over to feel for Debbie. Nothing. He reached further. Absolutely nothing. He was alone.

He rolled out of bed slowly, stretched and moaned again. The second moan was purely a natural response to an aching body that comes with age. 'Must go swimming soon,' Sutton said to himself as he pushed his arms up towards the ceiling, causing further unwanted pain. He drew back the curtains to see a clean, fresh frost leaving its mark on the surroundings.

Geoff had awoken just in time to see a glimpse of his Debbie, wrapped up against the cold air, taking the short walk to the Parlour Cafe. He smiled to himself as she slipped on the ice but quickly recovered her balance. 'Apart from work, life is good,' Sutton said to himself.

After a quick shower Sutton was dressed and downstairs reading the note that Debbie had written for him that morning. Not only did it catalogue what had happened last night, but it also reminded him that she would be home late after another counselling session.

It was no understatement to say that these sessions had saved their relationship. Recovering from a previous violent and emotionally abusive relationship had been traumatic for Debbie. Matters had reached a psychological climax when she had become involved with Sutton. The therapy was part of Debbie's recovery process, and it had been an instant success.

His phone rang, instantly removing the memories of last night's intimacy and returning Sutton to reality.

'Hi Val, how is he?' Sutton said without thinking. He immediately recognised the caller and had been expecting contact from the McIntyres, but wondered why it was Val calling. 'Maybe Pete is still sleeping. That would be very understandable,' he said to himself.

'Geoff what do you mean by how is he? What the hell's happened?' Val said, sniffing down the phone. She was sitting in their bedroom, having recently realised that Pete hadn't returned the night before. Despite her blinding headache, the main component of a stinking hangover, Val was shaking with fear. Her natural instincts had informed her that Pete was in serious trouble.

'Val, I'll see you in twenty minutes.' Sutton didn't need to extend the conversation. Within moments he was out of the house and on the road without waiting for his windscreen to clear properly. It took a skid on one of the minor estate roads for Sutton to come to his senses and accept that the slippery road conditions required respect.

Val answered the door dishevelled, and in a state of obvious shock. Geoff took her in his arms and guided her back through the house. With yesterday's smudged mascara still smeared across her tearstained cheeks, Val was suffering, and it took Sutton some time before he could even prise her from his reassuring embrace. Geoff took his time. 'Where the hell do I start?' he said to himself, 'I haven't a clue where he is.' He manoeuvred Val to the sofa.

'I'll put the kettle on,' he said rather pathetically, but at least it bought him more time. When the tea arrived, Val clasped the plain white mug as if her life depended on it. She was desperate to speak.

'It was the first evening on his mental health counsellors' course, but he left here early. He got a call from Matt Galloway so he went to meet him at the usual place – Starbucks, in the precinct.' Val sniffed.

'His mental health counsellors' course?' Sutton said. He had not heard Pete mention this.

'It was after Roger's death. Pete felt he needed to do something positive. It was going to help him, help others and possibly help understand why on earth Roger died,' Val said impatiently, as if emphasising the merits of her Pete. Sutton knew she must be desperate to hear news of her husband.

'Val, Matt Galloway was shot at the precinct last night shortly after meeting Pete, who was first on the scene and who went with him in the ambulance. He phoned me and I met him at the hospital. I then dropped him off at the precinct, and the last I saw of him he was walking back to pick up the car from the multistorey. Val, I haven't a clue where Pete is now.' Sutton spelt out the last sentence very slowly, but he made his point emphatically.

Val looked directly at Sutton, took a sip of tea and slowly swallowed. 'The car isn't here, Geoff.' She stared at Sutton.

'I know, Val. It was the first thing I noticed when I arrived.' Sutton said quickly, 'I need to go to work. The first thing we need to do is to check the multistorey for the car,' he added. 'In the meantime, I'll ask Tina to pop round.' Sutton was referring to Stew Grant's wife. He knew he couldn't just leave Val to fend for herself when she desperately needed support. The spouse of his lifelong mate Stew Grant was the obvious choice. Due to the length of time they had all known each other, the wives were almost as close as the husbands.

'We will need a statement and an officer will be round later, Val.' Sutton gave her one final long hug, and again he was forced to prise himself away. Finally he moved to the front door and hesitated. 'Val, I'm sorry, but I have to ask you… There is no way that Pete could have gone somewhere else without telling you, is there?'

The look that Val gave him in response not only answered his query but also caused Sutton instantly to regret that he had posed the question. He closed the front door deeply upset, both at the way their conversation had ended but also at the thought of his missing friend.

Having confirmed the reg number with Val, he called the control room for the multistorey in the precinct to be searched for a silver VW Golf. He then called Tina and asked her to go and see Val that morning. Feeling sure she would get more than a full account from Val herself, he only gave her scant details.

At 8.30 a.m. Sutton had arrived at Parton Constabulary Headquarters, a building that was located adjacent to the city centre police station. After he reversed into one of the few parking spaces available Geoff took a phone call. A silver VW Golf had been located on the second level of the precinct multistorey and all relevant CCTV footage had been seized.

Sutton remained in the driver's seat as the implications of the update resonated through his troubled thoughts. 'Where the hell are you, Pete?' he said out loud, followed by something more sinister. 'Are you alive?' Geoff had a troubled look upon his face as he made his way to another meeting with Turner. Firth and Delaney had also been ordered to attend.

The door to Turner's office was open, which was unusual in itself. Sutton was the last to arrive, or so he thought, as Chief Constable Mayling followed immediately behind him and closed the door. Even in Turner's fairly spacious office it was quite cramped.

Turner remained behind his desk while the others faced him in something resembling a semicircle. While the chief constable was present there was only one person in charge of this briefing. Turner began speaking.

'Last night, Wendy Galloway's son Matt Galloway was shot in the precinct by persons unknown riding a motorcycle. It was another professional hit, identical in many ways to the Lucifer's job. Matt had received a text from PC Robbie Hanson just as he was leaving the cafe, where he was a meeting a guy called,' Turner paused momentarily, 'Pete McIntyre. Matt had only just moved in with Hanson. Apparently they are long-time mates. Coincidence or not, but Bill Rudding was also seen in the area immediately prior to this shooting. That's where we are,' he said with some finality.

'Not quite, sir,' Sutton said politely. He solemnly updated the audience with the fact that Pete McIntyre, the primary witness to the previous night's shooting, was now a missing person who in all probability had been kidnapped. Turner stared at Sutton and, unusually for him, looked distinctly nervous.

'Right, where do we go from here?' Turner said, recovering his composure while turning a page in front of him. He continued to make copious notes. 'Do we really think that Wendy Galloway would authorise her son's shooting?' He repeated the question posed last night by Trish Delaney. There was tension in the air, complete silence. No one wanted to speak.

It seemed like an age before Turner spoke again. 'We have surveillance on Hanson today, and a covert search team are attending the East Parton marina where Rudding had his meet yesterday, are they not?' It was a question, not a statement, and was immediately picked up by Firth.

'Yes, sir, I briefed the search team an hour or so ago. They will be on the plot by now and the surveillance operation is already underway,' she said immediately.

Chris Mayling spoke. 'We could arrest both Hanson and Rudding. It will be exceptionally damaging to the force's reputation, but we could try and publicise some positive spin about how proactive we are regarding corruption. But it will still cause serious problems,' she said without conviction. 'I will also need time with our media officer before any press release. Any arrests of serving police officers are always leaked,' Mayling added in a disappointed tone.

Ron Turner knew that this course of action would be the last thing Mayling would want but it was becoming inevitable. The chief constable sighed to herself. She knew that following Operations TRUST and PROOF, whatever the outcome of RESOLVE, Parton Constabulary would be back in the national spotlight. And not for the right reasons.

Turner hesitated and looked directly at Sutton. 'Have we had any contact regarding … McIntyre?'

'Absolutely nothing,' Sutton said quickly.

'A kidnap with no bloody demands,' Turner said out loud to no one in particular. 'Geoff, I want you and Jo to look at this aspect. We have proactive work going on with Hanson and the search is being carried out with regard to Rudding's activities,' he added.

'Let's run with the operations as planned today and assess developments. We will review at 6 p.m. here,' Mayling said emphatically.

There wasn't a single word spoken as they left Ron Turner's office. To say that they all had other things on their minds was an understatement.

***

At the same time as the Operation RESOLVE briefing ended Chief Superintendent John Dexter was seated behind his desk when the ever-faithful Shaun Adams brought in yet another cup of hot black coffee and placed it on his desk.

'Are your teeth OK, sir?' Adams asked politely.

'Pardon?' said Dexter, as he sought to stifle a yawn. It had been an early start.

'Yesterday's dental appointment,' Adams continued.

'Yes, fine now, Shaun, thanks,' Dexter said dismissively, indicating it was time for him to leave.

Once on his own, Dexter reflected on his morning's work. It would have been almost at the same time as when Debbie was opening the Parlour Cafe that Dexter had returned to the east marina in his BMW. It was approaching daylight when, dressed as smartly as ever, he returned to the disused unit, the scene of yesterday's meeting.

'It was bloody freezing.' Dexter thought back to the morning. Using the torch from his mobile phone, it hadn't taken him long to find what he was looking for. His silver pen top glinted against the small beam generated by the phone.

He was never the earliest to arrive for work, and when his subordinates had arrived they were surprised to see the boss's immaculate Beamer parked in its designated bay. Now, sitting alone in his office, he was attempting to restore the renowned shine on the Dexter footwear. Through the open door he would never have noticed Shaun Adams quietly documenting another piece of unusual timekeeping.

'More crap,' Dexter said to himself while reviewing the large amount of paperwork mounting up on his desk. It included a vast number of vetting forms. Professional standards were given the role of vetting by the force, and while there was a small department responsible for carrying out the basic checks, the forms always came to John Dexter for the final endorsement. There was no doubt that vetting was an important aspect for the force and getting it wrong could cause not only embarrassment but also significant reputational damage. Not only did they have responsibility of ensuring that new appointees, whether police officers or civilians, were fit and proper people, but they also maintained a protocol with the local authority to assist in their licensing enquiries for pubs and taxi firms.

To his colleagues Dexter was diligent to the point of being obsessive when it came to vetting. It was a responsibility he would never delegate. Even if he were on annual leave, vetting forms would be kept for his personal attention. For John Dexter it was the most important aspect of his job. And in the case of Art Gormley, Dexter's signature, written with his unique silver pen, kept his thriving business on track.

'Life is back on an even keel,' Dexter said to himself before pausing, taking a deep breath and adding, 'For now.' Then he exhaled.

There was time for a further moment of reflection and a sip of his thick black coffee before the unmistakable ringtone of his other phone instantly returned him to the here and now. It rarely rang during his working hours and produced a shiver down his normally arrow-straight spine. It caused him to gulp his hot coffee, which instantly scalded the back of his throat. He checked the contact. It was a pseudonym. Wendy Galloway never phoned him directly.

Dexter took a risk and didn't answer. It was a tactic to give him time, but it would only work once.

Wendy Galloway didn't make just one phone call, and while John Dexter was the most senior and her longest-running asset she had more than one option within Parton Constabulary, and she wasn't going to wait.

15

Bob Hope

Sutton had emerged from Turner's briefing with his head in a spin. He desperately sought a coffee and some seclusion and so, now that Firth was involved in the search, he returned to their empty office. It was a safe environment. He knew he would be alone.

Sutton rummaged in his Barbour to recover his informants' phone. He had procrastinated for too long and, while he hated the thought, if it were Vern Edwards on the other end he wouldn't be ringing to ask about the weather and he wouldn't go away. Such was Edwards's influence, even when incarcerated, that Geoff knew it was a distinct possibility that he had some information regarding the Parton shootings. He looked up the Bob Hope contact and rang the number.

The phone rang once, twice. Geoff swore inwardly at his weakness as he felt his hand shaking. 'About fucking time too, Sutton. Just hold on a minute.' Geoff immediately recognised the voice. It was unforgettable, as far as he was concerned. Now Sutton had made contact he imagined that the incarcerated Edwards had an empire similar to that of Grouty in Ronnie Barker's *Porridge*, but minus any humour.

'What the fuck's happening in Parton, Sutton? The

filth need to get a grip,' Edwards said with some authority. Geoff didn't reply. He needed to hear what Edwards was about to say. There was a prolonged silence between them. It was patently obvious to Sutton that despite the prison regime Vern Edwards had changed little, was still very much his own man and was totally in control. A bribe or two here and there would enable him to operate much as he wished, without the obvious freedom. Having a phone, and using it almost when he wanted, would not only allow him control of any existing outside assets but would enable him to organise deliveries that would make life inside bearable.

'What's fucking happening, Sutton?' Edwards menacingly repeated his question. Silence again. 'Sutton, I've got some info on the shootings,' Edwards added. No response.

Geoff was almost beside himself, such was his impatience to ask the questions that would ascertain if Edwards did really have a nugget of intelligence, or was he just bored and increasingly bitter? Did he just want retribution against Wendy Galloway? Geoff knew it was a grudge that would only die with him.

'The thing is, Sutton, if you had called me back earlier Matt Galloway wouldn't be in hospital now.' Edwards continued his one-way conversation. He knew the score. Just release the reel. Give him some line. Add some bait. Vern was in his element, similar to a skilled fisherman searching for a bite.

'What do you want, Vern?' it was Sutton's first contribution to the call, and he needed to know from the outset what Edwards's motivation was, other than his lifelong vendetta with Wendy Galloway.

'I need a fucking script,' Edwards said quickly. 'My

fucking parole board is not too far away. Something about me being a fucking hero, helping the police to bring an end to the shootings, might help in getting me out of this shithole. Reformed character and all that crap.' Edwards the career criminal, as eloquent as ever, had made his pitch.

'Vern, any information will have to be official. These phone calls are unlawful. It will all require taping on an authorised prison visit,' Sutton said, trying to take control of the situation and also to sound confident. This time it was Edwards who was the silent partner in the call as Vern considered all his options.

'I will see the fucking governor today and will request a prison visit. It will be high-priority because I can protect life,' Edwards boasted, and ended the call.

Sutton scanned the bare walls of his new office. He needed the time to reflect on the phone call. There was no doubt in Geoff's mind that in the next hour or so, Vern Edwards would be appearing before the governor, demanding his prison visit. Despite his current circumstances Edwards had some influence.

'Forget the call,' Geoff said to himself. He could try and ignore the content and merely document an intelligence report sheet stating that he had received an unauthorised contact from Vern Edwards but there was nothing of note. But the recent shootings needed a breakthrough and Edwards, as dangerous and manipulative as they come, could potentially provide this.

He required authorisation and so rang Ron Turner's extension. Sutton used the pseudonym and quickly relayed the recent history he had had with Bob Hope, culminating in his most recent phone call a few minutes before. Turner knew exactly who Bob Hope really was.

'What's his bloody motivation, Geoff? Revenge? And does he really have something we don't know?' Turner repeated the questions that Sutton had already asked himself.

'I can't answer that, sir. But, knowing Edwards, I feel sure we will get the prison visit request today, and realistically I don't think we have anything to lose,' Sutton said earnestly.

'We can discuss it at tonight's briefing.' Turner ended the call and pondered over Sutton's conversation. He paused just for a moment with the palm of his hand still resting on his telephone receiver. Turner knew that the matter of a prison visit with a dangerous informant had to be discussed with Chris Mayling. Despite his vast experience, Ron Turner had learnt a significant lesson from Operation PROOF, and his chief constable deserved respect.

Once Sutton had finished his conversation with Turner he travelled to meet Jo Firth, who was liaising with the search team. When he parked he heard the instantly recognisable noise of his informants' phone. It was the call he expected.

'I've seen the fucking governor, Sutton. I will be seeing you soon.' Edwards chuckled down the phone and ended the conversation as another shiver was sent down Sutton's spine. He hated Vern Edwards and, if he was honest, was frightened of him. Past history had left an indelible scar deep in his mind.

While the search was taking place on the east side of the marina, Sutton and Firth decided to meet in one of the few low-profile cafes on the west side. Firth was due to meet with the search team supervisor who, dressed as a site worker, wouldn't look out of place in an area that seemed to be constantly under development. Sutton was eager for her to know about his recent contact with Edwards.

'Jo, I hope you've got no plans for tomorrow.' Sutton added, 'I think there is every chance that we will be off to HMP Wassingham.'

Firth couldn't hide her curiosity. 'Why? Who?' The words really didn't make sense together. There were two questions in two words. Sutton gladly explained his association with Vern Edwards, and that he was his former handler. Firth was wide-eyed with amazement. When she was a mid-career officer she had been on Crown Court security during the infamous Vern Edwards trial. It had been a real eye-opener at the time for an officer who was relatively young and new in service to see the circus coming to town.

There was a perverse awe attached to Vern Edwards, a fact that wasn't lost on Firth. And now potentially she was to have the opportunity of meeting him. Her feelings quickly changed to those of apprehension and vulnerability, 'If the visit happens, will I be up to the job?' Firth asked herself. In former times she would have looked to a bottle of vodka for some comfort. There had always been plenty close by.

Their conversation ended abruptly when they were joined by the search team sergeant. His hands were gripping a hot cup of coffee as he warmed himself after the freezing cold of the previous two hours. 'Sorry, Jo. We found absolutely nothing, other than a few ancient lobster pots,' was his brief update.

'Are you sure you checked the correct unit?' Firth asked, thinking they had missed something.

'Jo, not only did we do the one with the overhanging

sky-blue door, but we also searched every bloody unit,' he said, taking a long, slow mouthful of coffee, which brought feeling back into his previously freezing bones.

'Thanks for trying.' Firth failed to hide her disappointment. He left their table to join the rest of the team, who had just arrived for some well-earned refreshment.

Jo's phone rang. Rory Lomas and his operatives were back on Parton Constabulary territory. Another early start. This time it was a different target, but it was yet another police officer. 'They must have some serious problems,' Lomas said to himself.

They had plotted around the subject's block of flats after first identifying Robbie Hanson's distinctive black Audi A3 Sportback in an allocated parking bay that indicated the flat number of the vehicle's owner. It was approaching mid-morning and there had been had no movement whatsoever. 'Never mind. There are worse jobs to be on,' Lomas said to himself. He wondered if this enquiry might be a runner, meaning a weekend deployment and some much-wanted overtime for him and the team.

He couldn't help thinking about the investigation. The briefing they had been given had been restricted to their target. But the fact that they had been tasked outside their Borrington force area and the subject was, for the second time in two consecutive days, a serving cop, was enough to suggest that the job was extremely sensitive and quite possibly linked to their two recent shootings.

It had been a sleepless night for their target, Robbie Hanson. Matt Galloway hadn't returned as expected. Consequently, Robbie felt compelled to walk towards the city centre precinct. He knew where they would be – at the usual meeting place for Pastoral Pete, and with so much going on in his young life the fresh air would do him good.

As he neared the city centre he saw from a distance the blues and twos. Call it a sixth sense, but Hanson went no further on his intended the journey and returned home. With shaking fingers he opened up his Twitter app to access the latest news. No names were mentioned regarding the victim of another shooting, but Hanson's knowledge and instinct told him it was Matt Galloway.

After grabbing his car keys Robbie made the short trip in his Audi to the infirmary. The sight of armed police confirmed his thoughts. Reverting to his police way of thinking as opposed to that of a concerned friend, Hanson wondered how any mother could shoot her son. He knew full well about the friction between Matt and Wendy.

'It's an off, off, off.' Lomas heard the news. 'At last,' he said to himself, 'some movement.' One of the major problems he had as a supervisor was the boredom that caused drifts in concentration for his team during prolonged periods of inaction.

It was another couple of hours before Lomas took the opportunity to update Firth while she was at the marina. 'Nothing of great interest, Jo. He's been out at his parents' farm this morning. Due to the terrain we couldn't get too close without compromise. Got a couple of pictures when he came out. He looked pretty upset. He's back home, and we are now plotted outside his flat.'

'Subject on the move.' Firth heard the background radio transmission from one of Lomas' operatives. 'Shit, go,' she heard, and Lomas was gone.

No sooner had one conversation ended when another began as Sutton's phone rang. It was Trish Delaney,

'Geoff, can we meet in your office at HQ? I've got some news that I need to give you in person,' she said quietly.

'Twenty minutes,' Sutton said immediately, and finished the conversation, 'Drink up,' he told Firth. The two were on their way.

Delaney had arranged to meet Sutton and Firth in their small office on the same floor as the command suite at Parton HQ. Delaney looked agitated, to the extent that even her normal tidy appearance was suffering. She brushed away some loose strands of her normally very groomed black hair out of her eyeline. She looked as though she couldn't contain herself and talked quickly.

'We took some extended CCTV footage from yesterday's surveillance around the marina. If you remember, there was a BMW involved. At the time an unknown individual alighted from the white van associated with Wendy Galloway at the birdwatchers' car park. That individual then drove off in the Beamer. There are a couple of posh restaurants on the west marina that have their own private state-of-the-art CCTV. It clocked the Beamer and the van. It's cracking footage. Not only does it show the reg number, but it also captured the image of the driver of the BMW. It's bloody Dexter, John bloody Dexter.'

There was silence between the three. Delaney was standing, awaiting a response, with Firth and Sutton staring at her, occupying the only chairs available.

Sutton broke the silence. 'Dexter, our John Dexter?' He repeated Delaney's comments. It was a meaningless statement, merely confirming their incredulity that the force's head of professional standards had now become part of the enquiry. 'Does Turner know?' he added in a far more measured tone.

'Not yet, but the enquiry team do. It was a delegated action prompted from yesterday's surveillance on Rudding. Everyone in the bloody force knows John Dexter and his posh cars,' Trish said emphatically, again trying to flick those annoying strands out of her eyeline.

The conversation was interrupted as Ron Turner entered their office. He didn't bother to knock. 'Geoff, the prison has been on, and I have a meeting to confirm a visit with the chief at 1 p.m.,' he said, and was about to walk away when Sutton spoke.

'You might like to update her about this, sir.' Not wishing to steal Delaney's thunder, Sutton looked across at his colleague. Delaney imparted her information about how Chief Superintendent John Dexter had now entered the investigation picture. If Turner was surprised, he didn't let on. 'I may need to speak with her earlier than I thought,' Turner murmured to no one in particular, in a direct reference to his lunchtime meeting with Chris Mayling.

He exited their office almost as quickly as he entered, giving nothing away to his present audience. When he left their company a broad grin appeared across his face. 'It couldn't have happened to a nicer chap,' said Turner to himself. 'Dexter involved with Galloway.' He chuckled.

16

Stew Grant

On that Friday morning Rita left her car at home and walked from her small bedsit to her place of work at Art Gormley's. 'Another day, another dollar,' she said to herself, walking briskly to keep warm.

She lived alone, had done for years, and had worked for Art ever since she had lost her domestic cleaning job some time before. She didn't particularly enjoy her role of part cleaner, part taxi driver, but she had been loyal to Art over a period of time. And he, in recognition, paid her more than his other employees, apart from the skilled Jonta Roberts. Rita saved earnestly. It was a simple way of life that, given her current circumstances, suited her for the time being.

Art Gormley sat in his usually bloated state, surveying his empty desk. It was cleaned daily, and always by Rita. It was a functional necessity, such was the mess that Gormley would leave when he finished work for the evening. It was an unwritten rule that no one was allowed entry into Art's office unless invited. That said, the only time Art's office was anything other than a complete tip was when Rita had completed her first job of the day. Today was no exception.

'Morning, Art,' Rita said politely. She knocked and

opened the door, then presented him with a huge white mug of coffee with the word *BOSS* emblazoned on it in large red capital letters. That was her second job of the day.

'Ta,' Gormley replied, without looking up.

He arrived for work just before the nightshift raced away and shortly after Rita had cleaned his office. His timing was important, and he started at that time so he could count the takings over the previous twenty-four hours on a tidy desk.

Today Art was troubled. The kidnap wasn't the problem, but he knew that keeping the victim would be a nightmare. Dexter would give no idea of timescales. Art regarded John Dexter as a necessary associate, although he had no time for him. Sadly, without Dexter's support, Gormley wouldn't have a business. It was as simple as that.

Despite his natural and regular dishonesty Art's criminality was at a low level. He was more a Del Boy character, not a kidnapper or murderer. Gormley turned white as thoughts echoed around his mind. Holding someone against their will was a different ball game. He tried to console himself with the fact that personally he was not involved in a hands-on way. It made him feel slightly better. 'John Dexter is just some corrupt shit,' he said to himself. 'Nevertheless, I need to make sure the bastard's OK,' was a promise he made to himself about his new tenant in Norfolk Street. The thought emanated from his dubious conscience.

***

Art's prisoner had different issues. Pete McIntyre had spent a horrendous night trussed up. His mind was still racing as he drifted in and out of consciousness.

The sun started to make its appearance through the threadbare curtains. Despite having submerged himself under the rank duvet he was still freezing. When he was alone the previous night he had mentally tried to come to terms with his circumstances. But now his mind was slowly beginning to play games. Pete was shivering, not helped by the fact that he had wet himself. Most notably his breathing became shallower, in part due to a developing cough. The gaffer tape around his mouth and the broken nose just added to his problems.

Some twenty minutes later Jonta Roberts was the passenger in the rear seat in the Honda, whose blacked-out windows obscured the view inside from any prying eyes. Rita was driving them to The Counties suburb of the city, on their way to Norfolk Street. Being the chosen two, selected by Art, they talked. Well, Jonta talked, and Rita listened. Having often been tasked by Art to complete some of his less honest activities, the pair had struck up a solid relationship over time.

Rita knew Jonta to be very much a family man. He doted on his partner Gemma and, the apple of his eye, their two-year-old daughter, Kate. Rita politely endured the weekly update of Kate's latest exploits, together with the associated video clips on his smartphone. She had forgotten the times that Jonta had said these immortal words, 'I'm stopping the bad stuff, Rita,' as they embarked on another one of Art's enterprises. The previous jobs had been chicken feed compared with the paydays offered to him for the shootings.

Gemma may not have been fully aware of her partner's extracurricular activities, but she had more than an inkling. 'When you don't want to know the answer, don't pose the question,' she often said to herself, as yet another normally unaffordable gift arrived for both her and Kate. Yet Jonta was a troubled man.

On Art's instructions the Honda had been fully valeted by the night shift, and before they had travelled Rita had popped out for some necessary provisions. From the lost property area in the office she had been able to collect some items of miscellaneous clothing that customers had discarded in the rear of Gormley's fleet of taxis. What was left in the back of taxis never ceased to amaze the staff. Jonta also took the opportunity to discreetly arm himself with a small cosh.

On their way to Norfolk Street the pair discussed that morning's job. Rita was more than happy with the get in and get out strategy. She had made it clear to Jonta that she didn't want to see their subject or be in his room.

Rita cleverly parked the vehicle, again as close as possible to the front door. Not that there was a significant need to do so. The majority of The Counties residents tended not to rise before twelve noon.

'Watch the stairs, Rita,' Jonta said, donning his black balaclava, as the two made their way into the house that had become McIntyre's prison.

Upstairs Pete heard the guests arrive. His heart started racing and his nose started to bleed again as his blood pressure rose. With an unwanted cough and splutter he struggled to move around the mattress but was only able to wriggle onto his side as he awaited his captors' appearance.

Jonta took the clothes from Rita and entered McIntyre's room. He bent down, and with only a minimum of difficulty manoeuvred Pete onto his back. Then he placed his small cosh across the base of his neck. He bent over the prone body and tried to avoid the stench of urine. He spoke to McIntyre in hushed tones.

'I'm going to fucking cut away the tapes so you can sit up. The cosh is the start.' Jonta gave him a sharp, painful reminder with a short rap across his shins. His actions were to ensure that McIntyre remained under his complete control. As soon as all the bindings were cut away, McIntyre immediately breathed more easily. He wasn't about to shout out or take on his captor, whose eyes seemed to burn through him from out of the sinister black balaclava. Pete thought that his second unseen guest may well be armed.

'Can I stand?' McIntyre asked, even though he didn't know if he would actually be able to get to his feet. His request was greeted by a masked nod of the head, and Jonta casually threw a white plastic bag over to him containing the lost property clothing. McIntyre looked down at his maroon Wolsey trousers and despite his plight, coughed and smiled inwardly. 'Better times,' he said to himself, and slowly undressed. He knew he couldn't afford any modesty.

There was a knock on the door, which was then opened. And without a word a plate of sandwiches and a large bottle of water were pushed by unseen hands along the bare floorboards. The refreshments appeared from behind the opening door. There was never any chance that Rita would enter, either with or without a mask. A long time had passed but she had immediately recognised McIntyre's voice, and it confirmed her first thoughts following the sighting of him the night before at the infirmary.

McIntyre didn't ask questions. There was no point. But at least he was now dressed in more ill-fitting but thankfully dry clothes. In addition, to the rasping cough he couldn't ignore, he had developed a sore throat. As Pete sat his ankles were bound again, this time with white plastic grips. His left wrist was tied to the small supporting leg of a strong bedside cabinet, the one piece of furniture in the room, which had the added advantage of being bolted to the floor. His free right wrist would allow him at least to eat, drink, urinate and potentially sleep more easily.

As this process was taking place McIntyre's mind was racing. 'What will happen to me?' He hardly dared to think what might become of him. Should he shout out? A waste of time. He correctly thought that his prison had been carefully chosen. Even if someone passing heard his screams absolutely nothing would happen. The fact they had visited and given him food was in his mind a positive. 'So far they want me alive,' he said inwardly. Then he coughed loudly. His condition was getting worse.

Pete heard his captors leave almost as soon as they had arrived. Mentally he felt better in himself, and with his right hand he immediately reached for a bottle of water. He almost gagged and gulped at the liquid. He desperately needed hydrating. Pete placed the bottle down and gagged again as he shoved a sandwich into his mouth. 'God, I am hungry,' he said, and coughed loudly. The remnants of the sandwich acted like projectile vomit and landed on and beyond the stained duvet.

He looked across at the food, which consisted of sandwiches and a few chocolate biscuits. The refreshments and, perversely, the visit, had given him a lift. However, this short-term positivity quickly began to evaporate. The more he thought about his circumstances and, more importantly, the potential characters behind his kidnapping, McIntyre knew in his heart of hearts that time wasn't on his side.

Rita and Jonta returned to Gormley's and reported that his prisoner had been given food and clothing. Jonta returned to his day job and serviced a couple of motorcycles from the fleet, while Rita began to address her only source of disagreement with Art, which was her time off. She insisted that every Saturday should be her day off. Art had absolutely no idea why it was such an important day for Rita, and the next day was no exception.

The early starts enabled Rita to finish work by mid-afternoon at the very latest. She made her way out of the office and into the city centre precinct, which had the best shopping area. Middle age had been kind to Rita. Her short, well-groomed hair and smart appearance gave the distinct impression that she liked and could afford the good things in life. She was definitely someone who looked out of place when working at Art Gormley's. But Rita kept herself to herself, with very little known about her as far as Gormley's was concerned.

Art had quickly taken to her, despite the fact that she had knocked him back after a couple of attempts at early morning fumbles when she was cleaning his office. In reality it was easy for Rita to find favour. Most of Art's employees were students or people on some benefit swindle. Apart from Jonta and Rita they were self-employed and most had their own vehicles, which was less hassle for Art, who didn't need to know much about their circumstances.

She bounced along the precinct cobbles. 'Some special perfume. It always makes an impression,' she said to herself after purchasing some Clive Christian X Parfum. Nothing but the best she could possibly afford.

Before finishing her retail therapy Rita treated herself to a Mulberry scarf, which would perfectly finish off tomorrow's intended outfit.

Life had changed completely since she had lost her job as the McIntyres' cleaner, when without a by your leave they had left the area. The manner of their departure hadn't been lost on Rita, and she had not been best pleased. She had given Pete and Val loyal service over a prolonged period of time. But thanks to that morning's scribbled note, one of many on Art's desk that she had surreptitiously read as she diligently went about her duties, Rita now knew the identity of their new resident at number 56 Norfolk Street. She wasn't the only individual not upset about McIntyre's current predicament.

Importantly, there was further information discovered during that morning's cleaning. Another note, with more information, had been safely pocketed by the diligent Rita. 'Art is such an untidy slob,' she said and smiled, knowing full well that the information she had obtained could be important to someone very, very special as far as Rita was concerned.

While Rita was completing her shopping, McIntyre's lifelong mate Stew Grant was at home, having a little bit of me time as he sat in their new orangery with a cup of tea in one hand and that day's *Daily Telegraph* in the other. The orangery was Tina's latest expensive house project. Stew could finally understand the benefits, despite the cost, as he cast his eyes out across the frost-bound lawn.

The clear skies outside prompted him to think about the next day's golf with McIntyre and Sutton. He'd got a confused message from his wife Tina as she flew out the door. 'Got to go and see Val McIntyre, love. Some sort of crisis.' There was no time for him to give a response. Stew knew that his wife had a nail appointment later and would now be out of his hair for most of the day. He breathed a deep sigh of peaceful relief.

Before he got to grips with *The Telegraph*, Stew had phoned Pete. Strange. No response, and he hadn't even been able to leave a voicemail. When the process was repeated some five minutes later Stew shuddered, thinking back to the Roger Strong scenario when neither he, Pete or Sutton had been able to make contact with their stricken former friend.

He rang Geoff, whose phone rang out. Stew couldn't hide his disappointment when he then received a Sutton text: *Sorry, Stew. Busy at work. No chance of golf tomorrow. Working. Maybe the rugby club later on.* Realistically, Sutton hadn't a clue how his Saturday would develop.

Stew paused and sent Geoff a further text, asking if he'd heard from Pete, before returning to *The Telegraph*, although he knew that he wouldn't be unable to concentrate fully until McIntyre had made contact.

A couple minutes later he sighed deeply and reached for his pen. 'Now it's time for the crossword,' he said to himself. He had just received a further text from Sutton to say that he had to pop round, hopefully to see Pete when he finished work. Stew therefore wrongly presumed that everything was OK in the world and that McIntyre would be good for Saturday. It would then be a matter of confirming the usual routine with Tina.

She knew that Saturday's golf with Stew, Pete and Geoff, then going to watch Upper Parton RFC, their beloved club, was like a religion as far as the three friends were concerned. Tina also saw something strangely comforting in meeting up with her husband and his closest mates at the club on a winter Saturday night after they had consumed a few beers. She would have a quick half of lager before performing her taxi duties.

Then they would go back home and have some much-needed therapy in the form of a takeaway that her husband was only just capable of organising after those beers as she settled down to her weekly dose of *Strictly*. A perfect evening.

17

Hanson, Rudding and Dexter

'Make sure they both attend,' Wendy Galloway shouted down the phone at one of her henchmen as she paced around the kitchen. Time was moving on, and she hadn't had a suitable response. Wendy alone would deal directly with Dexter. She tasked others to deal with the lower ranks of her paid police contacts.

'Get them there.' Unusually, she found herself repeating instructions. Wendy's face was drawn. She was focused. Her son had been shot, but rather than attend the hospital or even ring to ascertain Matt's current condition, what really frustrated her was a complete blank from her contacts. If truth be told, the fact that her son was critically ill wasn't of particular interest to Wendy Galloway. It was that someone else had dared to shoot Matt in her city centre. She wanted to know who and why. And she wanted the answers now. After all, she paid good money for information and expected results.

'I'm not waiting. Same place as yesterday. Bring the gear,' Galloway added. Fortunately, her daughter Toni was still in bed, oblivious to her mother's increasing agitation.

While Wendy Galloway was on the proverbial warpath, surveillance on one her protégés was continuing.

'The target has just arrived at the hospital and has received a call.'

***

Rory Lomas was in the process of providing Jo Firth with a surveillance update when one of his officers transmitted a report. 'Sorry, Jo, I've got to go,' he said, and Lomas, for the second time that day, ended his call to Firth as the surveillance target Robbie Hanson responded to his recent contact.

'Phone call ended. Subject is now reversing out of the parking bay and making his way to the exit.' The surveillance team went mobile, and for the next ten minutes they tracked Hanson driving his black Audi Sportback to the car park at the east marina. Although the weather was better, the team still encountered the same problems as the day before in terms of attempting to observe the target as opposed to potential compromise.

Lomas's operatives were as creative as they had been twenty-four hours earlier, but on this occasion better equipped. Rory had prepared well and had decided to use their Mercedes Sprinter PURE Panel Van, with its in-house CCTV system, to record activities, particularly if a static observation point was needed. It proved to be an excellent call.

DC Helen Ives and her partner took a calculated gamble as they began to approach the marina. He drove the Mercedes to the west side, repeating the route Ives had taken yesterday, and they arrived at the conservation area car park. The officer's heart sank when she saw numerous twitchers scanning across the vista. Ives grabbed a pair of binoculars and looked across towards the east side, where she had a clear sight of the subject's vehicle.

'Subject has alighted from the Audi and is walking towards the harbour area. We have a loss of our target,' she said and sighed, knowing that it was impossible for anyone from the team to get any closer without showing themselves. She then scanned the car park.

'I've got another vehicle of potential.' Ives continued her commentary. 'There's a Ford Focus parked at the south end of the car park. Shit, sorry … hold on.' She took a deep breath, altered the lens and zoomed in. 'It's the same Focus from yesterday.' Ives held her nerve. 'It's Bill Rudding's vehicle already on the plot.' The officer repeated her words for the benefit of the loggist, and then obtained confirmation that her transmission had been received.

She jumped down from the van with her binoculars still around her neck and renewed acquaintance with her twitching friends. Her partner for the day remained in the vehicle utilising the recording equipment.

***

At exactly the same time that DC Helen Ives was discussing the latest feature in November's publication of *Bird Watching* magazine John Dexter's burner phone rang. He knew it would be Wendy Galloway. The colour drained from Dexter's face. He knew that he couldn't ignore Galloway on a second occasion. Fortunately when the phone rang his office door was closed.

'Wendy…' Dexter said, trying desperately to be upbeat, but he knew the call was never going to be pleasant. She would only contact him if it was a necessity. As far as Galloway was concerned John Dexter was her chosen one – by far her best ever recruit in terms of Parton Constabulary – and she knew that having the head of professional standards on her payroll was corruption at the highest level.

'Dexter, who shot my son?' Wendy said sharply.

'I don't know, but I may be able to have an idea soon.' Dexter knew he could put in a call to the relevant senior investigating officer, in this case DCI Trish Delaney. There was always some professional standards angle he could spin that would justify an update on the enquiry.

Wendy ignored his response. 'Dexter, usual place in ten minutes. Or you can say goodbye to your pension,' she added. There was only one person in control. Without thinking, Dexter grabbed his coat. 'Shit, she doesn't know the bloody half,' he said to himself as he opened the door to see the ever-diligent Shaun Adams appearing with another cup of coffee for his boss.

'Sorry, Shaun, that bloody tooth again. I've got an emergency appointment,' Dexter said as he flew out of the door. Shaun Adams merely nodded politely.

John Dexter's mind was racing as he drove to his destination. His normally calm and calculated exterior had completely disappeared, and he was gripping the steering wheel as if his life depended on it. It was purely by good fortune that he avoided an accident.

Once he had parked up as near as possible to the harbour of the east marina Dexter sat in his vehicle, trying to project a calm appearance that would reassure Wendy Galloway that he would, given the time, be able to provide a name and some background into Matt's shooting. Such was his focus Dexter completely failed to notice Hanson's or Rudding's vehicles. He walked slowly with some trepidation to the chosen meeting point.

Meanwhile, ten minutes seemed a lifetime for surveillance operative DC Helen Ives, who was trying every tactic in the book to change the subject away from birds to a topic she had at least more than a very basic knowledge. The phrase, 'I'm new to this game,' made absolutely no difference to these ardent twitchers.

Then Ives thankfully received a text from her partner in the surveillance van. 'Cup of coffee for you…'

'Thank the Lord,' she said to herself, before crawling into the warmth of the Mercedes.

'Look at this vehicle. Do you recognise it?' Ives was asked, and with her binoculars she again scanned across the estuary to the east marina car park. Another car had arrived on the plot.

Ives began her commentary. 'A black BMW X5 has arrived on the plot. One occupant, a smart-looking male, looking around. He has ignored the other two vehicles. He's walking slowly towards the harbour area and it's a loss, loss, loss.' Ives was completely unaware of the significance of this sighting.

Rory Lomas was troubled. There were three vehicles in the car park, two of which he knew were of definite interest to their operation. He picked up his secure mobile and rang Firth.

'This can't wait,' said Lomas to himself and provided the details of their observations. 'The good news is that we will have some footage recorded from the Merc,' he added.

'Thanks Rory, keep in touch,' Firth said, trying desperately to contain her excitement. Lomas and his team were unaware of the development concerning John Dexter's BMW and, as far as Firth and Sutton was concerned, even at this stage they didn't need to know.

***

Wendy Galloway and three of her tried and trusted had arrived at the east marina well before the others. Her army attended in one large SUV, which was then instructed to leave the area and await contact for a pickup, just like any taxi completing a fare.

Sutton took stock. There was concern written across his face. All three police officers subject to the investigation were meeting, and the team had no control over the situation. It was obviously a significant development, but what really worried Sutton was that any one of them might be in danger.

In a few moments he had returned to Ron Turner's office and, as the senior officer, Sutton had told him about the dilemma. 'Thanks for this, Geoff,' Turner said, and smiled sarcastically at Sutton. 'Let the meeting run. My call,' he said decisively. 'I can't contact the chief. She's priming the head of media for the expected fallout. As soon as she's free I'll speak to her, and if she has a different view we will act. I'm not making the same mistake as on Operation PROOF,' Turner said emphatically. A decision made, oblivious to the fact that Galloway and her men were already on scene, significantly increasing the risk of violence to those attending.

*****

Dexter was breathing hard. Cursing, he accidentally stepped into one of the few remaining puddles after yesterday's heavy rain. As he approached the unhospitable-looking unit with its broken overhanging door he stopped momentarily as it briefly occurred to him that walking away from this meeting with Wendy Galloway might be an option. Then he thought again. It definitely wasn't. He took one final deep breath, not knowing who or what he would find inside. He didn't have to wait long.

Dexter straightened up after entering the unit, but a kick to his solar plexus took out whatever wind that remained in his lungs. He gasped desperately and bent forward, clutching at the area of contact. As he did so a knee was brought up towards his chin. He shrieked out in pain as his head shot up and back. Dexter recoiled after the second blow. Then some unseen hands, swiftly and expertly – and operating with both power and some experience – pinned his arms. He felt them stretched out on either side of him as if he were being crucified.

His eyes cleared enough for him to look up and see both Rudding and Hanson in similar positions, spread around the inside of what was in reality a deep cave. Hanson, who had suffered a similar violent entry, stared in amazement at the appearance of Parton Constabulary's head of professional standards, John Dexter. He could hardly believe his eyes.

Wendy Galloway strutted around, trying to avoid the drops of salty water that descended intermittently from the cavern roof onto her expensively groomed hair. She swatted away the annoyance as if it were an aggravating wasp. She addressed her captive audience. 'I have a major problem. A simple question. I want to know who shot my son.' She focused her piercing eyes on the prize asset of John Dexter. Galloway paid Dexter more than the others, which reflected the officer's access to the very top echelons of the force.

Dexter returned her gaze. He was determined to appear confident. 'If only she knew,' he said to himself. His mind briefly drifted back to last night's frantically planned activities. 'Keep strong,' he told himself. He needed time.

'I said before, Wendy, that I can access the officer in charge of the enquiry and find out what's going on.' Then Dexter had the temerity to make a suggestion. 'If there's anything from your contacts it would help.'

'Don't fucking call me Wendy. You're on borrowed time, Dexter.' It was the first time he had ever heard her swear and Dexter bit down on his lip knowing he had made an ill-judged comment. He desperately tried to muster courage and composure from somewhere, anywhere.

'I need more time...' Dexter paused, then added respectfully, 'Mrs Galloway,' formally emphasising the *Mrs*. He knew it sounded pathetic, but that didn't matter to Dexter. In fear of his life he did as requested, even though he sounded like a schoolboy formally apologising to a teacher.

Wendy didn't reply. She paced. The noise of her shoes was only interrupted by Bill Rudding who, in between snivels, tried to explain how he could save the situation.

'Give me that,' Wendy said to one of her subordinates and, without removing her black leather gloves, she took possession of a baseball bat. She walked over to the hanging and unprotected frame of Bill Rudding. 'Shut the fuck up,' Galloway said firmly. And, pitched forward, with her arms extended in front of her body and deliberately aiming for the fleshy part of Rudding's thighs, Wendy Galloway delivered a blow as good as any home run. Rarely did she mete out punishment, but circumstances dictated. A wide smile appeared on her face in both enjoyment and satisfaction.

Rudding was in agony and his face was twisted in pain. He couldn't help himself in letting out a yell that he failed to muffle. Not that it mattered, given their location. Tears began streaming down his face as Galloway returned the weapon to her henchman and checked her watch.

'We meet here tomorrow. Everyone. Dexter, you will have what I want. If not you will watch these two. Then you...' She looked across at Hanson and Rudding, whose face was still twisted in pain, then back to Dexter. Wendy Galloway had left them all in no doubt there would be a price to pay. 'You will leave separately.' She barked out her final orders, 'Hanson, go.'

A few minutes later Ives shouted in, 'I've got the eyeball. It's our subject walking from the harbour, heading towards the car park—'

Lomas deliberately interrupted her, to both encourage the officer and alert his team. 'Keep it going, Helen.'

'The subject is back at the Audi and sitting in the vehicle, now rubbing both wrists. I can see exhaust smoke, lights... Standby, standby. It's an off, off, off,' she continued, as Hanson engaged the gears and moved forward.

Rory Lomas had a difficult decision. Should he follow the original target? Or should he split the team and try and identify others if they returned to their vehicles? Rightly or wrongly, he decided to follow Robbie Hanson, the original target.

The surveillance operatives were well away from the east marina car park before Dexter was released and was walking thoughtfully to his vehicle. Rudding was last. Wendy had considered, for no good reason, leaving him in the freezing unit overnight. But on a whim she relented and ordered one of her men to release him.

Bill Rudding collapsed in a heap on the unit floor. It took him some time and a few more strategic kicks before he was able to drag himself out of the unit and finally back to his vehicle. A horrible dead leg coupled with his injured ankle made even the smallest of steps absolute agony. Finally, the convivial meeting completed, a call was made for Galloway's pickup.

***

Robbie Hanson's mind was in a total spin as he drove back home. The thought that John Dexter was also involved in Galloway's operation had left him in a state of severe shock. Hanson realised that he was just a minor player to Galloway and certainly, in his position, not someone who had much influence. For Robbie at least, today's meeting was a reminder – not that it was needed – of the ruthless nature and the extreme power of Wendy Galloway.

Tailed by Lomas's surveillance team, Hanson returned home, made a sandwich and tried to relax. *At least I am above Rudding in the pecking order*, Hanson thought. *Could I turn myself in, admit to everything and, in doing so, curry some sort of favour with my colleagues?* His mind tried to explore any and all options. But it always returned to the same issue. Ultimately Hanson knew that whatever information he could divulge, it would not and could not detract from or dilute his involvement in the shooting of young Simon Mather.

Robbie was between a rock and a hard place. He thought about the here and now, about trying to see Matt at the hospital. But with the amount of security around the place it was a non-starter. The most Hanson could hope for was an update from the incident log when he returned to work tomorrow for a 2 p.m. to 12 midnight shift. He felt completely helpless. Robbie was finished for the day and passed his time tending to the rope burns on his wrists and answering a call – an off-duty welfare check on the young officer from his supervisor, Sergeant Steve Barker.

***

It was early afternoon when Chief Superintendent John Dexter had returned to his desk at professional standards. He stared at the walls of his office with the door closed. It would remain so. His pulse had not returned to a comfortable resting rate ever since he had received the first contact from Wendy Galloway.

Dexter was fairly confident that he could supply Galloway with some information about her son's shooting. He knew Trish Delaney and could use his own robust reputation as an unofficial bully. 'She is only a chief inspector,' Dexter said to himself. First he needed to check the incident log in the hope that Matt Galloway had passed away.

What to do with Pete McIntyre was far more problematic.

18

Chris Mayling

Pete McIntyre was also top of Geoff Sutton's priorities as he and Jo Firth worked away in their bare office during the afternoon. Firth liaised with the surveillance operation while Sutton focused his enquiries on his good friend's movements of the night before. His VW Golf had been forensically recovered but nothing had been found that would lead to Pete's whereabouts. The only breakthrough had been via the car park's CCTV system, which had located a Honda SUV leaving the car park soon after McIntyre had entered.

Geoff actioned an immediate enquiry with the registered keeper. It was an identical vehicle from down south, a scrapped vehicle. *Shit*, thought Sutton as he received the update. *That's our vehicle with those plates.*

Extensive searches via the city's automatic number plate recognition system had proved negative. The Honda had in effect disappeared after leaving the multistorey. He contacted Val, who had tried phoning and texting him for any updates. He had little positive in the way of an update on Pete's whereabouts, which only caused her greater upset. Thankfully, he could hear the reassuring voice of Tina Grant in the background.

'Val, have you received anything from Pete, or any

strange calls?' Sutton asked as discreetly as possible. It was deliberately phrased to avoid asking if she had received any ransom demands.

'No, nothing,' came the stuttering reply.

'Do you want another cup of tea, love?' Tina Grant could be heard saying in the background, and thankfully for Geoff the conversation was ended.

Sutton was momentarily dazed, but then reality was restored by a knock on their office door. It was Trish Delaney. She had arrived after spending the remainder of the day at the incident room. Firth had briefed her with the sighting of Dexter's vehicle during the surveillance. The Dexter angle had brought some excitement to the enquiry and Sutton could feel the gathering momentum, rumblings similar to the start of an avalanche.

'I'll just help myself,' Delaney said and headed for the kettle. She had a moment or two to relax, or so she thought. Sutton had other ideas.

'Please listen,' he politely asked Firth and Delaney. Sutton rang a number and placed his phone on loudspeaker for their benefit.

For Shaun Adams it had been a quiet afternoon and he was able to answer without delay as his phone rang. 'Shaun, can you speak?' Adams immediately knew both who it was and the basis for the question. But was he alone?

'Two minutes. I will ring back,' he replied. He picked up a couple of files and walked through the open-plan office then down the stairs to the secure storeroom, which was used to archive some of the force's most sensitive documentation. Even in a digital age there was still a requirement to keep hard copies. When Shaun was on duty, the only set of keys remained with him. It had been an outdated custom during his thirty years of service, but it ensured complete integrity. Once settled he rang Sutton, who answered immediately.

'Shaun, we have an ongoing enquiry, which I hope you can assist us with. The chief constable is aware of this investigation.' Sutton highlighted the importance and also hinted at the need for secrecy. 'Can you give me an account of where Mr Dexter has been over the past couple of days?' It was a direct blunt question. There was a short silence as Shaun Adams reviewed his conscience, as well as his utter respect for Geoff Sutton and his total loyalty for Parton Constabulary.

'Geoff, Chief Superintendent Dexter was out of his office this morning for a couple of hours. He was also absent from the office during some of yesterday. For all these instances he stated he was having dental problems. On each occasion he used his own vehicle.' Adams sounded as though he was giving evidence in the Crown Court. 'I don't believe him, Geoff.' Adams repeated himself. 'I don't believe him.' This was said very quickly, as if he was relieved to have imparted this information. 'If I can help in any way…' Adams added for good measure.

'Thanks, Shaun. I will come back to you,' Sutton replied and ended their short conversation. He looked at Delaney and Firth. 'Further confirmation. I know we have him on CCTV on one occasion. Dexter now can't say someone else was using his vehicle and this is proof of his deceit,' Sutton updated his two colleagues.

Firth checked her phone. 'Speaking of the Devil… Time we made tracks.' The three of them took the short walk to the Turner's office. Delaney left another half-drunk cup of coffee, but they couldn't be late for their prearranged meeting.

This time Chief Constable Mayling, in full uniform, was sitting behind the desk in Ron Turner's office. She was now in charge. 'Rightly so,' said Sutton to himself, with the force's head of professional standards now heavily implicated in a web of corruption. Turner, relegated, stood slightly uncomfortably by her side, while the others took their seats facing them both.

Turner began walking and talking. Starting from his initial position, he circled the room while Mayling made copious notes. Turner began the briefing using short statements of fact. 'Matt Galloway's condition has taken a turn for the worse. There's some internal bleeding. The day's surveillance involved a meeting of Hanson, Rudding and Dexter. And so far there are no demands from the captors of Pete McIntyre, although a Honda has been identified leaving the car park at the same time as the subject returned to collect his vehicle.' Turner returned to concentrate on John Dexter. Everyone listened intently.

'We now know that Dexter has been at the east marina on two occasions over the last two days. We know on the first time that there was an association with Wendy Galloway.' Turner continued. 'Today's surveillance involved Hanson, Rudding and Dexter only, as far as we know,' he added.

'There is also intelligence from a previously registered dangerous informant using the pseudonym Bob Hope, that he has information pertinent to the recent shootings. So I've authorised a visit to HMP Wassingham at 10 a.m. tomorrow.' Turner finished, after adequately summing up the salient points.

There was a silence around the room. 'Where the

hell did you get Bob Hope from?' Mayling said and laughed, referring to the nickname. 'Showing your age.' The comment broke the ice.

'Right,' Mayling said. 'We will lock up our men tomorrow morning and we will open a gold command room to coordinate their arrests, with ACC Turner in charge.' Mayling was making a direct reference to apprehending Rudding, Hanson and Dexter. 'By the time they are in custody it will also allow us to act on anything we may get from Bob Hope. But let's be realistic about him. There's only one person he will be looking after.' This was a direct warning to Sutton and Firth regarding their forthcoming prison visit. 'We need to act now. These arrests may give us a lead to the whereabouts of Pete McIntyre.'

Ron Turner looked on with some particular concern. It was nearly twenty-four hours since Pete had gone missing. 'A lot can happen in twenty-four hours,' he said to himself.

A frown appeared on his face as Mayfield continued. 'I need to address the press at some stage tomorrow – the later, the better – in the hope of some positive news. I am afraid that, whatever happens, Parton Constabulary are going to take a good kicking over the arrest of three serving officers. I will be speaking to the Home Office on Monday.' At that, the chief constable gathered her papers and left the room.

'She is absolutely spot on,' said Sutton to himself. He desperately wanted to go home and see Debbie, but first he needed to speak to Val McIntyre. He made another call, but her phone went to voicemail.

Sutton finalised the next day's prison visit arrangements and ensured that there was recording equipment available at the prison. Everything that Bob Hope – aka Vern Edwards –said would be recorded there and then.

He made his way through the long corridors to the building exit. Once outside he looked upwards and shivered. It was a clear, starry night. He rang Debbie. It was so good to hear her voice. He just smiled and giggled like a naughty schoolboy while they talked. A delivered curry was the order of the day. Debbie would organise it while Sutton made a necessary detour to check on Val McIntyre.

Despite the commuter traffic it took Sutton a mere fifteen minutes to arrive outside the McIntyres' house. After a couple of unanswered doorbell rings, Val finally emerged and for the second time that day Sutton took her in his arms on the doorstep, manoeuvred her back through the house, back-heeled the door shut then guided her into the living room. Once on the sofa Sutton was able to take in Val's appearance. She looked awful. There were no other words to describe her.

'Geoff have you heard anything? Tell me he's rung.' She sobbed in his arms. Her mascara was running in a sprint down her reddened cheeks. It was worse than this morning, as the predicament of her missing husband had become a fast-developing nightmare. Matters didn't improve when Sutton informed her that he had no news whatsoever, even though he tried to make positive the sighting of the Honda and the enquiries regarding that vehicle.

He looked across from the sofa and noticed the prescription and the small bottle of tablets on the table. Apparently Tina had made her exit some thirty minutes previously. 'My nails will just have to wait,' Tina had sighed to herself earlier that day. She had also been reduced to tears at her friend's distress when she eventually closed the front door on her exit.

'She must have put in a helluva shift,' said Sutton to himself, trying to imagine what Tina had endured. He then heard someone enter the house.

'Mam, it's Henry,' came a call, at which point the voice became a person in the shape of Pete's son. Sutton had placed messages on his voicemail updating him on the family's nightmare situation urging Henry to ring back. However, Henry had just returned from an overnight business trip, and entered the living room with his overnight bag hanging loosely over his shoulder.

Sutton instantly went to make a cup of tea to allow Henry to join his mother on the sofa. They were still embracing warmly when Sutton returned with a mug in either hand. The tea caused them to release their grip on each other. Henry then took the opportunity to cleverly divert his mother's sobs with tales of Ben, their only grandchild. This was Sutton's opportunity, and he politely took his leave. There was no point in staying.

'I'll let myself out,' Sutton said quietly, and slowly made his way out of the living room. He silently closed the front door and activated the Karoq key fob to unlock his vehicle.

'Uncle Geoff, what the hell is happening? Where's Dad?' Sutton grimaced at hearing Henry's voice. The fact that Henry called him Uncle Geoff was an obvious sign of closeness between the families. He turned to face Pete's son and recognised the emotion, indicated by the fact there was always two questions in one sentence. Sutton repeated to Henry what he had already told his mother.

'Is that it?' Is that it?' Henry said incredulously, 'He's

your best mate,' he continued. Sutton knew he couldn't answer. It was the exact conversation he didn't want.

'I'm sorry,' Sutton said genuinely, but he also knew it was a pathetic answer. He could just about hear Val wailing as Henry went back inside the house and slammed the door. It hurt Sutton as he sat in the car, unable to move. A large part of him agreed with Henry's comments.

Kidnappings were always difficult, in particular keeping the delicate balance of secrecy while enabling negotiations to take place between the criminals and the authorities. But in Pete's case it had been nearly twenty-four hours since he had disappeared and there had been no negotiations. And no contact whatsoever. The questions that increasingly occupied Sutton's mind were, 'Is Pete still alive? Has he been taken away and killed? If so, why Pete?' Yes, he was the closest to being a material witness to Matt Galloway's shooting, but as far as Sutton was concerned Pete McIntyre was as much in the dark as anyone about who had shot his young friend.

A short time later Sutton turned into his cul-de-sac and saw Debbie's car on the driveway. 'The times they are a-changing,' Sutton said to himself. He was now relegated to parking on the road outside.

He walked up the driveway and placed his key in the door, hesitating momentarily as he did so. His world had changed completely since he had been with Debbie, and while he had recently enjoyed being in the field of battle, when it came to work, Sutton was in a fortunate position. Earning a wage wasn't a requirement, and financially he was able to retire. Sadistically, he had enjoyed Operations TRUST and PROOF despite the reputational damage caused to the force.

Work for him brought the necessary social interaction that he both enjoyed and appreciated but the Bob Dylan song, 'The Times They Are a-Changin',' again resonated through his mind as he entered the house. Sutton's thoughts changed instantly as he walked into Debbie's arms.

19

Toni and Kev

A little touch of expensive cologne and Kev Stryker stood back and admired himself one more time. 'Just the business,' he said as he looked at himself in the mirror and flexed his muscular frame. To say he rated himself was an understatement. It was a Friday night, city centre girls' night, as far as Stryker was concerned. The fact he had been grafting recently made him even more determined that tonight would be memorable. He enjoyed the female attention that his rugged good looks attracted, even though he had no interest in the finer points of romance. His normal Friday routine: straight into the centre of town, meet up at the Crop, some good real ale with his mates, before a trip to the inevitable nightclub and a piece of the action.

That night Toni Galloway had again narrowly managed to avoid an argument with her mother and escaped from the house. Unusually it had been fairly easy, as her mother seemed to have more pressing matters on her mind. She had left the house for a couple of hours in the afternoon before returning home and spending the majority of her time in the study.

Breathing a sigh of relief, Toni sat back in the taxi. Dressed to kill, or that's what she thought. She was wearing the same stilettoes and short black dress as the last time she went out, with heavy make-up and elongated eyelashes. She was meeting the girls at the west side of the marina before heading up town for the nightlife.

Toni Galloway and Kev Stryker knew each other from past encounters. They had met previously at the end of an evening, and after a couple of slow dances their drunken night had ended down some dark alley before they both made their separate journeys home. On one occasion they had swopped mobile numbers, but Kev had ignored the numerous texts Toni had sent him. While Stryker knew that Toni was Wendy's only daughter (everyone did), Toni hadn't a clue that Stryker had been her mother's hitman and had pulled the trigger in last Friday's shooting.

While Kev and Toni were preparing for the bright lights of Parton nightlife, Robbie Hanson was in complete darkness. Alone and helpless in his flat, Hanson looked at the photograph of his mother with his arm supporting her, shortly following the diagnosis. It was the time of his police passing-out parade. She looked so proud of her son in his full uniform. 'That has all gone,' said Hanson to himself. His career prospects had evaporated, and his mother's health had deteriorated further.

It was after 10 p.m. Robbie picked up his phone, scrolled through his list of contacts and found a name, someone he knew he could trust.

Steve Barker was about to turn in. This was his last free night before a series of 2 p.m. to 12 midnight shifts. It was well known that Saturday lates were one of the worst shifts in terms of demand for the force, and a decent night's sleep was to be recommended. He played around with the remote. There was nothing worth watching, and he had already made his way to the bathroom when his mobile rang. It was Robbie Hanson. Barker answered immediately.

'Sergeant, I'm in the shit.' Hanson stuttered and sobbed but remained polite and respectful of Barker's rank. It was difficult for Barker to hear what he was saying.

'Please can I come round?' Hanson asked quietly, searching for some composure. He knew that Barker lived in the development nearby, in yet another apartment block for key workers. Steve didn't know if Robbie had been drinking. He glanced up at the small clock on his bathroom wall, where the illuminated digits showed 10.30.

'Robbie, if it's that business with Rudding it's all sorted,' Barker said confidently, hoping to put his mind at rest.

'Sergeant, Rudding is the least of my problems. I've got real troubles,' Hanson stuttered, still addressing Steve as his sergeant. His voice broke, slightly out of control, followed by more sobbing.

'Come round,' Barker said without delay.

***

Toni Galloway was in full cry now. It was the usual crowd, who were hanging onto her every word, as she organised a couple of taxis for her group to quit the marina and head up town. She had forgotten that she had already paid for a couple of rounds of cocktails, and her generosity only increased the number of her so-called friends.

The destination was Lucifer's. 'It will be fine,' she assured her doubters. Despite the alcohol consumed, the recent shootings had naturally affected local confidence.

It was the same time of evening for Kev Stryker and his mates. A few pints of hand-pulled delightful real ale had set the tone. Now for some action. The heavily muscled Stryker reassured the group that the best place to go was Lucifer's, a five-minute walk from the Crop.

Stryker's group were shivering in the queue outside Lucifer's. Their night-time uniform, while maybe showing off muscles and tattoos, etc. wasn't the most practical on a frosty November evening.

When Toni's girls arrived they stumbled out of their taxis. Most were attempting to pull down their short skirts in an act of modesty. Kev saw the group arrive and Toni emerge, but he took no notice. He became aware that the team of bouncers had been supplemented by a few uniformed police officers. He thought it must be a show of public reassurance, but noticed as he moved towards the front of the queue that a couple were carrying clipboards.

'Excuse me, sir, we are making enquiries about last weekend's shooting and wondered if you were here last Friday,' the officer politely said to Kev.

'Nope, not last Friday, Officer,' Stryker said, lying politely as he shivered. The officer then completed a short descriptive form and moved on. Surprisingly, Stryker wasn't asked to explain his whereabouts on that night. But then, as Stryker rightly thought, it was merely an appeal for witnesses.

They then made their way into the premises. Lucifer's was simple in terms of design. The ground floor, housing one long bar, was for drinking, and the basement was for dancing.

'Time for a drink.' Stryker shouted to be heard above the nightclub noise and pointed to the area where they always gathered when the group entered Lucifer's. The beer – fizzy bottled lager – was always crap, and Stryker's crew usually took to gin and tonics. One of the group knew a barmaid who could always be relied upon to provide generous measures. The idea was to spend an hour drinking G and Ts and have a good look around before descending to the basement for some 'entertainment'.

Toni and the girls followed an identical pattern of behaviour, but chose a different location in the bar area. They would have a few more drinks and a look around for potential talent before descending the stairs to the dance floor. Last week's shooting had not diminished the popularity of Lucifer's. The place was packed.

'It is almost time to make a move downstairs,' Kev said to himself, a direct reference to the basement dancefloor, as he viewed a girl who had caught his eye. She was in a group of four who had located themselves next to Stryker's crowd at the bar. She had returned his stare before going back to the conversation she was having with her girl-friends. Kev was instantly attracted by her long hair and figure-hugging short dress. As the girl moved off with her friends, destined for the basement dance floor, she glanced over her shoulder. Stryker instantly recognised the knowing smile that followed.

'Let's go, lads,' Kev shouted as they went about draining a final gin. They were basement-bound. Now for the most difficult part. Kev and his mates made their way through the crowded bar area, which always involved a fair amount of jostling through the largely inebriated crowd.

'What the fuck?' Toni Galloway shrieked above the noise, as someone knocked her arm that was carrying her latest cocktail. 'Oh, it's you, Kev,' she said and looked directly into the eyes of Kev Stryker. She then placed her free hand lightly on his muscle-ripped bicep.

Toni shivered slightly and whispered in his ear, 'Time for a dance.' It was more of an instruction than a request and it caught Stryker completely off guard. Toni, slightly unsteady on her feet, put her drink down and linked arms with tonight's chosen partner, then guided him down the stairs and marched towards the misty dry ice and the blaring music.

Toni Galloway's timing was absolutely perfect. The pair hit the floor as a slow number was playing. It wouldn't matter if it had been a slow number or the liveliest disco recording. Toni was going to hold Kev close, very close. Stryker was equally as drunk. They stumbled around, clutching and being clutched. There was never any chance that he would have the opportunity to pursue the smiling girl from the bar, but he wasn't complaining.

Some thirty minutes or so later the pair were fumbling around in another alleyway adjacent to the nightclub. It was all over before it started, and Toni hailed a taxi. Kev decided that he would have maybe just one more drink and re-entered Lucifer's. 'Such is life,' he said to himself.

It was gone 3 a.m. the following morning when eventually Stryker kicked off his shoes and crawled under the duvet, still in his clothes. Just before he drifted into an unsatisfactory drunken sleep, the familiar ping of his phone caused him turn on to his back, reach into his pocket and, after two failed attempts, eventually pull out his mobile. He fumbled for his bedside reading lamp, spilling the glass of water on the cabinet as he did so. 'Shit,' Stryker said in a slurred voice. 'Shit.' He squinted, once, twice and then rubbed his red eyes while scrutinising the luminated picture message.

There was a grainy picture of him and Toni in the back alley taken an hour or so earlier by one of his group, accompanied by the narrative, 'Always a romantic bastard, Stryker.'

Kev smiled to himself and managed to punch in a line saying, *Bloody Galloways. Always a fucking easy touch.* He leant over, squinting, and pressed *Send* before replacing his phone and collapsing back under the duvet. He was snoring immediately, with his bedside light still on. Despite it being almost 3.30 a.m. Stryker was completely comatose when the texts started flooding back to him.

Kev Stryker hadn't just replied to the sender when he returned the message. *Bloody Galloways. Always a fucking easy touch*, it had been drunkenly sent to *All contacts*.

It was slightly earlier, closer to 2 a.m., when Steve Barker had managed to persuade Robbie Hanson to get some sleep. They were exhausted, and they also knew that tomorrow was going to be a major day for them both.

While Stryker and Toni had been enjoying the Parton nightlife Robbie Hanson had earlier arrived at Steve Barker's flat in a mess, snivelling and sobbing. It took an hour before Barker managed to get anything coherent from him. Finally, after a couple of glasses of Steve's best malt whisky, it was all explained.

Robbie started with his mother's illness and the associated problems with her increasing disability. Hanson retold that fateful shift night out, when Barker, as usual, had made his tactical early exit. Once he had started, Hanson was in full flow. Barker recognised the fact and just let him talk.

Hanson paused after he recounted how Rudding had led him into a well-planned trap. Then he progressed to the first request that Wendy Galloway had made: his first bribe, which had gone some way to paying for the house alterations in support of his mother. He continued, in what was tantamount to a confession with his involvement in the Lucifer's shooting, and finished with that day's meeting at the unit on the east marina harbour.

'Guess who was there?' Hanson asked an open-mouthed Barker. In reality it was a ridiculous question – all the more so because Steve could hardly believe what he was hearing. Without a clue about what to do next Barker took the opportunity to refill their glasses before Hanson continued.

'You will never guess,' Hanson said correctly. 'Chief Superintendent John Dexter, Wendy Galloway and that shit who started it all, Rudding. Galloway wanted to know who is behind the shooting of Matt,' he ended almost triumphantly.

While Barker was in shock at what Hanson had reported, it did at least explain why his attitude at work had deteriorated. Steve also realised the almost euphoric feeling coming from Hanson now that he had been able to confide in someone.

The problem for Barker was what to do next. 'Robbie, the bed in the spare room is made up. We can sort this out tomorrow,' Steve said comfortingly, but his voice lacked conviction.

'Thanks, Sarge. I don't want to be alone,' Hanson replied. He drained his glass. Then, with a massive sigh, he trudged off to the spare room.

Barker drained his own glass. He didn't immediately

want to go to bed, so completed two key tasks first. Armed with a pen and paper, he recorded their previous conversation. Although the pair had consumed a couple of whiskies he would ask Hanson to read and sign these notes for accuracy in the morning. It was the closest thing he could think of as a contemporary interview and could be put to Hanson later in more formal surroundings when he was in custody. He then sent a text to Geoff Sutton, just to warn him.

Barker's first job tomorrow would be to ring Geoff Sutton and inform him of an arrest. Police Constable Robbie Hanson, on suspicion of murder and corruption.

20

Alice Hanson

Saturday morning

Sutton woke with a start and looked across at the illuminated digital clock. It was 5 a.m. He'd been experiencing a bad dream. Much of the detail concerned Vern Edwards. He looked the other way and at the delightful Debbie. 'Good morning, beautiful,' Geoff whispered, careful not to wake her. He smiled in total satisfaction.

After the trauma of the visit to see Val McIntyre, Sutton had loved his evening watching three episodes of *Homeland*. But his continuous protestations, saying, 'That would never happen. She would never have done that,' as he remonstrated with the TV on some police or security procedure, annoyed Debbie.

'Geoff Sutton, will you just shut up?' Debbie remonstrated, before playfully planting a tender kiss on his lips. He got the message, smiled and remained in silent contentment.

Sutton spent another hour in bed staring at the clock and wishing the minutes away. It was one of those hours that seemed never-ending. The red digits turned to 5.55 and he quietly slid out from under the warm duvet. The night before they had agreed not to disturb each other.

Sutton dived into the shower, dressed quickly and made his way downstairs. A quick cup of coffee and a slice of toast would be the order of the day, although his stomach was churning slightly at the prospect of what lay ahead.

With his mouth full of toast and a mug in one hand, Geoff reflected. One of the strange aspects of growing older was that you tended to worry more, and usually concerning matters that were relatively trivial. He wondered whether the fact that he was becoming nervous – and yes – even slightly frightened about meeting Vern Edwards again was in part due to his age. Sutton picked up his two phones on the way out. 'Domestic bliss,' he said and smiled to himself as he passed Debbie's motor parked on the driveway.

It was a wet and dark November Saturday, and he had arranged to meet Jo Firth at Parton HQ before picking up an unmarked car for the ninety-minute journey to HMP Wassingham. Although he wasn't expecting any messages or calls before he set off, Geoff checked his phone. He looked away then looked back at his phone just to make sure his eyes weren't playing games. Sutton read the message from Steve Barker not once, not twice, but three times. He looked up. Any remaining frost had cleared, so with the wipers on it was safe to go. He plugged in his phone and put it on hands-free. Everything was now ready for Barker's call.

Sutton had just turned into Parton HQ when the young sergeant eventually rang. 'Hi, Steve, just give me a minute. I'm parking.' Only a few moments had passed before Barker had given Sutton the whole Hanson story from the previous night's meeting.

'Good stuff, Steve,' Sutton said enthusiastically, before there was a slight pause as he took in the implications of the call and Barker caught his breath. 'Did he say anything at all about Pete McIntyre's disappearance?' Sutton asked, beginning to sound slightly desperate.

'Geoff, I haven't finished. I haven't done such a bloody good job. Hanson's gone. He's not here. I'm just hoping he's gone back to his place. I'm off there now,' Barker said quickly. 'He should have been sleeping in the spare room. He could be in a right state,' Barker said, referring to Hanson's mental health. 'I should have brought him in last night ... I should,' Steve said, repeating himself, fully appreciating the potential consequences.

'Look, don't blame yourself, and now is not the time for self-recrimination. Go and find him and give me a ring back.' Sutton tried to sound positive and reassuring.

'OK, Geoff. Give me fifteen minutes or so. Just need to get dressed,' Barker said.

Sutton spotted Jo Firth across the car park with her umbrella up. She was shaking some car key or fob in his direction and walking towards a nearby Nissan. Minutes later Firth and Sutton exited Parton HQ, destined for HMP Wassingham. Firth took the wheel while Sutton brought her up to speed with the previous night's events concerning Robbie Hanson. Sutton was anxious. He hoped for God's sake that Barker had found Hanson safe and well.

He didn't have to wait long before his phone rang. He put it on loudspeaker.

'Geoff, he's not bloody here. He's not bloody here,' Barker said with urgency. The night shift concierge had been persuaded to allow him entry after he had produced his warrant card, coupled with his saying the words, 'Potential suicide.' However, Barker's normal calm and mature demeanour had completely evaporated.

'OK, Steve, just stop,' Sutton said. He was telling him, not asking him. He was hoping that Barker could recover something from his dealings with Hanson that would assist in locating him without the balloon going up in the form of another major incident and search.

The conversation between them stopped almost as quickly as it started. 'Geoff, I have an idea. I will keep in touch,' Barker said, recovering some composure as he ended his call with Sutton.

Firth drove for another hour or so as Geoff contemplated a difficult call to Ron Turner. There was little or no talk. It was approaching 9 a.m. when they took their pre-planned stop. They turned into a service station, an ideal location for reviewing their preparation for the meeting with Edwards.

All prisons operated a strict regime regarding visits. Sutton and Firth had an allocated slot between 10 a.m. and 12 noon., so there was absolutely no point in arriving beforehand. The satnav indicated another thirty minutes to their destination.

As Sutton and Firth made their final preparations for their prison visit, Steve Barker had already set off on his own mission. It didn't take him long to decide where to look first for his missing subordinate. Knowing Hanson as he did, the decision came quickly.

After travelling out of the city centre he headed for the countryside and to a certain farmhouse. Barker had never visited Hanson's family home. He had had no reason to. However, he had met Robbie's parents at the police station, under a scheme that Barker had initiated himself for new starters if their partner or immediate family wished to visit at an appropriate time. The close-knit Hanson family, despite the mother's difficulties, had been the first to partake in Steve Barker's innovative idea.

Barker had neither the time nor the inclination to take in the scenery. The view was obscured by poor visibility as the rain continued to fall. The Hanson farmland had earlier been covered in a crisp white blanket of frost, which was now fast disappearing.

Steve pulled into the farmyard and breathed a sigh of relief at the sight of Robbie's black Audi. Barker skated over the cobbles with their layer of black ice and used the large metal knocker hanging limply from the ancient red wooden door to knock. He had narrowly avoided treading over a pair of discarded manure-covered wellington boots. Barker wasn't nervous. As far as he was concerned, Robbie Hanson's time had come. 'He has to face the music,' he said to himself. He knocked again, this time louder than before.

Alice Hanson stood in front of him, her obvious beauty camouflaged by work clothes and the mud splattered across her left cheek. Barker recognised that Alice was an attractive girl, a fact already confirmed from their previous short meeting.

'Sergeant Barker…' Alice said. It was a statement of surprise. What she really meant to say was, 'Why the hell are you here?'

'Can I have a word with Robbie, please?' Barker said, hunching his shoulders and emphasising the miserable weather as he stood outside. There was a short pause while Alice considered a response.

'Come in. Coffee?' She politely held the door open to welcome Steve into the dry warmth.

'No thanks,' Steve said as he wiped his shoes and dived into the house.

Alice ushered him along the hallway and into the

kitchen. The room was dominated by the Aga opposite a long table, and chairs were scattered untidily around. *No doubt this was the scene of numerous large family feasts in previous times*, thought Barker, as he also took in the other members of Hanson's family. His father was half-way through a full English, while Alice returned to her muesli and fruit. However, what immediately attracted his attention was the sight of Robbie spoon-feeding his mother, who was currently occupying a wheelchair with a cairn terrier curled up contentedly on her lap. Barker now felt a real bastard.

He took a deep breath. 'Robbie, can I have a quick word?' Given the circumstances, it was basically a plea as opposed to a request. This wasn't going to be easy, as Hanson was looking pleadingly into his sergeant's eyes. For a moment Barker looked away as Robbie returned to his caring duties, picked up another spoonful of blended food and gently fed his mother.

It seemed like an age for Barker until finally Robbie put the spoon down. 'That's it, Mum.' He rose slowly, then bent down and kissed his mother on her forehead as tears appeared in his eyes.

Barker walked out of the farmhouse, closely followed by Hanson. They had already reached Barker's car when Alice caught up with them. Despite the cold and wet she was standing on the cobbles in her woollen socks covered by inappropriate slippers, having forgotten to put on her wellies in the confusion.

'What the hell is going on, Robbie?' Alice asked her brother, who ignored his sister's comments and opened Barker's front seat passenger car door.

'He's been arrested for conspiracy to murder and corruption. I'm so sorry, Alice,' Barker said officiously while opening the driver's door. He just wanted to get out of there fast.

He drove off with his prisoner. The sight of Alice's face through the rain-splattered car window would never leave Sergeant Steve Barker.

Once PC Robbie Hanson had been booked in at the custody suite, Steve updated a much-relieved Sutton. An hour or so later, with the custody sergeant as a witness, Robbie Hanson signed the notes his sergeant had made as a true record of their conversation last night.

Following his call from Barker, Geoff sat back in the diner and watched Jo Firth finish her scrambled eggs. He didn't feel particularly hungry, partly due to his early morning hurried slice of toast but more so because of the imminent meeting with Vern Edwards. He rang Ron Turner, who was made aware of Hanson's arrest and the circumstances.

21

Gemma

It was bloody cold. Art Gormley sat at his desk – which was likely to remain in its current untidy state, given that it was Rita's day off. He had few options but to allocate Jonta to attend Norfolk Street alone for the daily welfare check on McIntyre. What really concerned him was the complete lack of contact from bloody John Dexter.

Work was far from Jonta Roberts's mind. Minutes previously he had walked out of his rented flat feeling happier than ever. He had planned for this day. While he made his way to work, his partner Gemma was reading a story to their daughter Kate while they were still in bed.

Earlier that week he and Gemma had taken Kate to see the Christmas window display in one of the largest independent stores located in the new city centre precinct. It was the highlight of the year for many young families. The established store displayed an annual Christmas story, with accompanying music, across its main show windows. Kate, her eyes wide, had squealed with delight as Jonta, pausing at each scene, had pushed her buggy. As they passed the final display both parents were in tears at the delight shown by their daughter.

They walked as a family and were returning to the taxi rank when Jonta noticed that Gemma was distracted. She had paused momentarily at a jewellery shop. She looked again, obviously taking careful note of the prices, before making up the ground to join him and Kate. Today, after completing his shift at Gormley's, Jonta was planning a return to the precinct. His sole intention was to purchase an engagement ring, and, thanks to his recent ill-gotten gains, money wasn't a problem.

When he arrived at Gormley's it was the first occasion that day that he'd checked his phone. *Shit, he's pissed again*, Jonta thought, and read the text that his good friend Stryker had sent him in the early hours: *Bloody Galloways. Always a fucking easy touch.*

Jonta read the message twice. *He needs to be bloody careful*, Jonta thought, even though at this time he hadn't a clue that the message had been so widely circulated. He rang Stryker immediately. No reply. He sent him a text, the next best thing, requesting a call back.

Jonta arrived at 56 Norfolk Street using the same Honda. After parking he entered the property. Once inside he shivered at the cold, damp air permeating everything. He could hear coughing as he pulled on his balaclava. He carefully climbed the stairs before making his way to McIntyre's room.

'Shit, he's not well.' Jonta stated the obvious as he looked down at the visibly shaking McIntyre. His concern had nothing to do with the broken nose. It was McIntyre's distinctive pallor and his laboured breathing, punctuated with a repetitive cough. The prisoner had notably deteriorated. 'It's so bloody cold in here,' said Roberts to himself.

The only positive from Jonta's visit was that, given the release of one hand, McIntyre could just about use a bucket when he needed to urinate. Despite his condition that had proved a success, and another change of clothing wasn't required.

Jonta hunted around the house and ripped down a set of threadbare curtains from another room to provide McIntyre with another foul-smelling cover. Jonta had purchased a few more sandwiches and, given the circumstances, he made McIntyre as comfortable as possible. He then left him with another large bottle of water. Roberts descended the stairs, trying to ignore the sound of Pete's coughing. He reported back to the troubled Art, emphasising his concerns. Gormley scoured the garage for an electric heater.

A couple of hours later, with no reported mechanical problems from any of Art's vehicles, Jonta got a flyer from work and headed to the city centre precinct.

In his Norfolk Street prison Pete McIntyre began to feel life was closing in. The recent visit had failed to raise his spirits. He coughed loudly. It was accompanied by a tightening of the chest and an inability to get warm. No matter how he manoeuvred himself under the duvet and the curtains his shaking was becoming more violent. 'It is so bloody cold,' he said as he spluttered again.

Pete tried to take a bite out of a sandwich but spat it out after a reflex motion caused by another bout of coughing. With his teeth involuntarily chattering he said, 'We are heading for the warmest part of the day,' as he forlornly tried to comfort himself.

McIntyre peeped his head out from under the inadequate covers and looked up at the window, which was now completely frosted over. His mind wandered, trying to focus on happier times to boost morale. Yet he knew that his health was deteriorating rapidly.

The thought of another freezing night sent a shiver of a different nature flooding through his veins.

22

HMP Wassingham

Once their prison meeting was prepped Sutton settled the cafe bill while Firth went to warm the Nissan. He was walking across the small car park when a small dark blue Corsa with just the one female occupant pulled alongside them. 'I'm sure I know her from somewhere,' Sutton said, joining Firth. 'Do you know who that is?' Sutton asked his partner, thinking that it could be a work colleague.

'Never seen her before,' Firth said confidently, glancing across in a manner that made Sutton check his sanity.

'I'm sure I know her from somewhere, Jo,' Sutton added with equal surety as the pair continued the journey.

You could see HMP Wassingham from a distance, despite the poor visibility. It was a relatively new establishment, built within easy reach of main roads and transport hubs, but just far enough away from any major city. Now privately owned, it stood in an elevated position. The prison's huge metal perimeter fencing supported many strategically located floodlit pylons, which were currently beaming brightly in the gloom. The building itself was almost star-shaped, with each point of the star representing a prison wing.

From paedophiles to lifers, HMP Wassingham had

the lot, and on a daily basis the staff just about kept matters on an even keel. The vast visitors' car park was fairly empty when Firth parked the Nissan as close as she could to the main entrance and within scrutiny of a CCTV camera. The public visiting hours on a weekend were 12.30 p.m. to 2.30 p.m., and Geoff and Jo knew that they had to complete their business well before then.

After leaving their phones and all valuables securely in their car, Sutton grabbed their interview notes together with the prison visit authority and placed them into a plain wallet holder with an A4 pad and pen.

The entrance to Wassingham was grey, dismal and forbidding. A small clear tunnel, shaped like a bus stop, gave a false impression of welcoming before you then walked into a large entry hall whose walls were covered with posters and signs. Most of the instructions displayed warnings to individuals that they would be prosecuted if they even attempted to smuggle drugs or other prohibited items into the prison.

Sutton smiled ironically to himself as he thought of Edwards and the fact that he seemed not only to have a direct line to the governor but was able to make phone calls almost when and where he liked.

Within the entry hall there were five search stations, each similar to a turnstile entrance at a football match. As it was prior to the official visiting time, only one entrance was currently staffed.

Sutton and Firth approached and had their photographs taken separately. Firth looked nervously across at her partner and Sutton smiled back unconvincingly. It was a vain attempt to instil some reassurance, to try and combat the institutional atmosphere in their stark new surroundings. They produced their warrant cards. *Not good enough*, thought Sutton, as the somewhat bored-looking prison officer, dressed all in black, requested their visit authority too.

Firth looked over her shoulder to where a smart-looking male carrying a large briefcase was waiting. 'No doubt a solicitor-client meeting,' she correctly assumed.

'Phones or other sharp objects…' It wasn't a question. It was an order.

Moments later the seemingly bored prison officer had stamped their authority form and allowed them through, this time into another area similar to that of any international airport. Then he took another photograph and gave them a body search with an implement resembling a magic wand, which took place behind some discreet screens.

'Please walk this way,' another officer said, as she indicated where they should go. She was also dressed in an identical drab uniform, but she had a large bunch of keys hanging limply from a utility belt.

Now they were outside in the fresh air, walking in the rain from one building to another within the prison confines. Sutton took a deep breath of fresh air. His pulse was racing, but he needed to focus.

He heard a shout from one of the many rows of windows guarded by bars. 'Filth … pigs…'

They can pick us out anywhere, thought Sutton, as a steady and persistent banging could be heard from their cells. While it was obviously safe, the noise around them only heightened the intimidation they both felt. The sounds seem to echo as Sutton and Firth continued their journey.

Inside another building Geoff and Jo were led to a small basic interview room and the door was closed.

Other than the recording equipment there was absolutely nothing. There was a total of four seats all fixed to the floor, two each on either side of a table. Everything seemed to be painted grey, which only added to the experience.

'These two, Jo,' Sutton said to Firth as they took their seats on the side where Sutton had noticed the partially visible red panic button. Geoff took out their pre-planned notes and placed them on the table.

Sutton and Firth didn't speak but looked across at each other and waited and waited.

It seemed like an age before they heard footsteps. Then finally the interview room door was opened by an experienced-looking officer. With his free arm he guided the handcuffed Vern Edwards into the room.

For some unknown reason Sutton stood up immediately and took in the sight before him. He had to say that Edwards looked well despite his years of imprisonment. Clean and tidy, he was always a gym addict, a habit that had continued while in prison. Sutton wasn't the least surprised to note the prison issue tracksuit was typically drab, grey in colour.

'Get these fuckers off,' he ordered the officer, pointing to his handcuffs. Despite his muscularity Edwards wasn't a tall man, but in a strange way, being of average height only added to his physical presence.

The officer looked across towards Geoff, who nodded his approval. If he were honest, he thought he didn't have a choice. Being in Edwards's presence took Sutton immediately back to the time when he was his handler and Vern was registered as a dangerous informant. On meeting him again Sutton was as nervous now as he had been then. Nothing had changed. He hated being in

Vern's company, but desperately tried to hide his feelings of intense vulnerability.

'I will wait outside.' The officer made his exit as Edwards extended his hands and arms, displaying a full range of tattoos. He rubbed his wrists, which were now free from the heavy metal cuffs.

'You've put on a bit of weight, Sutton,' Edwards said, pointing towards him while patting his six-pack and taking immediate control of the interview.

'Vern, before we formally record this conversation, tell me what you want from this. There are no promises,' Sutton said quietly, trying desperately to sound relaxed.

'I've already fucking told you, Sutton. A glowing report for my parole board.' Edwards smiled, totally ignoring Firth. 'I want out of this bastard place.' He turned his head slightly and spat on the floor. It was another gesture of intimidation and it caused Sutton to look away in disgust. It was a gesture meant to emphasise just how desperate Edwards was to end his time in custody.

Sutton could feel his skin crawl, purely as a result of being in the presence of Edwards. 'I pity his cellmate,' he said to himself.

Geoff turned on the recording equipment, went through the preliminaries and then introduced those present. 'This meeting is purely voluntary and has been organised at the prisoner's request. He also has the right to terminate proceedings at any time.'

As the formalities had now been covered Sutton then looked across the table at Edwards, who was staring at him. He felt Vern's eyes piercing his own. Geoff licked his dry lips and continued slowly, with an obvious open question. 'You have requested this interview because you have some information regarding the recent shootings in Parton city centre. Is that right?' Sutton summoned the courage to stare back at Edwards.

'For years me and fucking Wendy Galloway have been at war. That's what got me in this shithole.' This time Edwards didn't spit, but his red eyes flickered around the room. 'Galloway organised the bouncer kid getting shot outside Lucifer's the other week, but she wasn't involved in either the shooting of her son or the kidnap that happened on the same night.' His eyes refocused on Sutton. 'The person behind Matt Galloway's injuries isn't his fucking mother. The shooting and kidnap are down to one of yours, Sutton. He's a bizzie, an old-fashioned rozzer,' Edwards said, very slowly and deliberately.

'Despite the fact that two different people organised the fucking shootings they were committed by the same person, who was riding pillion on a motorbike. The same shit pulled the trigger, Sutton. The same shit.' At that Edwards simulated firing a gun with his raised right hand. His fingers formed the barrel, which he aimed directly towards Sutton's head. He mimed the word *Bang*, and slowly dropped his hand.

There was a moment's silence between them as if Edwards, like an actor, had delivered a classic line then waited for his audience to appreciate the significance of what he had said. Edwards had finished for now. He sat back and just stared.

Sutton felt his palms. They were both sweaty and shaking, but thankfully out of Vern's sight. 'We strongly believe that there is a possibility of police involvement,' Sutton said, trying to sound suitably unimpressed.

Edwards interrupted him by saying, 'This prick is high up, Sutton. John fucking Dexter – head of your complaints, Sutton. It's a fucking joke,' Edwards said. He was making it personal, and Geoff knew it. 'Good press,' Vern continued sarcastically. He spoke with absolute certainty, his burning eyes never leaving Sutton, who on this occasion looked down.

Geoff summoned his nerve and forced himself to return the stare but said nothing and wondered. There was a silence, it seemed like forever, 'How the hell does Edwards know this? How does he know about Dexter's involvement?' Sutton said to himself.

He tried to gather his thoughts. 'Take control, take control,' Sutton repeated to himself, nipping the fleshy base of his right thumb with the index finger and thumb of his left hand. The ensuing sharp pain enabled him to swiftly focus.

'Who pulled the trigger, Vern? Who pulled the trigger?' Now it was Sutton repeating himself.

'Not sure, Sutton, not fucking sure, but I'm working on it and I'm your fucking best bet.' Edwards smiled at him, but Geoff was shell-shocked. His hands were now gripping the fixed table that separated them. Sutton's white knuckles were an indication of his state of mind. Vern was in control, toying with him. Did he already know where Pete was?

'Edwards, do you know anything about a kidnapping following Matt Galloway's shooting?' Sutton asked a straightforward and direct question, almost through gritted teeth. Firth recognised the friction and put her hand on his forearm as a calming measure. The intervention wasn't lost on Edwards, who smiled sarcastically.

'I may find out and, if I do, I will be fucking ringing you. That's if you ever answer your fucking phone,' Edwards said, without the usual swagger. Sutton had asked a question that Vern couldn't answer.

'It might mean parole or no parole, Vern,' said Sutton with half a smirk, securing his advantage. Geoff's eyes swivelled around the interview room, now mocking Edwards's circumstances. The momentum had changed. The previously simmering atmosphere had now reached boiling point and they both knew it. Vern Edwards hated the police – always had, always would – and Sutton was a member of that organisation. It was their fault that he was doing his time.

He placed his tattooed hands firmly on the table and stood up. Determined that Edwards wasn't going to dominate him, Sutton did likewise. He knew that his final comment had ended the interview. From a standing position Sutton reached forward and switched off the recording equipment.

'Ready,' Edwards shouted, and the prison guard returned to the room. Vern presented his wrists and was handcuffed. As Edwards was led from the room he looked back and gave Sutton one final stare.

Geoff sat down exhausted, not because the interview had been prolonged. It was the effect of meeting Vern Edwards.

'You OK?' Firth enquired with some concern. Edwards had completely ignored Jo and had dismissed her presence throughout. 'What an evil bastard,' she added. 'He frightened me,' Firth said honestly, breathing deeply.

'He frightened me, Jo,' Sutton readily admitted.

They both smiled in relief. As Sutton looked down and extended the fingers of his right hand he could see that they were still shaking. Between the two of them they had vast experience in their respective roles, yet the interview with Edwards was a conversation they would always remember. Sutton picked up their prepared notes.

'Waste of time, this lot,' he said, and managed a laugh as their own prison officer escort arrived.

Sometime later they walked out of HMP Wassingham, relieved to be free again, although the sky was still dark and it was raining incessantly. While the interview had been relatively short, the process of getting in and out of the prison took longer than imagined, and by the time they walked back to their car the early arrivals for the scheduled visiting time had begun arriving.

'That's the Corsa we saw at the service station,' Sutton said to Firth, just as he was closing the passenger door, 'I am sure I know that woman, Jo,' Sutton added, looking at the driver.

'Let's just get out of here, Geoff.' Firth ignored Sutton's last comments and reversed the Nissan. Jo just wanted to leave the prison and their recent experiences well behind. She looked around. The gloom of the day was reflected on the walls of HMP Wassingham.

Rita sat in her dark blue Corsa and glanced down at her watch. Just another fifteen minutes to wait before her regular allotted visiting time. She pulled down the sun visor and released the enclosed mirror to check her appearance. She was excited. She always was at this time of the week. The visit to see Vern, her Vern, was the highlight, and today was no different. Their secret relationship had been going on for more years than she cared to remember.

23

Ron Turner

The historic Galloway and Edwards turf war had made an indelible mark on Ron Turner. He had played a major part in the enquiry as the force's head of intelligence, with John Dexter as his deputy. Turner was never entirely happy with Dexter, although it was nothing he could put his finger on. The flash cars and expensive holidays coupled with an obvious burning ambition... John Dexter always gave him concern. He knew that his own promotion to ACC had hurt Dexter a great deal.

On that previous Friday evening after their briefing Turner had taken the short walk to the chief constable's office. He needed her permission that he should be the arresting officer when Dexter was locked up the following morning. It was a request that was partly personal, but also because he believed it unfair that an officer of a lower rank should have to make an arrest of an individual who he knew would be both difficult and intimidating. Chris Mayling willingly granted this request.

The reappearances of Wendy Galloway and Vern Edwards were proving difficult for Ron Turner, as were his former suspicions concerning Dexter. At this stage of his career he was asking himself the question, 'Do I really need this?' He was visualising his favourite landscapes of the Lake District in the knowledge that he and his long-suffering wife had planned to buy a retirement home somewhere in Cumbria.

It was early morning when Turner received a call from Sutton giving him an update of Robbie Hanson's arrest and confession. He sighed to himself. From all accounts young Hanson had been a good cop who had been caught up in a myriad of unfortunate circumstances. 'He wasn't the first and he certainly won't be the last,' Turner said to himself as he made his way across the sodden car park at force HQ to meet the team of officers assigned under his command to arrest Dexter.

Then, with all previous thoughts banished, Turner mischievously grinned to himself. 'This should be good fun,' he mused. 'A bit of sport.' He eagerly anticipated John Dexter's wake-up call.

It took thirty minutes to arrive at a peaceful suburban estate where the home of Chief Superintendent John Dexter was located. The weather couldn't hide the comforts of a five-bedroom detached house. There were just the two vehicles in Turner's convoy: an arrest team consisting of himself and a couple of detectives, followed by a personnel carrier containing a search team. Turner's vehicle pulled up outside the target address, while the carrier remained out of view at a church car park half a mile from Dexter's residence.

'Right let's do it,' Turner said enthusiastically as the car drew up outside Dexter's house. He led them up the driveway past the BMW X5 and pressed the doorbell. The sound resonated, with Turner purposely maintaining pressure on the button before hearing a shout from a voice that was instantly recognisable.

'All right, all right, I'm bloody coming.' The large red

door was soon opened, and Turner was greeted with a familiar sight. Despite the early hour Dexter was up and already smartly dressed. His mouth opened as if he were about to say something, but there was only one person who was in control of this situation.

'John Dexter, I'm arresting you for conspiracy to murder and corruption,' Turner said with confidence, after reminding Dexter he was under caution.

'Cuff him.' Turner looked towards the two detectives while Dexter stood, mouth still open, standing bolt upright on his doorstep. Dexter was led to the car as Turner called up the search team. They quickly established that no one else was present in the property. Fortunately for Dexter his wife was absent, visiting their daughter in London. The new prisoner was initially stunned. It was only during the journey to the city centre custody suite that Dexter began his verbal attack on Turner.

'I'm coming after you, Turner, you bastard,' Dexter mouthed, sitting handcuffed, accompanied by a detective in the rear of their vehicle. There was no response. 'I'll fucking have you, Turner,' he spat out with venom. The lack of response didn't help Dexter's mood.

Ron Turner, pen in hand, remained in the front of the vehicle and ignored his obnoxious passenger. He had a broad smile across his face as Dexter continued his vitriol. It was purely personal, and all contemporaneously recorded by Turner. Throughout the journey Dexter never stopped.

Once his prisoner was booked into custody, ACC Turner opened the operations room. It was staffed by an experienced team of four. A detective hovered by a huge whiteboard, which covered the back wall and recorded the arrests and any immediate actions from the recovered evidence. The remaining three members of the team staffed the telephone extensions. One was a public hotline after yet another media appeal for information. This included both shootings, which the police had linked. The staff also had access to a couple of laptops on which they could monitor any social media platforms. The information they obtained was then relayed to SIO Trish Delaney and her team of investigators. Hanson and Dexter were currently in custody.

All staff stood as Chief Constable Mayling entered the room, in recognition of both her rank and the growing respect she had gained throughout the force. Mayling and Turner made a good team. Unlike his contemporary John Dexter, Ron Turner was Parton Constabulary through and through.

Turner's phone rang. It was the inspector from Bill Rudding's arrest team. 'Sir, Rudding has been detained. He broke down crying after attempting some sort of deal with us. He was pathetic, really, and put the blame firmly on Robbie Hanson, who he claimed had assaulted him. He's almost hysterical now, but he's on his way to custody and I'm remaining with the search team.' He ended his update by saying, 'I will let you know of any significant finds.'

'Thanks, Inspector. Keep in touch,' Turner replied, and within minutes the whiteboard was fully updated. He then turned to Mayling. 'Ma'am, can I have a word, please?' The look on his face indicated that it would be a private word.

Inside the welcoming office of Chris Mayling, Turner updated her on Sutton's prison visit. 'What do you think?' was her obvious response.

'It's typical Vern Edwards. Like a fisherman would,

he's cast us some bait. Enough to create an interest, but no more.' Turner stopped for a moment and summed up his thoughts. 'In my view, if Edwards comes up with further intel – which he has suggested – we can reassess the situation. I don't consider what he has told us to date merits any favourable report to the parole board. But currently he isn't to know that. Let's just see what develops,' Turner added, giving Mayling a knowing wink. A most unusual Turner response.

'I'm happy with that, Ron. Now what about Pete McIntyre? The force are about to take a public hiding over the arrest of corrupt coppers. The saving of a life through the release of a hostage could assist in restoring some public confidence,' Mayling said with some urgency.

24

Kev Stryker

On the Saturday morning Wendy Galloway woke following a restless night. For a split second she thought about ringing the hospital to check out Matt's condition, but it was a fleeting concern that was quickly forgotten.

As was her custom when she went to bed, Wendy turned her phone off. During her restless tossing and turning she heard Toni make her normal chaotic return home from a night out. 'Pissed again,' said Wendy to herself and wrapped a pillow around her head in a vain attempt to drown out any further noise.

At approximately 8 a.m. she turned on her phone and read the text that had been forwarded during the early hours: *Bloody Galloways. Always a fucking easy touch.* She forced herself to read the message twice before her hand began to shake with pure anger.

***

Sutton and Firth may have thought they had experienced a traumatic morning during their prison visit, but it was nothing compared to the physical pain that Kev Stryker was suffering. At approximately 9 a.m. three of Wendy Galloway's finest had demolished the back door of his small, terraced house. They had parked their van and entered the property via the unadopted cobbled lane at the rear of the premises. It gave access into the backyard and was away from public view.

Stryker didn't hear them. He was still comatose from the excesses of the night before. His plan was to wake around lunchtime and have a shower and some brunch before making his way to the leisure centre to instruct a self-defence class

Two men ran up the stairs, while one kept watch in the lane. The two visitors dragged Stryker out of bed before the kicking began. A sober and alert Stryker might have been a match for the two, but while still drunk he just couldn't react until it was too late.

Their feet rained in on Stryker. Careful to avoid his head, they thoughtfully pinioned his arms and legs instead. Kev groaned, incapable of shouting, and began vomiting. 'Dirty bastard,' one of his attackers murmured, while taking a break from the gratuitous violence. It didn't last long. It was enough to know that they had subdued their prisoner. Positioned either side of Stryker, they each linked an arm underneath either shoulder. Kev was dragged down the stairs head first and placed in the rear of the empty van, accompanied by his two assailants. The third member of Galloway's gang returned to his position behind the wheel.

The pain of Kev's severe hangover had been super-seded by the punishment he had just received. He remained in last night's clothes and his phone remained in his pocket.

They had been travelling for ten minutes or so before Stryker began asking himself, 'What the fuck is this all about?' He began sobering up as his phone rang. It was ignored by his captors. Answering the damn thing was impossible, and his whole body throbbed constantly from top to bottom. Even the slightest piece of uneven road impacted upon the pain coursing through the body of Kev Stryker.

Wendy Galloway was in her element, secreted away in her study and directing operations that usually resulted in somebody's pain or death. Knowing Toni wouldn't surface until sometime that afternoon, she knew she wouldn't be disturbed.

She had received a further text saying, *Package has been secured and is now en route to delivery point.* For the first time that morning Wendy Galloway managed to smile. 'Time to check when the swimming pool opens,' she said to herself and began to surf the Internet. Within a couple of minutes she had checked the tide times. High tide would be at 6 p.m. She smiled again.

Unbeknown to Kev Stryker, he was the package being transported to the delivery point. On this occasion Galloway's men drove through the car park on the east marina and ignored the harbour, taking instead a small track that travelled parallel to the barren coastline. It was one of those little-known coastal tracks that take you to nowhere.

A mile or so later they had arrived. Gull's Point was a small inlet, a classic smugglers' cove in days gone by, immediately south of the desolate East Parton marina. The perfect spot, as far as Wendy Galloway was concerned.

After parking they remained in the van for a couple of minutes. Stryker could hear the constant sound of rain on the van roof, like a never-ending beat from some eighties disco classic. He heard the van door open and close. The driver was out and about, completing a final recce. A couple of minutes later he returned and was now standing outside the rear doors of the van.

The journey to the location had at least enabled Stryker to sober up and make an assessment. The very fact he had been dragged out of bed and kicked to hell was a strong indication of his desperate plight. Now they had stopped and with his senses alive, he heard the unmistakable sound of the sea. Stryker rightly guessed that he would be leaving the vehicle. That in itself would provide him with an opportunity of escape.

Lying prone, face down, with a foot across the back of his head and another in the middle of his back, Kev tensed his aching muscles. 'Shit, I am sore,' he groaned inwardly, pushing the pain to the very back of his mind. 'I need to have a go,' he said to himself.

Stryker heard the back doors swing open and a waft of freezing air and rain entered the van. One of Galloway's army jumped out and joined the driver, leaving just one of them inside the vehicle. His foot remained on the back of Kev's head.

Stryker then felt himself being dragged out of the van by his legs while still face down. He placed his hands down to break his fall as his upper body fell. Kev hit the ground. His legs were still being dragged backwards as if he were a rag doll, splashing in and out of puddles on the rain-soaked ground.

Summoning all his strength and agility, Stryker pulled his knees up towards him in an effort to release the grip of the men dragging him. As he did so he twisted, making it even more difficult for Galloway's men to keep their hold.

Success. For just a moment Stryker was free and in a split second he was lying prone on the ground, hardly believing his luck. It was a split second he would live to regret as the final member of Galloway's team, having anticipated Stryker's move, jumped from the van, made up the couple of yards and landed a size ten boot across Kev's right shoulder.

Stryker heard the crunch accompanying the searing pain. That broken right shoulder had ended his escape plans. He couldn't stand, never mind fight back. Writhing in pain and clutching at his shoulder, he screamed out as the filthy brown water pooled into his mouth. The fact that no one was around to hear his screams only added to his agony.

Ten minutes later Kev Stryker was secured around a single wooden post, one of the last remnants of a former landing area within the inlet. The fact that he had been bound with his arms to the front made it marginally less agonising for his right shoulder. Kev felt his bones crunch with every minute movement within his bindings.

Through the bitter cold and driving rain Kev Stryker soon became aware of his intended fate. He managed to focus on a very small shallow rock pool a few yards from his feet. 'Which fucking way is the tide travelling?' he mouthed in desperation.

Wendy Galloway received the call she was expecting. 'Package has been delivered.' She checked her watch. 'Time to change my outfit,' she reminded herself.

Meanwhile Kev Stryker looked down at the now brimming rock pool. He knew the answer to his question.

25

Rita

Saturday afternoon

Ron Turner paced the floor of his command room, his eyes glued on the whiteboard. He was more than satisfied with the results so far. Hanson had been interviewed almost immediately after his detention had been authorised. He didn't want a solicitor and effectively told his story, covering his mother's illness, the fateful shift night out with Bill Rudding and his involvement in the first shooting outside Lucifer's. He ended his account in tears as he talked about his relationship with Matt Galloway. His interview included everything the enquiry team had hoped it would.

All efforts to interview Rudding and Dexter had so far been thwarted. Rudding requested a police surgeon to examine his injuries. Dexter had made a similar request. This was due to the fact that he wished to make a formal complaint of assault by his arresting officer ACC Ron Turner. It came as no surprise that Dexter had requested the same firm of solicitors used by members of Wendy Galloway's operation.

As for Rita, she waited patiently and passed through the mundane ritual of security procedures at HMP

Wassingham. Past experience told her to carry as little as possible when she went to the prison. On this occasion she had just a couple of scribbled notes that were not likely to attract attention, but hopefully contained enough to give Vern what he wanted.

Much had happened since Vern Edwards had been sentenced. His subsequent divorce a couple of years later from his long-suffering wife was inevitable. Their marriage was a sham, and Rita had been on the scene long before Vern's final arrest. She was captivated by the man and ignored his infamous violent past.

Rita's past love life, just a couple of unsatisfactory relationships, was hardly worth a mention. Then she had gone on a chance night out, a highly unusual occurrence for Rita, and had tagged along reluctantly at her niece's hen do. She even had to be forcibly pushed onto the dance floor. But the feel of Vern's muscular body caused her to melt. It took one dance. One dance led to two and the rest is history. Rita often thought back to that night.

Her blind love meant that she didn't believe anything said during the course of his criminal proceedings. It was a complete farce as far as she was concerned. Sitting discreetly in the public gallery, she watched everything. And as for that so-called supergrass, she felt complete hatred for him. Rita had never felt such feelings of resentment.

Looking back, it was a difficult time for Rita. A short time before Vern's trial she lost her regular cleaning job. Without letting her know they were going, her employers had quit the area without having the decency to inform their loyal housekeeper. Needing work, she then knocked on Art Gormley's door, not once but twice. Everyone in Parton knew that Art Gormley employed casual staff on a regular basis, but for one reason or another they usually didn't last long.

On the second occasion she gained admission and tried to ignore the smell of his disgusting office. But Rita's persistence brought dividends. She proved her worth to Art, who recognised Rita's quiet and efficient loyalty. Her diligent cleaning of Art's office also provided Rita access to crucial information. Never more so than the present day. The timing couldn't be better, as the matter of Vern Edwards's forthcoming parole board had been mentioned. Rita would do literally anything to secure Vern's early release.

Every Saturday since his sentence, Rita had attended whichever prison Edwards was incarcerated. The day when Vern would be released was the light at the end of a very long tunnel, but that light was becoming brighter each day and the possibility of a life together was rapidly becoming a probability.

Through the search stations Rita felt her heart beating. It always did at the prospect of meeting Vern when she arrived at the visitor's room, which was similar to a small airplane hangar. There was no decoration and absolutely no welcome, just signage explaining the do's and don'ts and the maximum punishments should these rules be ignored. Prison officers took up their designated positions, assisted by strategically placed CCTV cameras, before the prisoners were eventually led into the room.

Rita sat patiently at her allocated table on her fixed chair. There was the noise of people gathering, usually the regulars, who also took up their designated places. The general buzz was punctuated by crying babies or toddlers who arrived in numbers. Some were at an age where they could formulate short sentences. 'Mam, can

I have this? Mam, can I have that?' They were no doubt wondering what this was all about. Rita, knowing them by sight only, smiled or nodded her head at one or two people. She completely avoided conversation, even when pressed.

Whenever Rita sat waiting for Vern to arrive for their visit her mind drifted back to the identity of the super-grass. It was something that had always haunted her. At the trial she had listened to the testimony, desperately trying to identify the distorted voice. It was crucial evidence that had sent her Vern down.

A bell rang and the prisoners entered. Her heart skipped more than a beat when she saw Vern approach and instantly reminded her of that first dance. Even when dressed in the drab grey tracksuit, Rita considered him the most attractive man in the world. She always stood as he approached and reached across the screen for his hand. She couldn't help herself, even though she knew it would always attract some form of rebuke from the officialdom. And right enough, a prison officer began moving towards them and told her to take her hand back.

Suitably admonished, Rita sat down. Vern looked around, a final visual check to make sure there was absolutely no interest in their conversation. Everyone seemed engrossed by the person or persons in front of them. They were clear, and Vern sat forward with his elbows on his side of the desk and his hands supporting his unshaven chin. He began talking and recounted his earlier visit from Sutton and Firth. Rita listened excitedly.

'Do you think it's enough?' Rita asked, in a direct reference to his parole report.

'Probably not,' Vern admitted. 'Have you fucking got anything?' he asked, with some urgency. Despite the number of years they had been together, Rita always cringed at his swearing. Initially she had naively tried to correct him but had quickly realised it was a complete waste of time. Rita looked around and noted that the same prison officer who had admonished them had begun to take an unusually keen interest.

She leant forward. 'Vern love, I've got what you wanted on some notes. Maybe give me a ring later.' Her eyes rolled upwards in the direction of the attentive officer.

'Just tell me, Rita, please. I will fucking remember,' Edwards said, hardly hiding his anticipation. He glanced to his right and noticed that the officer had been suddenly deployed to a quarrelling couple. It had all the hallmarks of a potential domestic.

'For whatever reason, Jonta confides in me. I've known him a while. He told me about the money he and his mate Kev Stryker have made recently from a couple of jobs. He says they were driving jobs. They would be. He's mad about motorbikes, and Stryker would be the one who pulled the trigger. According to Jonta, Kev Stryker has some big ideas about becoming the local hard man,' Rita said, desperately trying to say calm, speaking quietly and slowly.

'The confirmation came from one of Art's scribbled notes I recovered from the junk in his office. It shows their names and a scrawled drawing of a motorbike. Typical Art. It's the only way he can remember things in that tip of an office.' Rita cleverly paused, allowing Vern to digest the information she had provided. He gave a further glance around. The nearby domestic had escalated, requiring the attendance of other officers seeking to defuse the situation. And Rita took full advantage.

'Art's had a busy week. He asked me to follow a guy from the hospital. The guy went to the precinct multi-storey, where he got kidnapped by Jonta and Stryker. The guy kidnapped is holed up in one of Art's rentals in The Counties. There's something very familiar about this bloke. I was sure I recognised him, but the clothing threw me completely. It just couldn't be who I was thinking of,' Rita recounted.

'What's the address, love? It's fucking important,' Edwards said, after listening intently.

'It's 56 Norfolk Street,' she said quietly, despite her pounding heart. They both sat back and considered what had been said. Then Rita continued, as if in deep thought. 'Why would Dexter task Gormley to carry out the kidnap? Art is a criminal, but kidnap? He usually handles stolen MOTs or shoplifted gear.' Rita knew her boss only too well.

Vern leant forward again. His elbows were back supporting his chin, 'I know exactly fucking why, Rita, all thanks to you,' he said with some satisfaction. 'You told me about the fucking notes you found a few years back. Well, it's all about Art's taxi operating licence. That's what John Dexter does in the police: he fucking confirms Gormley is an all-right guy and the council take his word. He authorises taxi operating licences and Art relies on fucking Dexter for his business.'

'But why has Dexter wanted this guy to be kidnapped?' Rita asked.

'I haven't a fucking clue, Rita, haven't a fucking clue.' Edwards repeated what he said to emphasise his point and sank back in his seat. 'And I don't think fucking Art even knows,' Vern said with some finality.

The remainder of the visit was uneventful, as the pair

were simply planning for the future. The alarm sounded to end visiting time. They again touched hands before their favourite prison officer, relieved the domestic was over, stepped forward. Edwards reluctantly turned away and exited the room while Rita recovered a tissue from her handbag to dry her eyes before joining the other visitors in a mass exit.

Edwards wandered back to his cell. Rita had given him almost everything he needed. He had the whereabouts of the kidnap victim as well as the names of those who were involved in the shootings. It was potential freedom for him, and he knew it was gold dust for Geoff Sutton. Vern ordered his cellmate to keep watch as he recovered his mobile.

***

Firth and Sutton were making good ground on their return to Parton. The rain had finally stopped and there was just the slim chance that the sun was about to make a rare November appearance. Geoff was deep in thought, still racking his brains in an effort to identify the female driver of the Corsa. He was brought instantly back to reality as his informants' phone rang. This time there was no hesitation. He didn't even need to check the screen for Bob Hope.

'Sutton, how you fucking doing?' Edwards's voice was only slightly less intimidating on the phone.

'What is it?' Sutton asked politely. His hand was clammy, and it had become glued to the phone when he heard Edwards's voice.

'It's called parole, Sutton. It's called fucking parole,' Edwards said in emphasis.

There was a prolonged silence between the two, while

Firth, sensing the importance of the call, pulled into a lay-by.

'Well, what is it, then?' Sutton tried to sound confident.

'Three things, Sutton, three things.' Vern knowingly prolonged the agony. He couldn't care less that his information was potentially life-saving. Sutton didn't respond. He put the phone on loudspeaker and looked across to Firth.

'Is the bitch listening, Sutton?' It seemed that whatever the circumstances Edwards would always be in control. Again Sutton didn't reply. He reached down into his folder and armed himself with a notepad and pen.

'The bloke from the fucking kidnap is at 56 Norfolk Street in The Counties, one of Gormley's properties. And Art organised the whole fucking thing on John Dexter's orders. Another thing, Sutton, for your parole report... The two people for the shootings are Jonta Roberts and Kev Stryker. It was Stryker who pulled the trigger. That's it, Sutton. That's fucking it. See you on the outside,' Edwards said in a threatening voice, and ended the call. Sutton noticed that his hand was still shaking as he recorded the details of their succinct conversation.

Without recourse to Sutton or any other supervision Firth glanced at her watch. It was approaching 2 p.m. and she knew he would be about to start duty.

***

Sergeant Steve Barker had secured his locker, picked up his radio and headed for the parade room. The young sergeant felt awful, and it wasn't just the lack of sleep. He was struggling to get the sight of an emotional Alice Hanson out of his mind, and as for her stricken mother... Not only that, but he also contemplated the tragic circumstances surrounding the arrest of Robbie Hanson – not that he could, or would, have dealt with the matter in any other way. His thoughts swung between thinking that Hanson deserved everything coming to him and a feeling of heartfelt sympathy. In marked contrast, the downfall of PC Bill Rudding hadn't even entered his mind.

Barker sat down at the head of the table in the parade room, awaiting the constables on his shift to report for duty. It was the same routine whatever the force. Officers were briefed with the latest intelligence before being allocated their duties for the forthcoming shift. A small TV screen gave officers a collective visual on the latest intelligence as Barker shuffled some additional notes. 'Right, listen in,' he said with authority before his mobile rang – an unforgivable mistake. Barker knew he wasn't on the ball because he always turned it off prior to a parade.

'Apologies,' he said and sighed as he looked down at his phone, 'I've got to take this,' he added, and without giving a second thought answered Jo Firth's call.

'Steve, get a team down to 56 Norfolk Street. Urgent. Just had some information that that's where our hostage is being housed.' Barker instantly recognised the urgency in Firth's voice and ended the call without uttering a word.

'Tom, Rocky, Sue, get the personnel carrier. Job on. We need the Enforcer and riot helmets. Carole, finish the parade, please,' Barker said to his acting sergeant.

He ran from the room, followed by the chosen three. Minutes later the liveried personnel carrier, with its blues and twos activated, waited impatiently for the electronic gates of the station backyard to pull back. Sue drove. Barker, the passenger in the front seat, felt adrenaline course through his body. All thoughts of fatigue had long disappeared. Tom and Rocky sat in the rear. The matt black door Enforcer had been placed carefully in the aisle of the vehicle.

'Right, listen in. Sue, take the shortest route to The Counties, 56 Norfolk Street.' There was only one person in charge as Barker shouted to be heard above the wailing sirens.

'Tom, the Enforcer, me and Rocky in first. We have just had some intel that the victim of Thursday's kidnap is at this address. We're going in under Section 17 of the Police and Criminal Evidence Act 1984 (PACE), to save life and prevent serious harm.' Barker never forgot the legislation. 'I haven't got a clue if there are other people at the address. Rocky, give Carole a shout back at the nick and just tell her we may need backup.' Barker ended the shortest of briefings as the carrier accelerated away from the police station.

Sue needed no further directions. The Counties was well known to them all, and she was grateful that the weather and the road conditions had improved. Barker, Tom and Rocky held on tight as the vehicle rocked and rolled its way to Norfolk Street. Sue's passengers maintained their balance as they struggled donning their protective headgear. Nothing further was said, and nothing further was needed as a buzz of nervous excitement drowned the noise of the vehicle.

'Thirty seconds,' Sue screamed as she took the final right turn with the tyres screeching. 'I'm going up on to the pavement,' she added, knowing that the side door of their vehicle would be adjacent to the nominated house door. Tom, his helmet visor down, nodded at Rocky to pull the door back to facilitate his exit. Barker, in the front, with his hand on the door lever, felt his beating heart ready to join the rest of his body and explode.

'Here we go,' Sue bellowed, ploughing up the kerb on to the pavement. Barker literally left his seat at the manoeuvre, just before the vehicle came to halt. Simultaneously, Rocky violently pulled at the side door as Tom athletically manoeuvred himself and the Enforcer out of the vehicle – where he was met by Barker, who had already alighted.

'Go Tom, go,' Barker yelled towards his colleague, who required no encouragement. He handled the Enforcer expertly. He wielded the menacing heavy black implement with both hands, first bringing it back to gain momentum before delivering the heavy round face at the target in a technique similar to a rocking Viking ship at a fairground. The sound of splintering wood greeted the first smash on the lower panel of the poorly maintained front door. Tom momentarily stood back while Rocky kicked hard at the remnants of a lock, which instantly gave way.

'Police,' they cried out in unison. Barker screamed as he ran upstairs, while Rocky and Tom cleared the ground-floor rooms. Barker heard the shouts of 'Clear,' emanating from his colleagues below. He had already checked the upstairs. It had only taken a matter of seconds to glance into the two bedrooms and the bath-room.

'Bloody nothing. Shit,' Barker shouted in sheer frustration as he reached for his phone.

Sutton and Firth remained in the lay-by. There was no point in moving, as they knew that Barker would call back immediately with a result. There was no conversation, just a gathering tension between them. They waited impatiently. Firth's phone rang. She answered and placed it on loudspeaker.

'The house is clear, Jo. It's absolutely clear,' Barker said with some dismay.

'The bastard,' Sutton said loudly in sheer exasperation. It was simply a reflex comment made with only one person in mind: Vern Edwards. Geoff banged his fist on the dashboard. 'Shit, where's Pete?' he said with emotion.

'Any sign of occupation?' Firth asked Barker after what seemed an age.

'One discarded mattress in an upstairs bedroom, but that's it. Could be just junkies, although the property seemed secure,' Barker replied. 'I will get SOCO to have a look,' he added, referring to a forensic examination. Sutton just stared through the windscreen while Firth ended Barker's desperate call.

'Where the hell is Pete?' Sutton said. His voice faltered as he looked across at Firth. He thought back to the face and previous words of Henry, McIntyre's son.

Without recourse to Firth or anyone else, for that matter, Sutton opened the car door. Moments later he stood in the desolate lay-by surrounded by the illegal waste dumped by fly tippers, his hands on his knees, with his back to the car and the fluctuating flow of traffic.

For the first time he fully realised the implications of Pete's kidnapping and that he may never see one of his best friends again. It was the obvious thought from the outset, given the nature of his disappearance. But, due to his total involvement in the investigation, this patently obvious realisation had never hit home. It did now. Sutton was violently sick.

He stood upright as Firth, who had joined him, handed over a tissue. Embarrassed, he couldn't look at her as tears began to well up and his body began to shake – not with the cold, but with the outpouring of emotion. *What on earth will I be able to say to Val or Henry?* he thought, in a fleeting moment of self-pity.

Firth let Sutton have his time. Then she reached around and placed an arm around his waist to guide him back to the car. As far as Sutton was concerned, the sound of passing traffic was drowned in a sea of emotions.

***

Prior to any subsequent police activity in The Counties, Art Gormley had sat in his untidy office. Jonta Roberts had given him the update on the prisoner at Norfolk Street. It was more than concerning. He didn't do this crap. Kidnapping was way out of his league. The possible consequences of him serving time frightened him more than anyone would believe. *Bloody Rita would know what to do*, he thought, looking again at his littered desk, and cursed her for having the temerity to take a day off.

Enough was enough. He rang Dexter, not once, but on several occasions, but his phone went immediately to voicemail.

It was lunchtime, and the rain had stopped when he drove the Honda back to The Counties. After an unsuccessful search for an electric fire Art had formulated a better plan. He'd already made a purchase at a nearby pharmacy and stopped at Suffolk Street, where he picked up Eric Bates. Eric was a large unit who acted as Art's enforcer for his tenancy properties in and around The Counties. His reward was rent-free accommodation.

The pair attended the end terrace that was 56 Norfolk Street, where they found McIntyre literally coughing his guts out. No disguises were required as he had begun to drift in and out of consciousness. Under the cover of the Honda, which was again parked on the pavement guarding that door, as well as the adjacent property, Eric carried and dragged their prisoner, while Gormley fumbled in his pockets and recovered the keys to number 54. It was another of his properties, and he knew that at least this place had a working and recently serviced gas central heating system.

Just in case, thought Art, as they returned to 56 and cleared any sign of recent occupation other than the lone mattress. 'They will think it's just a junkie,' Art said to Eric. 'And the mattresses are better next door,' he added.

Eric had by then secured McIntyre in another upstairs bedroom and administered some cheap cough medicine purchased on Gormley's visit to the pharmacy. Meanwhile, Art started up the central heating. They abandoned Pete, who was still coughing, secured the front door and drove off. Art deposited Eric back at Suffolk Street and gave him the keys to the new property. He was ordered to return to the address in the early evening to check on McIntyre's condition.

A breathless and exhausted Gormley hauled himself back into the Honda. He was beyond panic. 'The bloke's bloody dying,' he said to himself on returning to work. As he left the area, Art was oblivious to the sound of wailing sirens of a marked police carrier making its way towards their location. Gormley had more important matters to attend to. He needed to speak with Dexter. Now.

***

Rita was dreaming her life away as she made the return journey from HMP Wassingham to Parton. She drove along, singing happily along to the radio. 'Hopefully not much longer,' she said to herself as she contemplated the life she and Vern would have upon his release from custody. The time was getting closer and closer.

Rita had never knowingly met Tyler Eastlake. He was similar to any other six-year-old. Saturday football training with Parton AFC juniors was the highlight of his week. After training, carrying a ball, with Dad Keith holding his other hand, he waited impatiently at the pedestrian crossing. Once the green man was illuminated the intermittent pips began, and the pair received all the signs that it was now safe to cross the road.

Rita failed to see the crossing, let alone the father and son. At speed, straight through the red light, she took them both out, but young Tyler took the greater impact, crashing against the windscreen before going up and over her vehicle. He died instantly, while his dad survived but received life-changing injuries.

It was a cut and dried case of death by dangerous driving. By the time Vern Edwards would have been eligible for parole Rita would be beginning her time in custody.

26

Kate

Kev Stryker could only shiver and stare at the rising water. His aching broken shoulder was the least of his problems. He couldn't divert his gaze from the incoming tide as his phone rang out and messages pinged. He had made repeated attempts to manipulate his injured torso into a position that would enable him to extricate his mobile, but these attempts only caused greater pain and increased frustration.

While Kev suffered, Wendy Galloway waited for her car to arrive. It was early afternoon. Toni had still not surfaced from the previous night. Wendy, as ever, had prepared, this time with a smart pair of Hunter welling-ton boots. Her tailored denims were tucked neatly inside. A Volvo XC60 with blacked-out windows appeared on the driveway. She regularly changed vehicles. This afternoon she had ordered an army of two for the job she had in mind.

The Volvo set off and Wendy smiled contentedly. Although she needed to complete a couple of errands along the way, her final destination would be the day's highlight.

Galloway began her journey at the same time as Jonta Roberts was visiting the jewellers in the city centre precinct. His pocket was jammed full of the £20 bank notes made from his recent criminal activities. It didn't take him long. He had a very good idea of what to look out for when, as a family, they had visited the Christmas displays. He also had an idea of Gemma's ring size, courtesy of her mother's jewellery, which she only wore on special occasions. Jonta had crudely measured one of the rings during an evening while she was bathing Kate. Like a military operation, Jonta had been planning his proposal for some time.

The purchase took place minutes after he had entered the shop and zoned in on the display that had previously caught Gemma's attention. With the deal completed, Jonta eagerly handed over the notes to a surprised shop assistant, who had already returned not only with a small decorative box but also the card reader machine.

Unusual... The young assistant kept any suspicious thoughts to herself. This purchase would help her sales target, and a good Christmas bonus was just around the corner.

Jonta floated out of the shop and drifted along the pedestrianised thoroughfare. He would have been on cloud nine but for the fact that, despite his repeated attempts, there was still no response from Stryker. With the ring box securely tucked inside his leathers he sat astride his favourite mode of transport and checked his phone again. Nothing. He was almost sick with excitement about proposing to Gemma, but yet at the same time he was becoming increasingly concerned about Stryker. He always answered his phone and either made a return call or sent a text if he couldn't speak.

Ten minutes later Roberts arrived outside Stryker's house. Jonta was one of the few who would use the rear entrance. He could always leave his bike securely in the backyard. After removing his helmet Roberts saw the remnants of the back door hanging limply from its hinges. He walked cautiously towards what remained of the entrance after placing his helmet and gloves on the ground. For some reason Roberts placed his hand tightly over the pocket containing Gemma's newly purchased engagement ring. Gingerly he pushed open the groaning timbers of what was the back door, then ducked underneath the shattered wood to gain access to the untidy galley kitchen.

'Kev?' it was more of a polite enquiry, an ask, as opposed to a shout. Jonta walked through the living room and the diner. He was conscious of the thudding sound made by his motorcycle boots on the hard wooden floor. He called again. 'Kev?' but this time louder and with more urgency and climbed the stairs, taking them two at a time, now with a degree of panic. He entered into Stryker's infamous bedroom and noticed the tangled duvet, half on and half off the bed. An upturned glass was nearby.

Jonta, his heart pounding, slowly retraced his steps and returned to the living room. He sat down on the large sofa, which apart from the giant TV hanging on the wall was the only furniture available. Stryker took minimalistic to the extreme.

Roberts looked around the room, with nothing to focus on. His eyes were glazed. He hadn't a clue what to do next. He was a follower, not a leader. That was Stryker's role. Kev's disappearance was completely out of character. He stared at his mobile and read though the original message that had caused him concern: *Bloody Galloways. Always a fucking easy touch.*

Despite being dressed in his motorcycle leathers, Jonta suddenly felt very cold. 'What if bloody Wendy Galloway had got hold of this?' he said to himself, and shuddered at the thought ... A smashed back door – the occupant missing – when usually, at this time on a Saturday, Stryker would be cooking a hangover recovery fry-up before attending the leisure centre to instruct his self-defence protégés.

Kev Stryker was in major trouble. Jonta recognised all the signs and began shaking. 'Would Gemma help? Could I risk asking her?' He gripped the pocket holding their engagement ring again. Jonta's perfect feeling on a perfect day had disappeared.

While Jonta considered his options Sutton and Firth barely spoke as they finally returned to Parton police headquarters. Geoff was still seething, and desperate to ring Vern Edwards to inform him about the failed police raid at 56 Norfolk Street.

The pair walked across the car park on their way to meet Ron Turner. Sutton looked across at the adjacent city centre custody suite. His mind wandered while he thought that Hanson, Rudding and Chief Superintendent John Dexter were all currently housed in their small concrete cells. 'How the mighty are fallen,' Sutton said to himself. His mind particularly focused on Dexter.

They gathered in Ron Turner's office, away from the command room, to discuss the intelligence that Vern Edwards had provided. Chief Constable Mayling was already in attendance. As senior officers they had already been informed of the failed raid in Norfolk Street.

Could they still believe Vern Edwards? Not only had he supposedly given the location of the hostage, but he had also supplied the names of the gunman and the motorcycle rider, in Kev Stryker and Jonta Roberts. A number of background enquiries on both Roberts and Stryker suggested they were more than capable of being involved. Stryker had his violent pre-cons and an indirect link to Wendy Galloway. The link to Roberts was more tenuous. Although he was known as Stryker's best friend he had nothing in his past history to suggest involvement in violent crime, even though there were numerous intelligence reports of his criminal involvement with vehicles, particularly motorbikes. What had been established, though, was their current addresses.

Turner paced around his office, head down, circling Firth and Sutton, who were seated in the two chairs opposite his desk, where Mayling was scribbling some notes on an A4 pad. There was absolute silence in the room. The problem was simple. Did they continue to act on the intelligence supplied by Vern Edwards, given the abortive raid in Norfolk Street?

Ron Turner, relying on his experience, broke the silence. 'We've got to go with him,' he announced. It was a direct reference to Edwards. Turner had stopped his pacing and his eyes were piercing as they darted between all those present. 'There's still a weapon outstanding. As a matter of public safety, we need to try everything to recover that gun. This is intelligence we need to eliminate, even though the bastard might be leading us up a blind alley,' Turner announced forcibly.

Sutton nodded his head. 'I totally agree, sir. Whether we recover a weapon or not, by arresting Stryker and Roberts and searching their addresses we can confirm that we are acting on every lead, spurious or not. We can potentially secure their phones and do some financial checks. And also, to be brutally honest, what else do we have?' Sutton added.

Chief Constable Mayling lifted her head. 'Agreed. But it will be my entry in the secret intelligence log. It is my responsibility, and ultimately my decision,' she added.

'At least we're doing something positive,' said Sutton to himself.

It was a crazy hour or so before two search and entry teams assembled. Sutton was allocated to the team attending Jonta Roberts address, while Firth, accompanied by armed officers, was on her way to Kev Stryker's. There was no necessity for warrants, officers would use PACE legislation.

Before the arrest teams were deployed in the latest stage of Operation RESOLVE, Jonta Roberts made his way slowly home, weaving in and out of traffic. He almost rode with one hand, as with the other he grasped Gemma's engagement ring. His mind was in turmoil, drifting between the excitement of his imminent proposal to Gemma and his concerns over Stryker's disappearance. *Perhaps Gemma will be able to help*, he thought, with hope in his heart. *After I have proposed.*

Jonta arrived home and secured his bike. He unzipped the pocket containing the ring, reached inside and withdrew the small, neatly decorated gift box. He nervously inserted the key in the back door and jiggled with the lock while the fingers of his other hand were gripped tightly around the gift box.

Jonta entered their rented house, which was almost identical in terms of layout as that of Kev Stryker's. His daughter Kate, face smeared with her recently consumed lunch, ran to him through the galley kitchen. She was at the stage of life where walking wasn't an option. Jonta quickly placed the gift box back in his pocket before effortlessly lifting her up with both arms high above his head. Then, after lowering her, he placed a big kiss on her right cheek before hugging her close.

'Where's Mummy?' Jonta could hear the TV. No doubt it was another rerun of *Peppa Pig*. With Kate in his arms, he walked towards the living room.

Gemma was on her hands and knees, clearing up the array of toys scattered around. She looked up at Kate smiling brightly in the arms of her doting father. Gemma stopped what she was doing, stood up and hugged them both. It was purely a reflex response reflecting the idyllic setting of mother, father and daughter. Gemma returned to her knees and carried on clearing the room as Jonta bent down carefully, briefly relinquishing his hold of Kate. He placed her down as if she were the most delicate, cherished and expensive article that had ever existed.

Jonta crouched on one knee. At the same time he produced the gift box containing the engagement ring. They were both on their knees when Jonta proposed. 'Gemma, will you marry me?' he stuttered as Kate, standing beside them, giggled, happily showing the teeth she currently possessed.

There was no immediate reply from Gemma. She reached out, took the gift box and slowly began to remove the packaging. Once the paper and the small pink bow had been removed, Gemma's shaking hands opened the maroon and gold miniature box. Jonta thought his heart would burst. The beautiful silver ring sat proudly on its tiny white presentation pillow. The small diamond literally lit up the living room. Kate stopped her giggles and just stared at the bright light reflecting from her mother's engagement ring.

***

With near perfect timing the Enforcer made a satisfy-ing crunch, a clean hit to the brass Yale lock of the front door. It gave way instantly. The previous idyllic setting was instantly destroyed, Kate cried out and clung to her mother as screams of, 'Police, Police,' rang out.

It was a small house and the main action was over almost as quickly as it had begun, although the conse-quences would linger – in this particular case, for a lifetime. Half a dozen officers clad in riot gear, with visors down, had secured the premises. As expected, there were only the three occupants present.

Sutton followed the entry and search officers into Jonta's house and stepped over the debris caused by the Enforcer. There was mayhem in the front living room. Kate was sobbing in Gemma's arms, clinging to her mother as if her life depended on it. Jonta, who had been handcuffed and searched, was currently lying face down.

Amid all this chaos he was confused. From a prone position his eyes scanned the room frantically as he tried desperately to work out what happened to the engagement ring. Fortunately it had already been safely pocketed by Gemma. He seemed almost oblivious to the police presence and was in total shock at what had just occurred.

A female member of the search team calmly guided Gemma and her daughter into the kitchen, leaving Sutton to deal with Roberts as officers began the search of the premises. With the assistance of another officer Sutton hooked Roberts under his arms and pulled him back and upwards before settling him onto the sofa.

Sutton was momentarily distracted by a phone call. It was an update from Jo Firth at Kev Stryker's address. Due to the subject being suspected as the triggerman Ron Turner had authorised an armed deployment, but forced entry wasn't required. The back door was still swinging back and forth on its hinges. There was no one present. The property search was underway, and the team would, as a matter of procedure, also conduct a few hopeful house-to- house enquiries. Firth ended the call.

One of the officers entered Jonta's living room, and said, 'Geoff, can I have a word?' Sutton joined him. He was happy to leave his prisoner in the company an allocated officer. He wasn't going anywhere. Sutton looked at Jonta and thought, *Like a startled rabbit trapped in the glare of the headlights*, an expression he'd seen and recognised over the years.

They moved into the small hallway. 'We have found a large amount of cash hidden in his side of the wardrobe. There must be thousands of pounds there,' the officer said.

'Get forensics down, photograph it *in situ* and we'll have it fingerprinted,' Sutton said, before returning to the sight of Jonta Roberts, who was sitting transfixed on the sofa.

'Jonta where's your mobile?' Geoff asked quietly as he sat down next to him. Roberts just stared ahead, seemingly oblivious to the question. Sutton repeated the question, this time louder. It was more of a request now, and any empathy he may have had was receding.

Jonta managed a nod in the direction of three shelves near the large living room window. Geoff followed the indication and recovered the phone, which had been placed there to avoid any distractions prior to his planned proposal. He seized the item, thinking he may need the phone during an interview rather than leaving it for the search team. Due to the way he was behaving, any further conversation with Roberts – other than the formal protocol of an arrest – seemed a complete waste of time.

A couple of yards away in the kitchen Gemma was looking on while trying unsuccessfully to calm Kate's endless sobbing. She stared angrily at the constable assigned to them. 'Jonta promised—' she muttered.

'Promised what?' the officer asked quickly.

'Nothing, bitch.' Gemma spat out her reply as if her daughter weren't present.

27

Dave Ryan

Sutton gently ushered Roberts out of the house to an awaiting car. The assigned driver, Dave Ryan, was a probationer constable who had only recently passed the force's driving test. As far as Sutton was concerned, given his current transfixed state, Jonta Roberts posed no threat.

They had travelled a short distance when Roberts spoke. It was as if his voice came from nowhere. 'Can I have a tab, please? Is it Geoff?' He must have picked up Sutton's name from one of the search officers. Geoff looked across at Roberts, then down to where his now manacled hands were shaking uncontrollably. The request for a cigarette was an old-fashioned ask, and they were the first words uttered since his arrest. The glazed eyes had disappeared. He was now looking at Sutton, not through him.

Geoff took his time and studied Roberts closely. He tried to assimilate the current state of the investigation and Jonta's involvement. Despite the seriousness of the alleged offences, and his key role, he wasn't the trigger-man, and crucially he had never yet served a custodial sentence. He remained untainted by the institution of prison.

'It's a bloody chance.' Sutton swore to himself. 'A bloody chance, Sutton,' he repeated, calling on all his experience. An opportunity to speak with Roberts beckoned before the formalities of custody and of legal representation. He recognised the moment. Sutton looked into his eyes and instantly recognised that Jonta fully understood his circumstances. There remained a further fifteen minutes of journey time before their expected arrival at the Parton city centre custody suite.

'Can I have a cigarette, please?' Jonta repeated his question in a quiet, stuttering voice while again actually looking at Sutton. For Roberts it was a strange request. He had quit smoking five years previously when he had made another promise to Gemma. Now it was Sutton making the requests to the young constable driving their vehicle. They made a quick change of direction and indicated right.

A few minutes later, after a short detour via a convenient Tesco Express, Sutton clumsily opened a packet of twenty Marlboro Silver cigarettes. He was still recovering from paying the shocking price of the product when he offered Roberts a light. His next problem was to remind the fledgling constable that just for a few minutes he could forget his recent training and the force's orders regarding smoking, and the rule that prisoners should remain handcuffed at all times. He emphasised that Jonta Roberts remained Sutton's responsibility.

Despite the continued protestations from P.C. Ryan the detour continued under Sutton's directions before he and Roberts got out of the vehicle. Geoff had purposefully directed their driver to a side road, one of many in an industrial estate on the outskirts of the city that was named Parton Works. It was another council-backed regeneration scheme. The side road gave access to those areas of deserted wasteland often found in industrial estates and commonly punctuated with the debris from fly-tipping.

'It's a while since I've had a prisoner ask for a cigarette,' Sutton said. It wasn't a question, just some small talk in an attempt to establish rapport.

Having had his handcuffs removed, Jonta took a long, slow drag on his cigarette, blew out the white smoke and looked over the barren surroundings. 'I love Gemma and Kate,' he said with conviction. Sutton didn't answer. 'I'm in trouble, Geoff, deep trouble,' Roberts continued. It was another statement and again it attracted no immediate response, just silence, as Jonta took another long drag and felt the soothing effects of the nicotine slowly making its way through his body. He shivered against the cold.

Sutton was thinking on his feet. He had a serious dilemma, although he didn't want to stop Jonta from saying whatever he wished to impart. Thinking ahead, he needed to ensure anything that was said now would be deemed admissible in any subsequent court proceedings. He was out on a limb and pushing the legal boundaries to the very limit. The only way he could protect himself and also – hopefully – allow this conversation to be admissible as evidence, would be to caution him now.

'Jonta, I have to remind you that you're under arrest for murder,' Sutton said firmly before reciting the caution and adding Jonta's entitlement to legal advice. He completed the formalities, knowing that nine months or so later, under cross-examination, he would honestly be able to relate this occurrence in front of any jury.

'I was the fucking bike rider on the two shootings, Geoff. I also kidnapped a bloke.' Roberts's eyes never wavered as he stared over the wasteland, which was strewn with litter. 'I've ruined everything, Geoff, fucking ruined everything. Gemma and Kate—'

Without any warning Jonta violently kicked out at one of the black refuse bags scattered around where they were standing. It was an action born out of both frustration and realisation, but for Sutton it meant much more and he couldn't help himself. He had to speak. Jonta's declaration of involvement in the kidnapping ignited Sutton into trying to locate his best mate. He couldn't just leave Roberts to wallow in his own thoughts.

'Jonta, where is he? The bloke you kidnapped. Where is he?' Sutton demanded.

'Gemma and Kate, fucking gone.' Tears rolled down Jonta's cheeks as his focus remained with his family.

Sutton moved directly in front of him and reached out with both hands as he tried unsuccessfully to gain some purchase on Roberts's studded black leather jacket, 'Where is he, Jonta?' Any thoughts of sympathy were banished. His thoughts were trained on finding Pete McIntyre.

'Where the bloody hell is he?' Sutton repeated his question, but now louder and with increased frustration. His flattened hands moved upwards, towards Jonta's neck. Sutton pushed his hands forward, causing Roberts to stumble backwards over another black refuse bag. Jonta somehow recovered his balance, but the look on his face remained unchanged. He was simply wallowing in self-pity.

Sutton pursued him with his right arm pulled back, cocked like a trigger, and his left foot forward in a boxer's stance, pointing at his intended target. At that moment there was nothing more Sutton wanted than to sink his fist into the face of Jonta Roberts.

Sutton let go and unleashed his right fist into nothing more than fresh air. His momentum followed his fist, causing him to stumble forward. Roberts had anticipated the blow and had taken evasive action by neatly side-stepping the predictable punch. As he tried to recover his balance Geoff glanced to his right, only to see that Roberts was already pinned with both arms around his side by the recently trained constable, who had swiftly and expertly handcuffed the prisoner. Before asking for any advice Dave Ryan had taken control while Sutton looked on, foolish and embarrassed at his actions.

Geoff had lost it. And he knew it. His rule, which said that you never lower yourself to the behaviour of others, was broken.

A couple of minutes later Roberts had been returned to the rear of the vehicle and was sitting next to an embarrassed Geoff Sutton who, ignoring Jonta's presence, quietly apologised to the young officer.

They had only travelled one mile further when Roberts spoke again. It was as if his scuffle with Sutton hadn't occurred. 'It's 56 Norfolk Street, in The Counties. That's where he is,' Roberts said confidently.

'I've got to remind you that you are still under caution, Jonta.' Sutton still felt remorse at his previous actions, but they had acted as a reality check and had reminded him of the need to follow the correct procedures. With Dave Ryan present he now – crucially – had a material witness to what was being said.

'Jonta, he's not at 56. The police raided that address a couple of hours ago,' Sutton said firmly.

'He was, Geoff. He fucking was. I saw him. Art must have moved him. The poor bastard was in a bad way,'

Roberts continued, as Sutton once again clenched his fists.

'We are talking about Art Gormley, aren't we?' Sutton said. Geoff, while desperately trying to contain his emotions, needed to hear from Roberts about the Art Gormley connection.

Jonta went back to bemoaning his fate. 'Gemma and Kate... I've bloody messed up everything.'

'Who's bloody Art?' Sutton spat out, feeling the skin stretching over his increasingly white knuckles.

'He's the taxi man. I do his fucking servicing. He organised the job,' Jonta said quietly as tears continued to roll down his cheeks.

Sutton knew that this latest piece of intelligence, which had now been confirmed, gave the information from Vern Edwards much better provenance. Sutton was on his phone almost before Roberts finished his sentence, organising the arrest of Art Gormley. Everyone in Parton knew Gormley's Taxis. He ignored Jonta's tears. His focus was on locating Pete McIntyre.

The police vehicle idled as they waited for the security gates to open, which would give them access to the custody suite at the Parton city centre station. It was at that point, out of nowhere, Jonta began speaking again. It was if something had taken him away from his domestic circumstances and the continual thoughts of his beloved partner and beautiful daughter.

'Kev Stryker,' Jonta said loudly. 'Kev Stryker, Geoff. He's in trouble, fucking big trouble,' Roberts continued with some urgency.

'What was Stryker's involvement, Jonta?' Sutton was desperate to know the facts. Meanwhile PC Ryan reversed into one of the allocated custody parking bays.

Roberts looked desperately across at Sutton. 'Fuck off, Geoff, he's in trouble. Get my phone. Get my fucking phone,' Jonta shouted, as Sutton removed the mobile from his Barbour pocket. After obtaining the relevant password Sutton, as requested, began to scroll through the messages. 'There's a recent one about Galloway,' Roberts said, still agitated.

A voice came from the front of the vehicle. 'We need to take him into custody,' Dave Ryan said with some concern as he looked over his left shoulder at his two passengers. He had been briefed regarding a simple transport job as one of his first tasks as a qualified driver, but as far as he was concerned the simple job had turned into a nightmare. Sutton ignored him and scrutinised Jonta's phone.

'Bloody Galloways. Always a fucking easy touch,' Sutton said, reading out the text before looking directly at Roberts

But before he could speak Jonta interrupted him. 'I think he must have sent it to everyone when he was pissed,' he said. 'And when I say everyone, I mean everyone.'

'So that's why Stryker has disappeared.' It was Sutton's turn to interrupt. No wonder the back door of Stryker's house had been demolished.

The rear door of the car was opened by PC Ryan, who was relieved that his ordeal was over. He'd had enough of this personal torment. Sutton led the handcuffed Roberts and made the short walk to the custody suite.

Once Jonta had been housed Sutton went to a vacant interview room, where he quickly recorded his recent conversation with Roberts. It is safe to say that no mention was made of Geoff's failed assault. Jonta

Roberts was brought from his cell. After the formalities, he signed Sutton's notes. Geoff thought ahead and sighed to himself. *It's going to be another difficult Crown Court appearance.*

A very dejected-looking prisoner was being led back to his cell by the female detention officer when he suddenly stopped, turned around, 'Geoff, I think Stryker might have his phone. He sometimes sleeps with it when he gets pissed.' With that he turned away and was led to his cell.

Once the heavy door had been locked shut behind him, Roberts looked around and took in his new surroundings. It dawned upon him that a desolate cell like this was to become his new home for more than the next few years.

As for Geoff Sutton, he knew exactly why Jonta had told him that Stryker may well have his phone.

Just as Jonta was hearing the banging of his cell door behind him, Gemma sat holding Kate with her right arm as they sat on the sofa in their living room. The search had ended. They were finally alone, and tears rolled down her cheeks as Kate clung to her mother. The poor young girl, a sad and innocent casualty, was still traumatised by her father's arrest.

Gemma looked down at her left hand and opened the small decorative box that Jonta had given her during the interrupted proposal. While she would always have her doubts about other things, Gemma now knew for certain how her beautiful engagement ring had been financed.

'I told him,' Gemma said loudly, causing even greater distress to her young daughter. 'Goodbye, Jonta bloody Roberts and bloody good riddance.' Gemma grabbed the ring and hurled it into the living flame of the gas fire.

28

Art Gormley

Sutton removed himself from the unique atmosphere of the custody suite. He was in possession of Stryker's number, which he had obtained from Jonta's mobile contacts. He updated Jo Firth on her return from the fruitless search of Kev's property. Then, armed with Stryker's mobile number, she began preparing the authority required in order to ping the phone so that the satellite masts near Stryker would be able to provide an indication of his whereabouts. She emphasised the fact that the request was in order to save life.

Both Sutton and Firth knew that the process was never an exact science, and it would totally depend on Stryker still having the phone in his possession. While Firth completed the paperwork Sutton went to Art Gormley's office to join the already deployed arrest and search team. He desperately needed to get Pete back.

McIntyre, half-alive and half-dead, was drifting in and out of consciousness. Wherever he was, at least it seemed warmer. It was usually a coughing fit that roused him out of his comatose state.

He began retching and slowly reached out from under the blankets. His ribs ached from the torment of the continual violent movements of his chest. After summoning whatever strength remained in his rapidly deteriorating body Pete attempted to locate some water, which would ease his condition and soothe the feeling of grated sandpaper emanating from an area between the back of his throat and his upper chest.

While grabbing forlornly at random his flailing hand collided with the plastic bottle, and the water spilled out over the warm blanket wrapped around his weakening body. Another violent cough was followed by more retching as something horribly acid and alien hit Pete's taste buds. He spat it out immediately in a reflex action. McIntyre briefly opened his eyes to a globule of phlegm and blood. He knew his time was slipping away.

It only took Sutton five minutes to travel to Gormley's Taxis, which was ideally located close to the city centre. He parked adjacent to the liveried police personnel carrier and walked past a couple of taxis heavily emblazoned with the Gormley name, accompanied by glitzy sponsored adverts. An identical taxi lamp was centred on the roof of each vehicle.

Sutton stormed into the scruffy premises after stepping to the side of a group of discarded tyres. The business hub was a converted garage, with the two offices along the rear wall. One was Art's and the other was for his team of despatchers.

Naturally, it hadn't been a softly-softly approach by the arrest and search team. Four officers had begun the search of the despatcher's room while two remained with a petrified Art Gormley. Sutton had known about Gormley for years, and the fact that he had so far escaped punishment was as much of a surprise to Sutton as it was to everyone else.

Geoff entered Art's grubby empire, where two officers,

thankful for their protective gloves, were just beginning to look through the documents stored in the four ancient green filing cabinets.

'Take everything. He's going the journey... VAT fraud, benefits ... anything. He's coming in whatever,' Sutton said loudly and with conviction, while a bloated Gormley sat behind his desk. He hadn't moved since the officers arrived, partly because of his immobility and partly because he was both somewhat stunned by and frightened of the potential consequences. His reciprocal relationship with Chief Superintendent John Dexter had guaranteed little or no police interference into his nefarious activities over the years. Indeed, Gormley's had always been a useful tea stop for the less than inquisitive city centre beat bobbies.

'But VAT is the least of your worries Art,' Sutton continued, as he paced around like a tiger stalking his prey. 'Try a bit of murder and kidnap, with you doing a thirty-year stretch as a minimum. Sharing a cell along-side those other lifers—' Sutton stopped in his tracks and reluctantly placed both hands on the filthy desk as he stared through Art's round-rimmed spectacles into his eyes, which were crusted with matter.

'Nothing to do with me,' Art said, trying to sound confident. 'Nothing to do with me,' he said again in a voice that was only slightly stronger. He had repeated the remark partly to reassure himself.

One of the search team interrupted their conversation. 'There are a few properties listed here. Bound to be some sort of tenant benefit fraud,' he added sarcastically.

That single statement gave Sutton an idea. 'Get the bastard handcuffed. We're going on a journey,' Sutton said.

'W-w-w-w-what? Where?' Art stuttered, but behind the glasses his eyes started watering.

'Leave that to me, Art. A little fresh air will do you no harm,' Sutton continued, smiling down at him.

It took a few minutes before a grunting, huffing and out of breath Art Gormley was placed, in the personnel carrier. Due to his size he was handcuffed to the front. A nominated driver and two other officers from the team accompanied Sutton and Gormley on their journey. Geoff sat in the rear of the carrier opposite Art, who had immediate company in the form of two uniformed personnel sitting by him, one on either side.

'The Counties, please,' Sutton said, once they were all on board. He looked across to Gormley. Despite the cold, Sutton could see beads of perspiration appearing through his receding hair. He looked down and averted his eyes from Sutton's gaze. As they approached the renown sink estate. Sutton gave the driver further instructions. 'Norfolk Street,' he said clearly.

Art felt awful. His mouth was parched and he was breathing heavily. He licked his dry lips in the knowledge that for the first time in his career of crime he was in serious trouble. On this occasion he wasn't trying to explain a pair of Nike trainers nicked from JD Sports. He now felt horribly sick and his feeling of nausea only increased at Sutton's last words, 'Norfolk Street.'

The personnel carrier made the final turn. Sutton gave the driver clear instructions as they entered the row of terraced houses and asked him to pull up outside number 56. The sweating continued for Gormley as the carrier pulled up outside the end house.

Now Art's chest tightened as an aching pain flowed down his left arm. It had been nagging him for a week or so but had suddenly got worse during the journey. Art tried and failed to reassure himself. 'Must be the handcuffs,' he said in desperation.

'Get him out,' Sutton ordered the two officers sitting next to Gormley. Geoff knew that Art was struggling. He intended to show him the damaged entrance door to 56 Norfolk Street in order to increase the pressure on Gormley, in the hope that he would break and reveal Pete's whereabouts.

Geoff opened the side door of the carrier and dropped down on to the narrow pavement outside the address while the two escorting officers were faced with the more difficult task of extricating Art from the vehicle. To assist in the process Art's handcuffs were removed. He shook his left arm violently to try and obtain some relief from the pain, which had worsened. With a struggle he stepped gingerly down from the vehicle.

It was to be Art Gormley's final step. He dropped. Not like a stone, more like a boulder, and filled the pavement.

'Shit,' Sutton said. He was already calling 999 as Gormley's escorting officers began CPR. It seemed an age waiting for the ambulance to arrive, and in the meantime the police driver, a trained medic, joined his team members in attempting to revive the stricken Art. He looked up at Sutton and shook his head, indicating to Geoff that Art wouldn't be making any further trips to The Counties. As the officer looked up, he noticed the door number over Sutton's right shoulder: number 54.

'He owned the one next door as well,' the same officer said to Sutton as he thought back to the search of Art's office only a few minutes previously.

The approaching ambulance sirens could be heard as Sutton turned around looking at the door of number 54.

Without any further thought of the dying Art Gormley, Geoff kicked hard at the cheap lock of the flimsy wooden entrance door at 54 Norfolk Street. After two kicks Sutton was joined by one of the officers, who had given up on his life-saving efforts. The young, athletic constable delivered one expertly directed strike with a large size ten boot. The poorly maintained door instantly gave way.

'Police,' the officer shouted, leading the way as he entered the address. He secured the downstairs. Sutton followed and climbed the stairs two at a time. His heart was beating hard, not necessarily from exertion, but from adrenaline. The thought of finding Pete was playing out before him. Entering this address was more than a hunch. It was a belief.

The first bedroom was clear. For some unknown reason Sutton hesitated, petrified at what he might find, before entering the second. He walked in and looked down at his comatose lifelong friend lying face up under a blanket on what appeared to be some grubby mattress.

'Get the medics,' Geoff screamed hysterically, while at the same time running the couple of yards to where Pete was lying. Without thinking Sutton knelt down and reached forward cradling his friend in a loving embrace, ignoring his bloody broken nose, before Pete coughed quietly and then groaned.

Sutton moved around the mattress to make them both comfortable. Moments later, after a couple of forlorn attempts to revive the now deceased Art Gormley, two paramedics arrived to find Sutton in tears, sitting upright on the mattress caring for and desperately hoping that Pete McIntyre would survive. It took medics some time before they could prise Sutton away from his good friend.

Some ten minutes passed before a second ambulance

briefly arrived and departed carrying the body of the late Art Gormley. Sutton had almost regained his composure before seeing Pete, with his eyes closed and his face drained of colour, being wheeled out of the house, lying prone on a gurney covered by a bright red woollen blanket. An IV drip was being held aloft by one of the medics. In moments the blue lights illuminated their dull surroundings and the sirens indicated a 999 journey to Parton Infirmary.

Sutton watched the ambulance leave, reached for his phone and rang Pete's home number. 'Val, It's Geoff,' Sutton said.

'Mam's in bed, Geoff. We've had the doctor out. She's been given something to help her sleep,' her son said.

'Henry, we've found your dad and he's been taken to the infirmary,' Sutton said slowly. 'He's not very well,' he continued, desperately trying to remain positive. But there was no answer from Henry, who had ended the call. Geoff knew exactly where he would be heading after waking his mum.

Sutton sighed deeply then shook his head as if to wake himself from a state of mild concussion, like a boxer trying to regain his senses from a knock-down. That brief moment allowed him to regather his focus as he stood with the three uniformed officers, who were all trying to come to terms with what had just occurred.

'We need forensics here asap,' Sutton barked out his orders. The mist was clearing. A radio request was quickly made as Sutton's mobile rang. It was Jo Firth.

'Jo, I was just about to give you a call.' Sutton was speaking too fast. He had so much to say but the adrenaline was taking over.

Firth interrupted him by saying, 'Geoff, quiet please.'

She knew there had been significant developments, as she had just been made aware of the most recent update at Norfolk Street by the force's incident log.

'There's so much to tell, Jo.' Sutton just wasn't listening.

'Geoff, I'll be at Norfolk Street in ten minutes.' Firth ended the conversation and equipped with an Airwaves radio set, she ran out of the office after grabbing a set of car keys on the way.

'Control … urgent. I need to speak to the critical incident manager (CIM).' Firth's operational mind was in overdrive as she blue-lighted her way to The Counties area of Parton. For what she had in mind she really needed to speak with the senior officer in the force's control room. She tried to concentrate on her driving, eagerly anticipating hearing her ringtone so she could activate the hands-free controls. Her sweaty palms gripped the steering wheel. *Thank goodness the weather has improved*, she thought. Her phone rang. Thankfully she recognised the voice at the other end. It always helps.

The calm, reassuring voice of the trained communicator spoke. 'Jo, it's Harriet. I'm currently the CIM on duty. How can I help?'

'Harriet, we need a major search coordinated for a high-risk missing person by the name of Kev Stryker. It's further complicated by the fact that he is wanted for murder following the two recent shootings. We believe he's still in possession of his phone and, if he is, it's pinging from the nearest mast to the east marina.'

Firth jammed on her brakes and screeched to a halt as a young mother, headphones jammed around her ears and oblivious to Firth's vehicle, pushed a buggy into the road.

'Jo, are you OK?' Davidson still calm, asked.

'Fine, Harriet, bloody fine,' Firth replied, inwardly cursing the woman as she moved off again at speed with her shoulders hunched over the steering wheel. It felt as though her nose was actually touching the windscreen.

'When you stop driving give me a ring.' Davidson gave Firth some sound advice. After all, Firth was only a couple of minutes from her destination in Norfolk Street.

In the interim Harriet Davidson brought up the relevant computer screen that displayed the force's protocols for a high-risk missing person. She started ticking off the actions and mobilised two dedicated search teams headed by their inspector, a highly trained police search advisor. They would be assisted by Parton's own search and rescue team of volunteers, in addition to the coastguard, given the nominated terrain. Then Davidson studied Google Earth after establishing the telephone mast location. She nominated the east marina car park as a suitable rendezvous point (RVP). The search would be coordinated from there.

Davidson swivelled in her chair, just like Captain Kirk in an episode of *Star Trek*, and scrutinised her staff before nominating an individual to monitor what would become a dedicated communications channel for this operation.

As one of a small pool of qualified officers, Harriet Davidson loved the high profile her CIM role provided, but that didn't stop the nerves. Prior to opening her own policy log, she spoke into the headset microphone that seemed to ambush her mouth like an annoying wasp and said, 'CIM to India 99.' Davidson also made direct contact with the air support unit that not only covered Parton Constabulary but also two other neighbouring forces. She needed to utilise the mutual aid available.

'Throw the kitchen sink at it,' Harriet said to herself

as the adrenaline began to rise.

'CIM to India 99. Can you have look at Parton incident log 552 of today and let me know if you can respond?' Davidson asked.

Moments later came the reply. 'India 99 to Parton CIM. We will be airborne and attending the area. ETA ten minutes,' the helicopter supervisor said. 'We will keep you updated on our progress,' and he calmly ended his transmission.

Davidson put both hands on her desk, took a deep breath, stared at the screen and rechecked the actions before reaching for her stress ball. 'When in doubt, throw the kitchen sink at it.' She repeated the mantra before adding, 'You can always tone it down,' and sighed to herself. Harriet was well aware that her senior supervisors would no doubt be scrutinising the incident log, ready to throw some mud her way if things didn't work out.

She sat back to await the call from Jo Firth.

29

Harriet Davidson

Wendy Galloway had completed her few errands, one of which was the purchase of a very expensive bottle of rare craft gin. She intended to celebrate tonight. She was accompanied by her henchmen, and they had only recently arrived at the car park in the east marina. The Volvo was being driven carefully, to avoid the numerous potholes.

'Stop here,' Galloway said. For a couple of minutes they parked and sat in the car and waited, just to ensure that there were no signs of any compromise. Wendy scanned the area. The potential significance of the recently constructed phone mast on an area of wasteland between the car park and the harbour was lost on Galloway and her men.

'Right, let's go,' Wendy said, and grinned as they moved off. The Volvo continued its journey and drove through the car park, ignoring the harbour, slowly travelling along the single-track road. The rain had stopped beating down overhead. They travelled slowly to their secluded destination. As far as they were concerned there was no need to rush.

***

Jo Firth parked on Norfolk Street and immediately contacted Harriet Davidson, who updated her with the plan of action. Firth was comforted to know that Davidson had called in the cavalry.

'Geoff, quick. Get in.' Jo didn't wait for Sutton to answer. They had another important journey to make.

'Just wait for forensics and then finish the search at Art's,' he reminded his uniformed colleagues before following Firth's orders. The pair sped away from The Counties to their destination, the east marina.

The navigator of the police helicopter reported in. 'India 99 to control…'

'India 99, go ahead,' Inspector Harriet Davidson said.

'We are two minutes away from East Parton marina. I intend to do a full sweep of the immediate area, report back, then await any further instructions from the search advisor when they arrive at the RVP. Visibility isn't perfect. It's currently overcast,' the team leader said. 'But we can still observe, and I'm doubtful if anyone on the ground could see us,' he added.

'That's all received, India 99,' came Harriet's reply. Davidson looked up at her dedicated operator and nodded her head so he could take over the comms while she commanded the operation from a strategic viewpoint.

Sutton had managed to provide Firth with the developments concerning Art, Pete McIntyre and the address at Norfolk Street. Jo reciprocated with her own update and the reasons why they now found themselves speeding off to the east marina.

A monotone, almost slightly bored voice, which was transmitted from the helicopter, made contact, 'India 99 to control. We have a sighting. One vehicle. Looks like a SUV – yes, a Volvo. Can't get the reg. There are three people out on foot walking towards the shoreline. There's a sighting of someone in the water.' There was a pause. 'Is the Volvo one of ours?' the same voice enquired.

'India 99, just observe please. The Volvo may well be a hostile,' Sutton shouted in urgently, using Firth's hands-free Airwaves network. Jo just glanced upwards in dismay at Sutton's actions and rolled her eyes to the back of her head. Geoff's interruption had completely disregarded all communication protocols. In a bid to remedy the error he scrolled down his mobile contacts and immediately rang the control room. Harriet Davidson answered immediately. 'Inspector—' Sutton began, but didn't finish.

'What do you think you're doing?' was Harriet's first response. She had immediately recognised the voice that had made the previous broadcast. Tensions were increasing.

'Inspector, I'm Geoff Sutton, working on Operation RESOLVE. We need firearms authorisation immediately. I strongly believe that the people walking from the Volvo are targets. In all probability it is Wendy Galloway and two of her associates. They have kidnapped an individual by the name of Kev Stryker, who we believe is the individual in the water. From previous intel Galloway does have current access to a Volvo. You've got to go with me on this one, Harriet.' Sutton had tried to keep it as a brief as possible, but it was an awful lot for the inspector to assimilate and ultimately make her decision.

Davidson ended the call by saying, 'I will ring you back.' She had little or no time to make the call. From her elevated position in the control room she looked across at her staff. Some glanced back at her, knowing exactly what was going through her mind. The fact that Davidson and her staff regularly dealt with major incidents never detracted from their fear of failure and subsequent recriminations. The entire control room could feel the tension building.

As was her custom when nervous, Harriett used the palms of her hands, running them back over her jet-black hair until they reached the scrunchie holding her neat ponytail in place. She repeated the process, then looked upwards. Her current role was critical in her own personal career development. Incidents such as this dictated whether Harriet Davidson would continue to climb the ranks or forever remain an inspector.

Due to Sutton's length of service, most people in Parton Constabulary had either worked with or knew of Geoff Sutton. Davidson was no exception but knew him by reputation only. Trusting him was for her a leap of faith.

Harriet returned Sutton's call. 'Geoff, I am authorising firearms and two armed response vehicles (ARVs) to attend. Both will have four officers, including the driver. They are close by,' Davidson said quietly and quickly, almost hoping that she wouldn't be heard, even though she was fully aware that every transmission she made was routinely recorded.

'Thanks, Harriet,' Sutton replied. Then, as Sutton approached the east marina car park, Harriet Davidson requested an ambulance to attend. This was one of the best decisions she ever made. She then turned to the console. Her hands noticeably hovered over the keypad before typing up her most recent actions.

While the police resources were gathering in the east marina car park, Wendy Galloway and her chosen two walked gingerly across the shale, avoiding the rock pools as they approached the captive Stryker. The water circulated around him and was now above waist height. Wendy remained in the shallow waters – dry, thanks to her expensive wellies, and a safe distance from getting soaked from the incoming tide but well within earshot of her victim.

Stryker was struggling both mentally and physically. Shaking violently from the icy waters, he knew there was no way out.

Not for the first time Wendy smiled. Her men had followed her instructions to the letter and had strapped Stryker to the post facing the shoreline, close enough for her to enjoy a front-of-house seat at her very own theatre. It would give her the perfect opportunity to administer her own version of the last rites to Stryker. She looked at him in his sorry condition and made sure that he could clearly see her.

'I just have the one thing to say, Kev.' Wendy glanced down at her phone, although she would always remember the words. 'Bloody Galloways. Always a fucking easy touch.' She laughed loudly and flashed the screen in Stryker's direction. Then she turned and began the walk back to the vehicle, laughing all the way. Despite the pain, Kev Stryker had got the message. With his teeth chattering he cursed loudly. 'Fucking Toni Galloway.'

Wendy couldn't hide her feelings of self-satisfaction. She looked back. The tide was moving in quickly. Stryker reminded her of a medieval witch about to burn at the stake. In this case the tide would extinguish any burning embers. She instructed the driver to move, and her small army began the return journey towards the harbour and the east marina car park.

***

While Wendy Galloway had been enjoying herself it had been fairly manic for Inspector Harriet Davidson and her control room staff. The ARVs were now in position. The hard stop would take place just as the target vehicle reached the car park. They were hidden from sight by the harbour wall.

The Volvo entered the car park to be met by the first ARV which blocked its route. Galloway's vehicle braked too late and collided head-on. The second ARV blocked the rear of the target car. Its driver had quickly realised that it was an ambushed hard stop and had begun to reverse. A further collision was inevitable.

It was all over in seconds. Galloway's driver had been hauled out of the vehicle and had joined his mate and their boss, and they were all now lying face down with their wrists bound by the white plastic cuffs used in such operations. Wendy looked particularly uncomfortable. Her face was partially submerged in one of those large water-filled potholes on the broken tarmac that populated the east marina car park. Ironically, broken glass littered the scene, and a torn label of a particularly expensive bottle of craft gin, the remnants of one of her recent purchases, lay on the ground.

The arrests had acted as a complete distraction to the ambulance and coastguard vehicles, which had been able to drive around the chaos and make their way to Kev Stryker's location, guided by the force's helicopter.

Stryker lifted his chin up one last time. It was merely a reflex action against the icy waters instead of a movement by someone who was still trying to survive. His eyes were closed as the salty water splashed across his face. Stryker knew his time was up. He took one last deep breath…

The coastline rescue was already underway as the

paramedics lined the shore with their resuscitation equipment. Three coastguard operatives, all with masks, were already in the water. Two were in possession of foam-filled life rings and one of them had a sharp cutting implement thrust securely into his waistband. They had waded to a depth that then became more comfortable to swim. For their own safety each individual was at the end of a bowline that was held securely by another team member who was safely on the shore.

The strongest swimmer reached their target. She immediately tilted Stryker's head upwards and reappeared from under the waterline. She manoeuvred herself into a position to begin mouth-to-mouth as the second coastguard arrived at the scene, a couple of metres from his colleague. Without hesitation he flipped down his goggles, dived down and reached into his waistband as he did so. The freezing sea water was relatively clear, and he immediately saw what was securing Stryker. It took only seconds to carefully cut through the bindings without causing any further unnecessary injury. By that time the final member of the team had arrived and the life ring was secured. The coastguards began swimming back to shore, where the resuscitation attempt continued.

A few minutes later Kev Stryker was in the rear of the ambulance, barely alive, as the paramedics fought to stabilise their patient.

'India 99 to control,' the eye in the sky transmitted.

'India 99, go ahead,' Davidson replied.

'The ambulance is moving away now. Permission to stand down...' the helicopter team leader said as he saw the blue light flashing down the coastal path.

Firth and Sutton were stationed at the east marina car park. Although they hadn't been able to observe Stryker's sea rescue they had seen at first hand the armed response hard stop and Wendy Galloway's arrest. The prisoners had previously been quickly and efficiently removed from the scene before the ambulance carrying Kev Stryker, sirens blaring, passed their location.

'Jo let's take a quick look at Galloway's car,' Sutton said, and zipped up his green Barbour as they walked across the car park. The Volvo's damaged doors were still open and a uniformed officer was protecting the scene while waiting for forensics to arrive.

Sutton knew he shouldn't begin a search before the experts arrived, but he couldn't help himself. His past experience had given him an insight into the mind of Wendy Galloway. After putting on a pair of gloves he began a search of the vehicle, ignoring the protests of both Jo Firth and the officer dedicated to securing the crime scene. It didn't take long before he found what he was looking for – a small handgun, which was lying underneath the car mat that Wendy's feet had rested on prior to her arrest. Geoff smiled smugly. 'Schoolgirl error,' he said to himself.

Sutton knew it would have been Galloway's weapon, and not necessarily for her own protection. Geoff had guessed that Wendy was more than capable of shooting Stryker if matters hadn't turned out as she had planned. If the tide had been further out she would have shot him – maybe not to kill but just to maim, probably in the leg. It would have added to Stryker's agony but also to Wendy Galloway's satisfaction. It was the twisted way she worked.

Firth updated the control room concerning the weapon found in Galloway's car and Inspector Harriet Davidson breathed another long deep sigh of relief as the palms of her hands moved back over her hair. She held her breath then exhaled deeply, her puffed cheeks deflated like a punctured balloon.

'A good job and a successful outcome,' she said to herself, but she knew that the next major incident was just around the corner.

30

Debbie Smith

'Just one more thing, and we've got time to do it,' Sutton said to Firth, just after they had received an instruction to attend a meeting with ACC Ron Turner in an hour's time.

They exited the east marina car park and headed for the Galloway residence. Sutton needed to have a quick word with Toni.

They could hear the dog barking after repeated attempts ringing the doorbell. 'Bones,' they heard Toni scream, 'shut the fuck up.' Sutton recognised the cultured tones of Toni Galloway. They'd had previous dealings.

Finally the large door was opened. Toni looked a sight with her smudged mascara partially hidden behind bedraggled hair. She was dressed in a yellow and black spotted animal print onesie. In her drowsy state she hadn't checked the CCTV system, which would have identified her guests. Toni tried to push the door shut but was prevented from doing so by Sutton's size tens. Her actions were predictable.

Without seeking further permission Firth and Sutton walked into the hallway, following Toni, who had a loose grip on the drooling Bones. Geoff didn't allow her to talk. 'Toni, you have two options. You either give a statement

266

regarding your mother's involvement or you get arrested for murder.'

It was short and direct. It was meant to be, and it had the desired effect. Toni released Bones then turned and stared at Sutton. It was if she had been instantly released from a hypnotic trance. Geoff had rightly assumed that when it came to the crunch Toni Galloway would only protect one person: herself.

'I don't give a toss about her. I knew that she got the kid shot.' Toni was making a direct reference to the shooting outside Lucifer's. 'It was me who wrote the note telling you she did. I didn't need that blubbing press conference, for what it's fucking worth. She made a career of paying you coppers. It was bloody obvious how she identified the lad. That shooting has got nowt to do with me. It's your copper. You're a set of bent bastards,' Toni said with utter disdain.

Sutton looked across at Firth. No one would have ever guessed that the original anonymous contact received by Parton Constabulary concerning a corrupt police officer being involved in the Lucifer's murder had originated from Wendy's very own daughter. The smart money would be on the injured Matt, but never Toni.

Five minutes later Toni Galloway was being transported to the Parton central police station, where two members of the Operation RESOLVE incident room were briefed to take her statement. Fortunately for them she had made a quick change from her leopard print onesie.

***

Sutton, Firth and Delaney all met with ACC Ron Turner in his office. It was almost a unique occasion, as Turner offered them all a cup of coffee. It was gratefully received by everyone apart from Delaney, who produced a bottle of Evian water. Sutton cheekily asked if he had anything stronger. They then all stood as Chief Constable Chris Mayling entered the room.

Once the pleasantries were over Turner gave Trish Delaney, as the senior investigating officer, the opportunity to provide an investigation overview.

'Let's start from the beginning. Wendy Galloway: we now have evidence of her conspiracy in the first shooting (of Simon Mather) outside Lucifer's, after recruiting Robbie Hanson – who, along with Toni Galloway, has fully implicated our Wendy. Hanson has admitted his own involvement and has given a statement about his recruitment after being blackmailed by Wendy. We already have CPS authority to charge PC Hanson.' She looked at Sutton. 'In addition, we also have the weapon recovered from Galloway's Volvo following her recent arrest.'

Delaney then took a sip of water before continuing. 'Bill Rudding refuses to say anything, but we have the surveillance logs and more from Robbie Hanson. For Chief Superintendent John Dexter, more surveillance, phone evidence, together with Hanson and Shaun Adams, his secretary, they can both testify.' Sutton and Turner glanced across at each other.

'In addition, the search at Gormley's taxi business revealed total admin chaos, but among the items we recovered there are some printed emails from Dexter's private account to Art Gormley that outlined their association. He's knackered,' Delaney said with finality. There was another glance between Turner and Sutton, but this time there was an accompanying satisfactory smile.

Delaney paused before continuing her summary. 'Jonta Roberts is a broken man, and he is singing like the proverbial canary. He has already admitted that he was riding the bike at the two shootings and that his best mate Kev Stryker was the pillion passenger. He confirmed Stryker as the individual who actually pulled the trigger. He also gave us the information concerning the late Art Gormley's involvement in the investigation.'

'What about our injured people?' Mayling enquired.

Jo Firth had just received the latest medical update from Parton Infirmary. 'Kev Stryker is in recovery. He will live, thanks to the coastguard and the paramedics at the scene. They got there just in time,' Firth added.

'Pete McIntyre…' There was a pause as everyone in the room looked towards Sutton. 'He has severe pneumonia. However, he's a fit bloke and the prognosis is good. He's going to be fine, Geoff.' Firth looked towards her work partner. 'However, Operation RESOLVE now includes another murder. Sadly, Matt Galloway passed away under an hour ago. He will be joining Art Gormley in the morgue.'

'Thanks, Jo.' Turner added, 'Let us be clear on motive. The first shooting occurred because Toni Galloway was rebuffed outside Lucifer's. The second shooting was organised by John Dexter because he rightly believed that Matt Galloway would have known from his mother about Dexter's ongoing corrupt relationship with Art Gormley. Once he returned to the area Dexter assumed that Matt, as he had done in the past, would report that fact in some way or another to the authorities. Had that occurred, Dexter would have been finished.

'Dexter kept the council onside so that Art could

apply for – and then annually endorse – his taxi business by confirming his operator's licence. Art was always in debt to John Dexter. And as for Stryker's kidnap, it happened because of his drunken late-night fumble with Toni, which was followed by a misguided text dissing the Galloways—'

'But why kidnap Pete McIntyre?' Sutton interrupted Turner, who looked away. It was patently obvious that he hadn't welcomed the question. This was totally out of character. There was silence around the room, broken only by the temerity of the chief constable pulling rank.

'Why Ron? Why Pete McIntyre? His involvement requires an explanation,' Mayling said with authority.

'I know why,' Turner admitted, and then paused. 'With Matt Galloway out of the picture, Pete McIntyre would have been the only one who could have possibly known about John Dexter's relationship with Art Gormley.' Turner added, 'Matt Galloway told McIntyre everything he knew. Pastoral Pete was a very apt nickname.'

Turner hesitated again. 'And there is another thing. Pete McIntyre, for the people in this room only, was the supergrass in the Vern Edwards trial.'

You could have heard a pin drop. Everyone stared at Turner. 'Despite the problems with his mother we could never persuade Matt to formally testify against her, but we had the next best thing. Dexter and I persuaded Pete McIntyre to become a protected witness and give evidence. It was third-hand evidence, but it gave a complete overview of the Galloway and Edwards turf war. Despite McIntyre's assistance the CPS considered we only had enough evidence for the one offence, and ironically it was Edwards who went the journey for torturing one of Wendy's main men. We failed to put

Galloway in the dock, but it did provide some all-important public confidence and a bit of respite for the force.' Turner stopped speaking and took a long sip of coffee.

'Apart from myself, John Dexter was the only other person in the force who knew all about Pete McIntyre. In the years after the trial ended Matt Galloway rang to try and contact Pete about an ongoing corrupt relationship involving a high-ranking officer. Dexter dealt with the matter and naturally kept the enquiry on file when he went to professional standards. He provided a full report and basically wrote it off. The matter was closed, after being endorsed by the chief constable at the time. When Matt returned to Parton Dexter panicked.' Turner paused in his explanation.

'Shit, Pete,' Sutton said aloud as he thought about his good mate. He remembered the strange and unaccounted for disappearance of the McIntyre clan some years back.

'After a few years he opted out of the contract in the witness protection scheme,' Turner added, second-guessing Sutton's next question. 'Once you were in the scheme you were in it for life. Pete's either a brave man or slightly foolish,' Turner continued. 'But he was under intense domestic pressure to return to Parton. He took the view, rightly or wrongly, that with Vern Edwards inside and Matt's circumstances changing, it was now relatively safe for them to return,' Turner added, before helping himself to another well-earned sip of coffee.

'Shit. Pastoral Pete,' Sutton almost repeated his previous exclamation. Despite their close relationship Geoff Sutton hadn't had a clue about this side of Pete McIntyre.

'Right, ladies and gents, there's a lot to take in, and

I have an Operation RESOLVE press conference in the next hour. It will be pretty uncomfortable, but at least we have some results to provide a positive spin. Trish, keep me updated with the investigation and more importantly the charges. Thank you all.' Chief Constable Chris Mayling made her exit.

Jo Firth turned to Sutton and gave him a huge hug. During Operation PROOF and now RESOLVE they had forged a successful partnership.

It was early evening as Sutton walked slowly across the car park towards the Karoq. All the adrenaline was rapidly receding and he recognised the signs of total fatigue. The effects from the past few days started to kick in, like the slow release of a syringe as a drug enters the body. He sat in his vehicle and closed his eyes but, rather than allowing his mind to drift, Sutton concentrated hard. His decision-making didn't take long.

Before he drove out of the Parton HQ car park he finally had the opportunity to scrutinise his phone, he knew that he had missed a few calls. 'Stew, poor Stew,' he said to himself as he looked at the contact name of the six missed calls from Stew Grant. His mobile rang again. Inevitably it was Stew.

'Are you OK?' Granty sounded frantic. 'I've been ringing all day. I even left a message at the police station,' Stew said quickly, 'And what about Pete? I've tried Val, Henry, everyone,' he continued, clearly upset by the lack of contact and recalling the tragic circumstances concerning Roger Strong's death. He'd obviously had a nightmare day.

'Stew, I'm sorry. There's loads to tell you, but everyone is OK.' Sutton tried to sound reassuring.

'Well, if that's the case, what about a beer down at the

club?' Granty was recovering quickly. He was referring to their weekly meeting point and regular watering hole at Upper Parton RFC. 'I couldn't watch the bloody match today because I was busy trying to contact the pair of you,' he added.

'Sorry, Stew. Believe it or not, I've got something more important to do,' Sutton said and laughed.

'Can't think that there could be anything more important that having a pint at the club on a Saturday with your best mate,' Granty said and laughed back. 'Speak soon, Sutton.' Stew had given up on his pint and ended the call.

Finally Sutton was on his way back home. It was Debbie's turn to cook tea. 'How life has changed since she arrived,' Sutton said to himself. He parked on the roadside outside his house. Debbie's vehicle was still occupying the driveway. Geoff opened the front door. The aroma of some Italian dish immediately hit him. He could almost taste dinner. Sutton hardly had time to remove his coat when Debbie approached him from the kitchen, wine glass in hand, with those gorgeous dancing eyes.

'Geoff Sutton, will you marry me?' Debbie said. 'I love you so very much.' She finished speaking. Her eyes were swimming as tears rolled down her cheeks.

Debbie's tears joined his. Sutton couldn't speak. He was silenced with emotion. Then his composure and his voice returned. 'Yes, Debbie… Yes, Debbie.' It was a burnt Italian dish that they both enjoyed later that evening.

That Sunday was as hectic as any he had endured on Operation RESOLVE. A FaceTime call to his daughter Maggie saw her replicating her father's tears, particularly when Debbie asked her to be bridesmaid. And an early contact with Val McIntyre confirmed that Pete was continuing to recover. She felt sure that news of Sutton's engagement would greatly assist the healing process.

The happy couple then headed out, arm in arm, but only after more phone calls, first to Debbie's brother, Billy and then, naturally, to Stew Grant. Their recently announced engagement had been well received by those who mattered.

Still arm in arm, the happy couple made their way to the city centre precinct, and carefully avoided the multistorey car park. Debbie was no shopper – never had been, never would be – and so the whole process of visiting jewellers and choosing a ring took little more than an hour. Most of that time was occupied by Sutton repeatedly posing the question, 'Are you sure? Are you really sure, Debbie?'

'I couldn't be more certain, Geoff Sutton. I love you,' Debbie commented, looking down at the glittering diamond ring as the happy couple returned to the car.

On their return home they saw that there were two gifts left for them on the doorstep. One was an unwrapped four-pack of Thwaites craft beer from Debbie's brother Billy, with a handwritten note saying, *Congrats, Geoff, you'll need these!* Of course there was no sign whatsoever of any sentiment towards his loving sister. Typical Billy.

In contrast, but equally typical, there was a meticulously wrapped bottle of Bollinger champagne from Stew and Tina Grant. A giant, expensive card accompanied the present.

31

Chief Constable Chris Mayling

Sutton's alarm pinged at 6.30 a.m. on the Monday morning. He looked across at his still slumbering fiancée. He took a deep breath. 'God, she is so beautiful,' Sutton said to himself, and then, with the greatest of effort, dragged himself out of bed. His second major life-changing decision beckoned.

He abandoned a half-drunk mug of coffee and closed the front door. His green Barbour was soon flapping against the cold winter wind. Although this wasn't a designated workday, Sutton drove directly to Parton Constabulary HQ with only one thing on his mind. He made his way to the secretariat area where the force's chief officers were located. It was approaching 7.30 a.m.

He walked purposely towards Chris Mayling's office. The door was slightly ajar, and he could see the chief constable at her desk. 'Perfect,' he said to himself. Full of confidence, he knocked and entered the room almost at the same time.

It was then that his cunning plan went slightly awry, as he could see Ron Turner seated in front of Mayling. Sutton had thought that by going to see the chief that early he would be able to see her alone, before the busy daily schedule kicked in.

'Sorry, ma'am,' he said with the utmost respect. 'I didn't think anyone was with you.' He turned to exit.

'Come on in, Geoff. Come in,' Mayling said. It was an order. 'Ron has something to say to you,' she said, smiling.

There was a pause while Sutton remained in the room feeling very uncomfortable. 'Geoff, I'm retiring,' Turner said without any hesitation whatsoever, and offered his hand. Typical Turner. There was not a flicker of emotion as Sutton grasped the hand of friendship and respect.

'Me too,' Sutton spluttered in response, and in a conclusive act, with his other hand he reached into his pocket and placed his informants' phone on Mayling's desk. The two words were all he could say. He became incapable of giving any further explanation and immediately looked away.

The significance of actually announcing his own retirement was just too much but, while Turner was oblivious to Sutton's body language, Chris Mayling thought and acted differently. She stood up and walked around her desk to give Sutton a comforting and warm embrace. Unbeknown to Geoff Sutton it was the repeat exercise of a few moments earlier when she had hugged an embarrassed Ron Turner.

A couple of moments later Mayling was back behind her desk. 'Now what the hell am I going to do without you two?' It was a question said with feeling. She knew that Turner and Sutton would be a tremendous loss to the force but all three knew it was also an opportunity for others. 'Policing, like life, goes on,' Mayling said to herself.

Some thirty minutes later, and after swopping a few war stories with Ron Turner in his office, Sutton realised that, with accrued time off and annual leave, this may well be his final appearance at Parton HQ. Tears flowed yet again as the security gates opened.

Geoff made the return journey home and, for the first time in a while, he stopped and purchased the local newspaper. He glanced at the front page, which was taken over by an account of a tragic road accident. A youngster knocked down on a pedestrian crossing by a motorist returning from a prison visit.

The picture of the offending driver had been published. While he didn't recognise the name, Sutton knew the face. It was the driver of the Corsa he had spotted on the day of his visit to HMP Wassingham. He looked again at the photograph. She had been the McIntyres' cleaner before they had disappeared. He folded the paper and continued his journey to the Parlour Cafe.

Geoff had taken the decision to retire without consulting his fiancée and he needed to inform Debbie immediately. The prospect of a full English was also an appealing prospect. After that, possibly a round of golf with Stew before the pair of them paid a visit to see Pete in hospital.

'Let the new life begin,' he shouted loudly to no one in particular as he parked in the lay-by close to the Parlour Cafe. Geoff almost ran into Debbie's establishment.

Some twenty minutes later Sutton returned to his car. This time he walked very slowly. Matters hadn't gone as well as he expected. It wasn't as if Debbie had disapproved of his resignation. She hadn't said as much. But Sutton could tell by those gorgeous eyes she had been shocked at his news. He made the short journey home.

As Sutton continued with his day Debbie tried to continue working as normal. With a worried frown on her face she placed some cutlery in the cafe's dishwasher.

She kept asking herself the same question.

'What the hell will Geoff Sutton do without the police force in his life?'

Epilogue

Some seven months later

She looked absolutely radiant. Debbie entered the upstairs room of Upper Parton Rugby Club, arm in arm with her brother Billy, followed closely by Sutton's daughter Maggie, who was equally as stunning in her role as bridesmaid.

The upstairs room, which had only recently become licensed to hold marriage ceremonies, was appropriately decorated to reflect the occasion. It was a far cry from the former club meeting room adorned with rugby memorabilia, but as far as Geoff and Debbie were concerned it was the only possible venue.

As Debbie approached Sutton took one step away from his two best men, Stew Grant and Pete McIntyre.

It was a small, intimate affair, exactly as the couple had wanted. Debbie's staff from the Parlour Cafe and Sutton's former colleagues were all present. Sutton had clocked some notable attendees, including Chief Constable Chris Mayling, together with Ron Turner, Jo Firth and Steve Barker. Geoff had heard on the grapevine that both Firth and Barker had recently received well-deserved promotions.

Apart from Ron Turner's, there wasn't a dry eye in the house as Geoff and Debbie made their vows. Following the service the couple had a few formal photographs taken before settling down to a buffet, based around produce freshly delivered from Debbie's Parlour Cafe. The relaxed atmosphere was punctuated by prolonged entertainment from Grant and McIntyre in their best man speeches, although Pete had to pause for a short coughing fit, a remnant from his traumatic kidnap. There was also a poignant pause when they respectfully remembered Roger Strong, lightened only by recounting his infamous hole-in-one story.

The occasion was over all too quickly, and people said their goodbyes. Tina and Val had to literally drag their respective husbands from the room. Maggie was loading up the taxi with gifts and slices of wedding cake when Geoff took Debbie's hand and led her through the open doors out on to the balcony that looked over the rugby pitches. The sun had begun to disappear at the end of their perfect day.

He paused for a moment and reflected upon the past few years of policing. They had coincided with his major role in the significant investigations that had been given the operational names of TRUST, PROOF and RESOLVE. These enquiries had run alongside the early part of his relationship with Debbie, who was recovering from the psychological problems arising from her former abusive partner. Geoff looked deeply into those eyes. 'I love you, Debbie Smith,' Sutton said with absolute conviction.

'To coin a phrase, young Sutton, let the new life begin.' Debbie smiled back and kissed her new husband. The kiss was also given with absolute conviction, but the phrase, 'Let the new life begin,' wasn't.

Debbie looked deep into Geoff's eyes and said, 'How can you ever leave the police, young Sutton?'

Previous titles by the author

TRUST

Retired DCI Geoff Sutton now works as a civilian at Parton Constabulary. Life is quiet as he follows his usual routine of golf and watching his beloved Upper Parton RFC - but all that's about to change...

Walking home one evening, Geoff sees a familiar van. When it's still there the next morning he decides to act - and what he and his colleagues find inside is beyond their worst nightmares.

Geoff's experience is needed and he soon finds himself playing an integral part in an investigation that rocks the local force.

A dead prostitute, a missing foster child, a senior police officer whose love affair makes her careless... Geoff and his colleagues reveal blackmail, murder and kidnap as they untangle a web of deceit and corruption.

And Geoff is forced to ask himself: who can you really TRUST?

PROOF

Geoff Sutton finds himself at the wrong place at the wrong time...

The retired DCI, now working as a civilian with Parton Constabulary, has a shopping trip cut short when he encounters an elderly victim of the Parton Smart Team, an organised crime group that is targeting older members of the community. Another death is the last thing the force needs as they prepare for a high-profile demonstration of right-wing extremists in Parton city centre.

Sutton's quiet life of playing golf and watching rugby with his lifelong friends is shattered as he plays an integral role in the murder investigation. As the level of fear rises, connections appear between the adolescent members of the PST, the extremists and the intelligence services. Can Sutton prevent a disaster? And can he also deal with a devastating personal tragedy at the same time?

This tense, fast-paced sequel to Colin Green's debut novel, TRUST, reveals the challenges that small towns face in maintaining law and order in an increasingly complex world.